Wings

to Laura,

Believe . . !

Aprilynne Pike

Wings

APRILYNNE PIKE

HARPER TEEN

AN IMPRINT OF HARPERCOLLINSPUBLISHERS

HarperTeen is an imprint of HarperCollins Publishers.

Wings
www.harperteen.com

Library of Congress Cataloging-in-Publication Data
Pike, Aprilynne.
  Wings / Aprilynne Pike. — 1st ed.
       p.   cm.
  Summary: When a plant blooms out of fifteen-year-old
Laurel's back, it leads her to discover the fact that she is a faerie and
that she has a crucial role to play in keeping the world safe from the
encroaching enemy trolls.
  ISBN 978-0-06-166803-6 (trade bdg.) —
  ISBN 978-0-06-166804-3 (lib. bdg.)
  [1. Fairies—Fiction.   2. Trolls—Fiction.   3. Plants—Fiction.
4. Interpersonal relations—Fiction.]   I. Title.
PZ7.P6257Wi   2009   2008024653
[Fic]—dc22   CIP
                                                      AC

Typography by Ray Shappell

09   10   11   12   13   CG/RRDB   10   9   8   7   6   5   4   3   2   1
❖
First Edition

To Kenny—the method behind my madness

Wings

ONE

LAUREL'S SHOES FLIPPED A CHEERFUL RHYTHM THAT defied her dark mood. As she walked through the halls of Del Norte High, people watched her pass with curious eyes.

After double-checking her schedule, Laurel found the biology lab and hurried to claim a seat by the windows. If she had to be indoors, she wanted to at least see outside. The rest of the class filed in slowly. One boy smiled in her direction as he walked to the front of the classroom and she tried to muster one up in return. She hoped he didn't think it was a grimace.

A tall, thin man introduced himself as Mr. James and began passing out textbooks. The beginning of the book seemed fairly standard—classifications of plants and animals, she knew those—then it started to move into basic human anatomy. Around page eighty, the text started to resemble a foreign language. Laurel grumbled under her breath. This was going to be a long semester.

As Mr. James called out the roll, Laurel recognized a few names from her first two classes that morning, but it was going to be a long time before she matched even half of them to the faces that surrounded her. She felt lost amid the sea of unfamiliar people.

Her mom had assured her that *every* sophomore would feel the same—after all, it was their first day in high school too—but no one else looked lost or scared. Maybe being lost and scared was something you got used to after years of public school.

Homeschooling had worked just fine for Laurel over the last ten years; she didn't see any reason for that to change. But her parents were determined to do everything right for their only child. When she was five, that meant being home-schooled in a tiny town. Apparently, now that she was fifteen, it meant public school in a slightly less tiny town.

The room grew quiet and Laurel snapped to attention when the teacher repeated her name. "Laurel Sewell?"

"Here," she said quickly.

She squirmed as Mr. James studied her over the rim of his glasses and then moved on to the next name.

Laurel released the breath she'd been holding and pulled out her notebook, trying to draw as little attention to herself as possible.

As the teacher explained the semester's curriculum, her eyes kept straying to the boy who had smiled at her earlier. She had to stifle a grin when she noticed him sneaking glances at her too.

When Mr. James released them for lunch, Laurel gratefully slid her book into her bag.

"Hey."

She looked up. It was the boy who had been watching her. His eyes caught her attention first. They were a bright blue that contrasted with the olive tone of his skin. The color looked out of place, but not in a bad way. Kind of exotic. His slightly wavy, light-brown hair was on the longish side and slipped across his forehead in a soft arc.

"You're Laurel, right?" Below the eyes was a warm but casual smile with very straight teeth. *Braces probably*, Laurel thought as her tongue unconsciously ran over her own teeth, also quite straight. Lucky for her, naturally straight.

"Yeah." Her voice caught in her throat and she coughed, feeling stupid.

"I'm David. David Lawson. I—I wanted to say hi. And welcome to Crescent City, I guess."

Laurel forced a small smile. "Thanks," she said.

"Want to sit with me and my friends for lunch?"

"Where?" Laurel asked.

David looked at her strangely. "In . . . the cafeteria?"

"Oh," she said, disappointed. He seemed nice, but she was tired of being cooped up inside. "Actually, I'm going to go find a place outside." She paused. "Thank you, though."

"Outside sounds good to me. Want some company?"

"Really?"

"Sure. I've got my lunch in my backpack, so I'm all set. Besides," he said, hefting his bag onto one shoulder, "you shouldn't sit alone your first day."

"Thanks," she said after a tiny hesitation. "I'd like that."

They walked out to the back lawn together and found a

grassy spot that wasn't too damp. Laurel spread her jacket on the ground and sat on it; David kept his on. "Aren't you cold?" he asked, looking skeptically at her jean shorts and tank top.

She slipped out of her shoes and dug her toes into the thick grass. "I don't get cold very often—at least not here. If we go somewhere with snow, I'm miserable. But this weather's perfect for me." She smiled awkwardly. "My mom jokes that I'm cold-blooded."

"Lucky you. I moved here from L.A. about five years ago and I'm still not used to the temperature."

"It's not *that* cold."

"Sure," David said with a grin, "but it's not that warm either. After our first year here, I looked up the weather records; did you know that the difference between the average temperature in July and December is only fourteen degrees? Now *that* is messed up."

They fell silent as David ate a sandwich and Laurel poked at a salad with a fork.

"My mom packed me an extra cupcake," David said, breaking the silence. "Want it?" He held out a pretty cupcake with blue frosting. "It's homemade."

"No, thanks."

David looked at her salad doubtfully, then back at the cupcake.

Laurel realized what David was thinking and sighed. Why was that the first conclusion everyone always jumped to? Surely she wasn't the only person in the world who just really liked vegetables. Laurel tapped one fingernail against her can of Sprite. "It's not diet."

"I didn't mean—"

"I'm vegan," Laurel interrupted. "Pretty strict, actually."

"Oh, yeah?"

She nodded, then laughed stiffly. "Can't have too many veggies, right?"

"I guess not."

David cleared his throat and asked, "So, when did you move here?"

"In May. I've been working for my dad a lot. He owns the bookstore downtown."

"Really?" David asked. "I went in there last week. It's a great store. I don't remember seeing you though."

"That's my mom's fault. She dragged me around shopping for school supplies all week. This is the first year I haven't been homeschooled, and my mom's convinced I don't have enough supplies."

"Homeschooled?"

"Yeah. They're forcing me to go public this year."

He grinned. "Well, I'm glad they did." He looked down at his cupcake for a few seconds before asking, "Do you miss your old town?"

"Sometimes." She smiled softly. "But it's nice here. My old town, Orick, is seriously small. Like five-hundred-people small."

"Wow." He chuckled. "L.A.'s just a little bigger than that."

She laughed and choked on her soda.

David looked like he was ready to ask something else, but the bell sounded and he smiled instead. "Can we do this again tomorrow?" He hesitated for a second, then added, "With my friends, maybe?"

Laurel's first instinct was to say no, but she'd enjoyed David's company. Besides, socializing more was yet another reason her mom had insisted on public school this year. "Sure," she said before she could lose her nerve. "That'd be fun."

"Awesome." He stood and offered her his hand. He pulled her to her feet and grinned lopsidedly for a minute. "Well, I'll . . . see you around, I guess."

She watched him walk away. His jacket and loose-fitting jeans looked more or less like everyone else's, but there was a sureness in his walk that set him apart from the crowd. Laurel was envious of that confident stride.

Maybe someday.

Laurel threw her backpack on the counter and slumped onto a barstool. Her mom, Sarah, glanced up from the bread she was kneading. "How was school?"

"It sucked."

Her hands stopped. "Language, Laurel."

"Well, it did. And there's not a better word to describe it."

"You have to give it some time, hon."

"Everyone stares at me like I'm a freak."

"They stare at you because you're new."

"I don't look like everyone else."

Her mom grinned. "Would you want to?"

Laurel rolled her eyes, but she had to admit her mother had scored a point. She might be homeschooled and a little sheltered, but she knew she looked a lot like the teens in magazines and on television.

And she liked it.

Adolescence had been kind to her. Her almost translucent white skin hadn't suffered the effects of acne and her blond hair had never been greasy. She was a small, lithe fifteen-year-old with a perfectly oval face and light green eyes. She'd always been thin, but not too thin, and had even developed some curves in the last few years. Her limbs were long and willowy and she walked with a dancer's grace, despite having never taken lessons.

"I meant I *dress* differently."

"You could dress like everyone else if you wanted to."

"Yeah, but they all wear clunky shoes and tight jeans and like, three shirts all layered on top of each other."

"So?"

"I don't like tight clothes. They're scratchy and make me feel awkward. And really, who could possibly *want* to wear clunky shoes? Yuck."

"So wear what you want. If your clothes are enough to drive would-be friends away, they're not the kind of friends you want."

Typical mother advice. Sweet, honest, and completely useless. "It's loud there."

Her mom stopped kneading and brushed her bangs out of her face, leaving a floury streak on her brow. "Sweetheart, you can hardly expect an entire high school to be as quiet as the two of us all alone. Be reasonable."

"I am reasonable. I'm not talking about necessary noise; they run around like wild monkeys. They shriek and laugh and whine at the top of their lungs. *And* they make out at their lockers."

Her mom rested her hand on her hip. "Anything else?"

"Yes. The halls are dark."

"They are not dark," her mom said, her tone slightly scolding. "I toured that entire school with you last week and all the walls are white."

"But there are no windows, just those awful fluorescent lights. They're so fake and they don't bring any real light to the hallways. They're just . . . dark. I miss Orick."

Her mom began shaping the dough into loaves. "Tell me something good about today. I mean it."

Laurel wandered over to the fridge.

"No," her mom said, putting up one hand to stop her. "Something good first."

"Um . . . I met a nice guy," she said, stepping around her mom's arm and grabbing a soda. "David . . . David something."

It was her mom's turn to roll her eyes. "Of course. We move to a new town and I start you in a brand-new school and the first person you latch on to is a guy."

"It's not like that."

"I'm kidding."

Laurel stood silently, listening to the slap of bread dough on the counter.

"Mom?"

"Yeah?"

Laurel drew in a deep breath. "Do I really have to keep going?"

Her mom rubbed her temples. "Laurel, we've been through this already."

"But—"

"No. We're not going to argue about it again." She leaned on the counter, her face close to Laurel's. "I don't feel qualified to homeschool you anymore. Truth be told, I probably should have put you in middle school. It was just such a long drive from Orick and your dad was commuting already and . . . anyway. It's time."

"But you could order one of those homeschooling programs. I looked them up online," Laurel said hurriedly when her mom opened her mouth. "You don't actually have to do the teaching. The material covers everything."

"And how much does it cost?" her mom asked, her voice quiet, one eyebrow raised pointedly.

Laurel was silent.

"Listen," her mom said, after a pause, "in a few months, that's something we can consider if you still hate school. But until our property in Orick sells, we don't have the money for anything extra. You know that."

Laurel looked down at the counter, her shoulders slumped.

The main reason they'd moved to Crescent City in the first place was because her dad had bought a bookstore down on Washington Street. Early in the year, he'd been driving through and saw a For Sale sign on a bookstore that was going out of business. Laurel remembered listening to her parents talk for weeks about what they could do to buy the store—a shared dream since they'd first gotten married—but the numbers never added up.

Then, in late April, a guy named Jeremiah Barnes approached Laurel's dad at his job in Eureka and expressed interest in their property in Orick. Her dad had come home practically bouncing with excitement. The rest happened in such a whirlwind Laurel could hardly remember what had come first. Her parents spent several days at the bank in Brookings and by early May, the bookstore was theirs and they were moving from their small cabin in Orick to an even smaller house in Crescent City.

But the months crept by and still things weren't finalized with Mr. Barnes. Until they were, money was tight, her dad worked long hours at the store, and Laurel was stuck in high school.

Her mom laid one hand over hers, warm and comforting. "Laurel, aside from the cost, you also need to learn to conquer new things. This will be so good for you. Next year you can take AP classes and you could join a team or a club. Those all look really good on college applications."

"I know. But—"

"I'm the mom," she said with a grin that softened her firm tone. "And I say school."

Laurel humphed and began tracing her finger along the grout between the tiles on the countertop.

The clock ticked loudly as her mom slid the pans into the oven and set the timer.

"Mom, do we have any of your canned peaches? I'm hungry."

Her mom stared at Laurel. "You're hungry?"

Laurel traced swirls through the condensation on the soda can with her finger, avoiding her mom's gaze. "I got hungry this afternoon. In last period."

Her mom was trying not to make a big deal of this, but they both knew it was out of the ordinary. Laurel rarely felt hungry. Her parents had bugged Laurel about her weird eating habits for years. She ate at each meal to satisfy them, but it wasn't something she felt she needed, much less enjoyed.

That's why her mom finally agreed to keep the fridge stocked with Sprite. She railed against the as-yet-undocumented detriments of carbonation, but she couldn't argue with the 140 calories per can. That was 140 more than water. At least this way she knew Laurel was getting more calories in her system, even if they were "empty."

Her mom hurried to the pantry to grab a jar of peaches, probably afraid Laurel would change her mind. The unfamiliar twisting in Laurel's stomach had begun during Spanish class, twenty minutes before the last bell. It had faded a little on the walk home but hadn't gone away.

"Here you go," she said, setting a bowl in front of Laurel. Then she turned her back, giving Laurel a modicum of privacy. Laurel looked down at the dish. Her mom had played it safe—one peach half and about half a cup of juice.

She ate the peach in small bites, staring at her mother's back, waiting for her to turn around and peek. But her mom busied

11

herself with the dishes and didn't look once. Still, Laurel felt like she'd lost some imaginary battle, so when she was finished, she slid her backpack from the counter and tiptoed out of the kitchen before her mom could turn around.

TWO

THE BELL SOUNDED IN BIOLOGY AND LAUREL HURRIED TO stow the evil bio book as deep into her backpack as possible.

"How was day two?"

Laurel looked up to see David sitting backward in the chair across her lab table. "It was okay." At least she'd heard her name the first time for roll call in all of her classes so far.

"You ready?"

Laurel tried to smile, but her mouth didn't obey. When she'd agreed to join David and his friends for lunch yesterday, it had seemed like a good idea. But the thought of meeting a whole group of complete strangers made her cringe. "Yeah," she said, but she could tell her tone wasn't convincing.

"Are you sure? Because you don't have to."

"No, I'm sure," she said quickly. "Just let me get my stuff." She packed her notebook and pens slowly. When she knocked one of her pens onto the floor, David retrieved it and handed it to her. She tugged on it, but he didn't let go until she looked up at him. "They won't bite," he said seriously. "I promise."

In the hallway David monopolized the conversation, rattling on until they entered the cafeteria. He waved to a group at the end of one of the long, thin tables. "Come on," he said, putting a hand at the small of her back.

It felt a little weird to have someone touch her like that but strangely comforting too. He guided her through the crowded aisle, then dropped his hand as soon as they got to the correct table.

"Hey, guys, this is Laurel."

David pointed to each person and said a name, but five seconds later, Laurel couldn't have repeated any of them. She sat in an empty seat beside David and tried to catch bits and pieces of the conversation around her. Absently, she pulled out a can of soda, a strawberry-and-spinach salad, and a peach half in juice her mother had packed that morning.

"A salad? It's lasagna day and you're having a salad?"

Laurel looked over at a girl with curly brown hair who had a full tray of school lunch in front of her.

David spoke up quickly, cutting off any response Laurel might have attempted. "Laurel's vegan—she's very strict."

The girl glanced down at the small peach half with one raised eyebrow. "Looks more than vegan to me. Don't vegans eat, like, bread?"

Laurel's smile was tight. "Some."

David rolled his eyes. "This person interrogating you is Chelsea, by the way. Hi, Chelse."

"You look like you're on some kind of mega-diet," Chelsea said, ignoring David's greeting.

"Not really. This is just the kind of food I like."

Laurel watched Chelsea's eyes return to her salad and could sense more questions about to erupt. It was probably better to just spill than answer the twenty questions. "My digestive system doesn't handle normal food very well," she said. "Anything except plain fruits and vegetables makes me sick."

"That's weird. Who can live on just green stuff? Have you seen a doctor about this? Because——"

"Chelsea?" David's voice was pointed but quiet. Laurel doubted anyone else at the table had even heard.

Chelsea's gray eyes widened a little. "Oh, sorry." She smiled, and when she did, it lit up her whole face. Laurel found herself smiling back. "It's nice to meet you," Chelsea said. Then she turned to her meal and didn't even look at Laurel's food again.

Lunch break was only twenty-eight minutes long—short by anyone's standards—but today it seemed to drag on endlessly. The cafeteria was fairly small and voices bounced off the walls like Ping-Pong balls, assaulting her ears. She felt like everyone was shouting at her all at once. Several of David's friends attempted to draw her into their conversations, but Laurel couldn't concentrate when the temperature in the room seemed to be rising by the minute. She couldn't understand why no one else noticed.

She'd chosen a full T-shirt that morning instead of a tank because she'd felt so out of place the day before. But now the neckline seemed to grow even higher until she felt like she was wearing a turtleneck. A *tight* turtleneck. When the bell finally rang, she smiled and said good-bye but hurried out the door before David could catch her.

She speed-walked to the bathroom, dropped her bag on the floor at the base of the windowsill, and pushed her face out into the open air. She breathed in the cool, salty air and fluttered the front of her shirt, trying to let the breeze touch as much of her body as possible. The faint nausea that had filled her stomach during lunch began to dissipate, and she left the bathroom with just enough time to run to her next class.

After school she walked home slowly. The sun and fresh air invigorated her and made the queasy feeling in her stomach disappear completely. Nonetheless, when she selected her clothing the next morning, she went back to a tank top.

At the beginning of bio, David sat down in the chair next to her. "Do you mind?" he asked.

Laurel shook her head. "The girl who usually sits here spends the whole class doodling hearts for someone named Steve. It's a little distracting."

David laughed. "Probably Steve Tanner. He's super-popular."

"Everyone goes for the obvious person, I guess." She pulled out her textbook and found the page Mr. James had written on the whiteboard.

"Want to have lunch with me again today? And my friends," he added hastily.

Laurel hesitated. She'd figured he would ask, but she still hadn't thought of a way to answer him without hurting his feelings. She liked him a lot. And she'd liked his friends—the ones she'd been able to hear over the din. "I don't think so," she began. "I—"

"Is it Chelsea? She didn't mean to make you self-conscious about your lunch; she's just really honest all the time. It's actually kind of refreshing once you get used to it."

"No, it's not her—your friends were all really nice. But I can't . . . I can't stand that cafeteria. If I have to be indoors all day, I need to spend lunch outside. I guess with all the freedom of homeschooling for ten years I'm having trouble relinquishing it so quickly."

"Do you mind if we come eat outside with you, then?"

Laurel was quiet as she listened to the beginning of the lecture on phyla. "That would be nice," she finally whispered back.

When the bell rang, David said, "I'll meet you out there. I'll just go tell the others so they can come if they want."

By the time lunch was over, Laurel remembered at least half of the kids' names and had managed to join in several of the conversations. Chelsea and David went with her to her next class and it felt natural to walk with them. When David made a joke about Mr. James, Laurel's laugh echoed through the halls. After only three days, the school was beginning to be more familiar; she didn't feel as lost, and even the crush of people that had been so overwhelming on Monday wasn't quite so bad today. For the first time since leaving Orick, Laurel felt like she belonged.

THREE

THE NEXT FEW WEEKS OF SCHOOL FLEW BY FASTER THAN Laurel would ever have imagined after those first awkward days. She felt lucky that she'd met David; they hung out often at school, and she shared a class with Chelsea too. She never ate lunch alone and felt like she had gotten to the point where she could call Chelsea and David her friends. And the classes were okay. It was different to be expected to learn at the same speed as everyone else, but Laurel was getting used to it.

She was also getting used to Crescent City. It was bigger than Orick, of course, but there was still plenty of open space and none of the buildings were more than about two stories high. Tall pine and broad-leafed trees grew everywhere, even in front of the grocery store. The grass on the lawns was thick and green, and flowers blossomed on the vines that crawled over most of the buildings.

One Friday in September, Laurel ran right into David as she ducked through the doorway of her Spanish class, her last class of the day.

"Sorry," David apologized, steadying her with a hand on her shoulder.

"It's okay. I wasn't paying attention."

Laurel met David's eyes. She smiled shyly, until she realized she was standing in his way.

"Oh, I'm sorry," Laurel said, moving away from the doorway.

"Um, actually, I was . . . I was looking for you."

He seemed nervous. "Okay. I just have to . . ." She held up her book. "I need to put this in my locker."

They walked to Laurel's locker, where she stowed her Spanish book, then she looked expectantly at David.

"I was just wondering if you wanted to, maybe, hang out with me this afternoon?"

Her smile remained on her face, but she felt nerves settle into her stomach. So far their friendship had been confined completely to school; Laurel suddenly realized she wasn't entirely sure what David liked to do when he wasn't eating lunch or taking notes. But the possibility of finding out held sudden appeal. "What are you doing?"

"There're some woods behind my house—since you like to be outdoors, I thought we could go for a walk. There's this really cool tree there that I thought you might like to see. Well, two trees, actually, but—you'll understand when you see it. If you want to, I mean."

"Okay."

"Really?"

Laurel smiled. "Sure."

"Great." He looked down the hall toward the back doors. "It's easier if we go out the back way."

Laurel followed David through the crowded hallway and out into the brisk September air. The sun was struggling to break through the fog, and the air was chilly and heavy with humidity.

The wind blew in from the west, bringing the salty tang of the ocean with it, and Laurel breathed deeply, enjoying the fall air as they entered a quiet subdivision about half a mile south of Laurel's house. "So you live with your mom?" she asked.

"Yep. My dad split when I was nine. So my mom finished up school and came here."

"What does she do?"

"She's a pharmacist down at the Medicine Shoppe."

"Oh." Laurel laughed. "That's ironic."

"Why?"

"My mom's a master naturopath."

"What's that?"

"It's someone who basically makes all their medicine out of herbs. She even grows a bunch of her own stuff. I've never had any drugs, not even Tylenol."

David stared. "You're kidding me!"

"Nope. My mom makes stuff that we use instead."

"My mom would freak. She thinks there's a pill for everything."

"*My* mom thinks doctors are out to kill you."

"I think both our moms could learn something from each other."

Laurel laughed. "Probably."

"So your mom never goes to the doctor?"

"Never."

"So were you, like, born at home?"

"I was adopted."

"Oh yeah?" He was quiet for a few moments. "Do you know who your real parents are?"

Laurel snorted. "Nope."

"Why is that funny?"

Laurel bit her lip. "Promise not to laugh?"

David raised his hand in mock seriousness. "I swear."

"Someone put me in a basket on my parents' doorstep."

"No way! You're totally messing with me."

Laurel raised an eyebrow at him.

David gaped. "Honest?"

Laurel nodded. "I was a basket child. I wasn't really a baby, though. I was, like, three and my mom says I was kicking and trying to get out when they answered the door."

"So you were a kid? Could you talk?"

"Yeah. Mom said I had this funny accent that stuck around for about a year."

"Huh. Didn't you know where you came from?"

"Mom says I knew my name but nothing else. I didn't know where I was from or what happened or anything."

"That is the weirdest thing I've ever heard."

"It made for a huge legal mess. After my parents decided they wanted to adopt me, they had a private investigator looking for my birth mother and all sorts of stuff about temporary custody and whatever. Took over two years before everything was final."

"Did you live in a foster home or something?"

"No. The judge my parents worked with was pretty cooperative, so I got to live with them through the whole process. A social worker came out to see us every week, though, and my parents weren't allowed to take me out of the state till I was seven."

"Weird. Do you ever wonder where you came from?"

"I used to. But there are no answers, so it gets frustrating to think about after a while."

"If you could find out who your real mom is, would you?"

"I don't know," she said, pushing her hands into her pockets. "Probably. But I like my life. I'm not sorry I ended up with my mom and dad."

"That's so cool." David gestured toward a driveway. "This way." He glanced up at the sky. "It looks like it'll rain soon. Let's drop our bags and hopefully we'll have time to see the tree."

"Is this your house? It's pretty." They were passing in front of a small white house with a bright red door; multicolored zinnias filled a long bed that ran along the front of the house.

"Should be," David said, turning up the front walk. "I spent two weeks this summer painting it."

They dropped off their bags by the front door and walked into a neat and simply decorated kitchen. "Can I get you something?" David asked, walking into the kitchen and opening the fridge. He pulled out a can of Mountain Dew and grabbed a box of Twinkies from the cupboard.

Laurel forced herself not to wrinkle her nose at the Twinkies and looked around the kitchen instead. Her eyes found a fruit bowl. "Can I have one of those?" she asked, pointing to a fresh green pear.

"Yeah. Grab it and bring it along." He held up a water bottle. "Water?"

She grinned. "Sure."

They pocketed their snacks and David pointed toward the back door. "This way." They walked to the back of the house and he opened the sliding door.

Laurel stepped out into a well-kept, fenced backyard. "Looks like a dead end to me."

David laughed. "To the untrained eye, perhaps."

He approached the cinder-block fence, and with a quick, leaping bound, he pulled himself to the top and perched there.

"Come on," he said, holding out his hand. "I'll help you."

Laurel looked up at him skeptically but extended her hand. With surprisingly little effort, they hopped over the fence.

The tree line came right up to the fence, so with that one small jump they stood in a forest with damp, fallen leaves forming a thick carpet under their feet. The dense canopy hushed the sound of cars in the distance, and Laurel looked around appreciatively. "This is nice."

David looked up with his hands on his hips. "It is, I guess. I've never been a big outdoors person, but I do find a lot of different plants in here that I can look at under my microscope."

Laurel squinted up at him. "You have a microscope?" She snickered. "You really are a science geek."

David laughed. "Yeah, but everyone thought Clark Kent was a nerd too, and look how that turned out."

"You telling me you're Superman?" Laurel asked.

"You never know," David said teasingly.

Laurel laughed and looked down, suddenly shy. When she looked up, David was staring at her. The glade seemed even quieter as their eyes met. She liked the way he looked at her, his eyes soft and probing. As if he could learn more about her just by studying her face.

After a long moment he smiled, a little embarrassed, and tilted his head toward a faint path. "The tree's this way."

He led her on a path that wound back and forth, seemingly without purpose. But after a few minutes, he pointed to a large tree just off the path.

"Wow," Laurel said. "That *is* cool." It was actually two trees, a fir and an alder that had sprouted close together. Their trunks had merged and twisted, resulting in what looked like a tree that grew pine needles on one side and broad leaves on the other.

"I discovered it when we moved here."

"So . . . where's your dad?" Laurel asked, sliding her back down a tree and settling into a soft pile of leaves. She pulled the pear out of her pocket.

David made a low laugh in his throat. "San Francisco. He's a defense lawyer with a big firm."

"Do you see him very often?" she asked.

David joined her on the ground, his knee resting gently against her thigh. She didn't scoot away. "Every couple of months. He's got a private jet and he flies into McNamara Field and takes me back with him for the weekend."

"That's cool."

"I guess."

"You don't like him?"

David shrugged. "Well enough. But he's the one who left us, and he never tried to get more time with me or anything, so I just don't feel like a priority to him, you know?"

Laurel nodded. "I'm sorry."

"It's fine. We always have fun. It's just—kind of weird sometimes."

They sat in a peaceful silence for a few minutes, the tranquil clearing lulling them into a relaxed state. But then they both looked up as thunder rumbled across the sky.

"I'd better take you back. It's gonna pour soon."

Laurel stood and brushed herself off. "Thanks for bringing me here," she said, gesturing at the tree. "This is pretty cool."

"I'm glad you liked it," David said. He avoided her eyes. "But . . . that wasn't really the point."

"Oh." Laurel felt complimented and awkward all at the same time.

"This way," David said, his face coloring a little as he turned away.

They climbed back over the fence just as the first drops of rain began to fall. "Do you want to call your mom to come pick you up?" David asked once they were back in the kitchen.

"Nah, I'll be fine."

"But it's raining. I should walk you."

"No, it's fine. Really, I like walking in the rain."

David paused for a second, then blurted, "Then can I call you? Maybe tomorrow?"

Laurel smiled. "Sure."

"Good." But he didn't move from the kitchen doorway.

"Door's that way, right?" she asked, as politely as possible.

"Yeah. It's just, I can't call you without your number."

"Oh, sorry." She pulled out a pen and scribbled her number down on a notebook beside the phone.

"Can I give you mine?"

"Sure."

Laurel started to open her bag, but David stopped her. "Don't worry about that," he said. "Here."

David held her hand and scrawled his number across her palm.

"This way you won't lose it," he said sheepishly.

"Great. Talk to you later." She flashed him a warm grin before letting herself out into the heavy drizzle.

Once she was down the street just far enough that the house was out of sight, Laurel pushed back the hood of her jacket and lifted her face to the sky. She breathed deeply as the rain sprinkled on her cheeks and trickled down her neck. She started to stretch her arms out, then remembered the phone number. She buried her hands in her pockets and picked up her pace, smiling as the rain continued to fall softly on her head.

The phone was ringing as Laurel walked into her house. Her mom didn't seem to be home, so Laurel ran the last few steps to catch the call before the machine picked up. "Hello?" she said breathlessly.

"Oh, hey, you're home. I was just gonna leave a message."

"David?"

"Yeah. Hi. Sorry to call so soon," David said, "but I was thinking that we have that bio test next week and I thought maybe you'd like to come over tomorrow and study with me."

"Seriously?" Laurel said. "That would be awesome! I am so stressed about that test. I feel like I only know about half of the stuff."

"Great." He paused. "Not great that you're stressing over it, but great that—anyway."

Laurel grinned at his awkwardness. "What time?"

"Just whenever. I'm not doing anything tomorrow except chores for my mom."

"Okay. I'll call you."

"Great. I'll see you tomorrow."

Laurel said good-bye and hung up. She smiled as she bounded up the stairs, taking them two at a time.

FOUR

SATURDAY MORNING, LAUREL'S EYES FLUTTERED OPEN at sunrise. She didn't mind—she was a morning person, always had been. She usually woke about an hour before her parents and it gave her a chance to take a walk by herself and enjoy the sun on her back and the wind on her cheeks before she had to go spend hours indoors at school.

After pulling on a sundress, she grabbed her mom's old guitar from its case by the back door before slipping silently out to enjoy the crisp quiet of the early morning. Late September had chased away the bright, clear mornings and brought instead the fog that rolled off the ocean and lingered over the town until early afternoon.

She walked along a short path that snaked through her backyard. Despite the small size of the house, the lot was fairly large and Laurel's parents had talked of possibly adding on someday. The yard had several trees that shaded the house, and Laurel had spent almost a month helping her mom plant bunches of flowers and vines all along the exterior walls.

Their house was one in a line of homes, so they had neighbors on both sides, but like many of the homes in Crescent City, their backyard ran into undeveloped forest. Laurel usually took her walks into the twisting paths of the small glen and to the creek that ran through the middle of it, parallel to the line of houses.

Today she wandered down to the creek and sat on the bank. She pushed her feet into the chilly water that was clear and cool in the mornings before the water bugs and gnats ventured out and dotted the surface, looking for bits of food.

Laurel set her guitar on her knee and began to strum a few random chords, picking out a bit of a melody after a while. It was nice to fill the space around her with music. She'd started playing three years ago when she'd found her mom's old guitar in the attic. It was in dire need of new strings and some major tuning, but Laurel convinced her mom to get it fixed up. Her mom had told her the guitar was hers now, but Laurel still liked to think of it as her mom's; it made it seem more romantic. Like an old heirloom.

An insect landed on her shoulder and began to walk down her back. As Laurel swatted at it her fingers touched something. She stretched her arm back a little farther and felt for it again. It was still there; a round bump, just barely big enough to feel under her skin. She craned her neck but couldn't see anything past her shoulder. She touched it again, trying to figure out what it was. Finally she stood, frustrated, and headed back to the house in search of a mirror.

After locking the bathroom door, Laurel sat on the vanity, twisting until she could see her back in the mirror. She pulled the top of her sundress down and searched for the bump. She finally spotted it right between her shoulder blades— a tiny, raised circle that blended in with the skin around it. It was barely noticeable but definitely there. She poked it tentatively—it didn't hurt, but poking it did provoke a sort of tingling feeling. It looked like a zit. *That's comforting*, Laurel thought wryly. *In a completely non-comforting way.*

Laurel heard her mother's soft steps creak down the hall and poked her head out the bathroom door. "Mom?"

"Kitchen," her mom called with a yawn.

Laurel followed her voice. "I have a bump on my back. Could you look at it?" she asked, turning around.

Her mom pushed on it softly a few times. "Just a zit," she concluded.

"That's what I figured," Laurel said, letting the top of her dress snap back up.

"You don't really get zits." She hesitated. "Have you started . . . you know?"

Laurel shook her head quickly. "Just a fluke." Her voice was flat and her smile was sharp. "All part of puberty, like you always say." She turned and fled before her mother could ask any more questions.

Back in her room she sat on her bed, fingering the small bump. It made her feel strangely normal to get her first zit; like a rite of passage. She hadn't experienced puberty quite like the textbooks described it. She never got zits and, although her chest and hips had developed the way they were supposed to—a little early, actually—at fifteen and a half she still hadn't started her period.

Her mom always shrugged it off, saying that because they had no idea what her biological mother's medical history was, they couldn't be certain it wasn't a perfectly normal family trait. But she could tell that her mom was starting to get worried.

Laurel dressed in her usual tank top and jeans and started to pull her hair into a ponytail. Then she thought of the irritated blemishes she occasionally saw dotting other girls' backs in the locker room and left her hair down. Just in case the bump developed into something ugly later on.

Especially at David's house. That would suck.

Laurel grabbed an apple as she walked out the door and called good-bye to her mom. She was almost to David's house when she looked up and saw Chelsea jogging the other way. Laurel waved and called to her.

"Hey!" Chelsea said, smiling as her curls blew lightly around her face.

"Hi," Laurel said with a smile. "I didn't know you were a runner."

"Cross-country. Usually I practice with the team, but on Saturdays we're on our own. What are you doing?"

"I'm headed to David's," Laurel said. "We're going to study."

Chelsea laughed. "Well, welcome to the David Lawson fan club. I'm already president, but you can be treasurer."

"It's not like that," Laurel said, not completely sure she was telling the truth. "We're just going to study. I have a bio test on Monday that I'm totally going to blow without some serious intervention."

"He's just around the corner. I'll walk you there."

They rounded the corner and heard the mower. David didn't see them as they walked up and they both stood there, watching.

He was pushing a lawn mower through the thick grass, wearing only a pair of jeans and old tennis shoes. His chest and arms were long and wiry but corded with lean muscle—his skin was tanned from the sun and glistened with a light sheen of sweat as he moved almost gracefully in the gentle morning sunlight.

Laurel couldn't help but stare.

She'd seen guys running around without shirts countless times, but somehow this was different. She watched his arms flex as he reached a particularly thick patch of grass and had to force the mower to keep going. Her chest felt a little tight.

"I think I've died and gone to heaven," Chelsea said, not bothering to hide the appreciation in her eyes.

As if feeling them watching, David suddenly looked up and met Laurel's eyes. She dropped her chin and studied her feet.

Chelsea didn't even blink.

By the time Laurel looked up again, David was pulling on a shirt. "Hey, guys. You're up early."

"Is it early still?" Laurel asked. It was almost nine o'clock, after all. "Oh," she said, embarrassed, "I forgot to call."

David shrugged with a grin. "That's okay." He gestured at the lawn mower. "I'm up."

"Well, I gotta run," Chelsea said, her breathlessness back rather suddenly. "Literally." She turned so only Laurel could see her face and mouthed, "Wow!" before waving at them both and sprinting down the street.

David chuckled and shook his head as he watched her go. Then he turned to Laurel and pointed toward his house. "Shall we? Biology waits for no man."

After the tests were handed in on Monday, David turned to Laurel. "So, how bad was it, really?"

Laurel grinned. "Fine, it wasn't that bad. But only because of your help." They'd studied for about three hours on Saturday and had talked for another hour on Sunday night. Granted, the phone conversation had nothing to do with biology, but perhaps she had learned something by osmosis. Osmosis over the phone. Right.

He hesitated for just a second before saying, "We could make it a regular thing. Studying together, I mean."

"Yeah," Laurel said, liking the idea of more quiet "study" sessions with him. "And next time you could come to my house," she added.

"Great."

It was raining by the time class let out that day, so the group gathered under a small pavilion instead. Almost no one ate there because there were no picnic tables or cement underneath, but Laurel liked the bumpy patch of grass that never seemed to dry all the way—even with the roof overhead.

When it rained, most of the group stayed inside, but today David and Chelsea joined her as well as a guy named Ryan. David and Ryan threw bits of bread at each other and Chelsea commentated—critiquing their aim, throwing form, and inability to keep from hitting spectators.

"Okay, that one was on purpose," Chelsea said, picking up a piece of crust that had hit her square in the chest and flicking it back over to the guys.

"Nah, it was an accident," Ryan said. "You're the one who told me I couldn't hit *anything* I aimed for."

"Then maybe you should aim for me so I can be assured of not being assaulted," she shot back. She sighed and turned to Laurel. "I was *not* meant to live in northern California," she said, pushing her hair out of her face. "During the summer my hair does fine, but introduce a little rain and *bam*! It turns into this." Chelsea had long brown hair with a tinge of auburn that fell in ringlets down her back. Soft, silky ringlets on sunny days, and jumping, coarse ringlets that bounced out of control around her face when the air was cold and humid—which was about half the time. She had light gray eyes that reminded Laurel of the ocean when the sun was just rising, and the waves had an endless quality to them in the murky half-darkness.

"I think it's pretty," Laurel said.

"That's because it's not yours. I have to use special shampoos and conditioners just to be able to brush through it every day." She looked over at Laurel and touched her straight, smooth hair for a second. "Yours feels nice; what do you use?"

"Oh, just whatever."

"Hmm." Chelsea touched her hair one more time. "Do you use a leave-in conditioner? That usually works the best with mine."

Laurel took a breath and let it out noisily. "Actually . . . I don't put anything on it. Any kind of conditioner makes my hair really slick and oily-feeling. And if I use shampoo, it makes my hair really, really dry—even the moisturizing kind."

"So you just don't wash it?" The idea was apparently beyond foreign to Chelsea.

"I rinse it really well. I mean, it's clean and everything."

"But no shampoo at all?"

Laurel shook her head and waited for a skeptical comment, but Chelsea just muttered, "Lucky," and turned back to her lunch.

That night Laurel examined her hair closely. Did she need to wash it? But it looked and felt the same as it always did. She turned her back to the mirror and poked and prodded the bump. It had been a tiny thing on Saturday morning, but over the weekend it had grown pretty big. "Hell of a first zit," Laurel grumbled to her reflection.

The next morning, Laurel woke up to a dull tingling between her shoulder blades. Trying not to panic, she hurried into the bathroom and craned her neck to look at her back in the mirror.

The bump was bigger around than a quarter!

This was no zit. She touched it carefully, and a strange tingling sensation lingered everywhere her fingers brushed. In a panic she clutched her nightgown to her chest and ran down the hall to her parents' room. She had just raised her hand to knock when she forced herself to stop and take a few breaths.

Laurel looked down at herself and suddenly felt very foolish. What was she thinking? She was standing in the hallway in little more than her underwear. Mortified, she stepped away from her parents' door and crept back to the bathroom, shutting the door as quickly and quietly as she could. She turned her back to the mirror again and studied the lump. She turned to view it from a few different angles until she convinced herself it wasn't nearly as big as she'd thought.

Laurel had been raised on the idea that the human body knew how to take care of itself. Most things—if left alone—would clear up by themselves. Both her parents lived that way. They never went to the doctor, not even for antibiotics.

"It's just a humongous zit. It will go away on its own," Laurel told her reflection, her tone sounding exactly like her mother's.

She dug into her mother's drawer and found a tub of the salve her mom made every year. It had rosemary, lavender, tea-tree oil, and who knew what else in it, and her mom put it on everything.

It couldn't hurt.

Laurel scooped up a fingerful of the sweet-smelling salve and began rubbing it on her back. Between the tingle of her hands irritating the bump and the burn of the tea-tree oil, Laurel's back was on fire as she pulled her nightgown over her head and, with her shoulders pressed to the wall, scooted to her room.

She chose a loose-fitting baseball-style T-shirt with cap sleeves and a full back for today. Most of her tanks would *probably* conceal the bump, but Laurel didn't want to take any chances. This thing couldn't get much bigger without becoming all gross, and when it did, Laurel would rather have it hidden beneath a shirt. It tingled every time anything brushed against it—her long hair, the T-shirt as she pulled it over her head—and, of course, every time she touched it, trying to remind herself it was real. By the time she headed downstairs, she was convinced every nerve in her body was connected to the bump.

By the time Thursday rolled around, Laurel could no longer deny that whatever this thing was on her back, it wasn't a zit. Not only had it continued growing the last two days, it seemed to be growing *faster*. That morning it was the size of a golf ball.

Laurel had come down to breakfast determined to tell her parents about the weird bump. She'd even taken a breath and opened her mouth to just blurt it out. But at the last second she'd wimped out and simply asked her dad to pass the cantaloupe.

Between the T-shirts she'd been wearing the last few days and keeping her long hair loose, no one had noticed the bump yet, but it was only a matter of time—especially if it kept getting bigger. *If*, Laurel repeated to herself, *if it gets bigger. Maybe Mom's stuff did the trick.*

She'd been putting salve on it for three days straight now, but it didn't seem to be doing much. But then, something that grew this big and fast couldn't be something that a little tea-tree oil could fix, could it? Maybe it was a tumor. Laurel was sure she'd read news stories about people having spinal tumors. Laurel took in a sharp breath. A tumor made too much sense.

"Hello? Are you even listening to me?" Chelsea's voice cut through Laurel's thoughts and she turned her face to her friend.

"What?"

Chelsea just laughed. "I didn't think so." Then quieter, "Are you okay? You were really spaced."

Laurel looked up and for a second couldn't remember which class she was headed to. "I'm fine," she muttered irritably. "Just thinking."

Chelsea scrutinized her face for a few seconds before one skeptical eyebrow poked up. "Okay."

David fell into step beside them, and when Chelsea peeled off to head to her own class Laurel tried to get ahead of him. He reached out and pulled her back. "Where's the fire, Laury? It's still three minutes to the bell."

"Don't call me that," she snapped before she could stop herself.

David's mouth bounced shut and he didn't say anything else as the flow of people slid around them.

Laurel searched for words of apology, but what was she supposed to say? *Sorry, David, I'm just on edge because I might have a tumor.* Instead she blurted, "I don't like nicknames."

David had already pasted on his brave smile. "I didn't know. I'm sorry." He ran his fingers through his hair. "Did you . . ."

His voice trailed away and he seemed to change his mind. "Come on. I'll walk you to class."

She felt awkward walking beside him now. She turned to him when they reached her class and waved. "See ya."

"Laurel?"

She turned back around.

"What are you doing on Saturday?"

She hesitated. She'd hoped that she and David could do something again. And until this morning, she'd been trying to come up with a casual way to ask. But maybe it wasn't such a good idea.

"I was thinking a bunch of us could get together and have a picnic and maybe a bonfire. I know this great spot on the beach. Chelsea said she'd come, and Ryan and Molly and Joe. And a couple other people said maybe."

Food, sand, and a smoky fire. None of those sounded fun.

"It's a little cold, so we can't really swim, but . . . you know. Someone usually gets pushed in. It's fun."

Laurel's fake smile melted away. She hated the feeling of salt water on her skin. Even after a shower she could still feel it—as if the salt had absorbed into her pores. The last time she'd gone swimming in the ocean, years ago, she'd been sluggish and tired for days afterward. And there would be no way of hiding her bump—or whatever it was—in a bathing suit, either.

She shuddered as she wondered how big it would be in two days! She couldn't go, even if she wanted to. "David, I—" She hated turning him down. "I can't."

"Why not?" David asked.

She could say she had to work at the bookstore—until the last couple of weeks she'd spent pretty much every Saturday down there helping her dad—but she couldn't bring herself to lie. Not to David. "I just can't," she mumbled, and ducked through the doorway without saying good-bye.

By Friday morning the bump was the size of a softball. It was definitely a tumor. Laurel didn't even bother to go in the bathroom to look. She could feel it.

No T-shirt was going to hide this.

Laurel had to dig into the back of her closet to find a fluffy blouse that would at least camouflage the lump. She waited in her room till it was time to go to school, then raced downstairs and out the door with only a yell of "Good morning" and "Good-bye," to her parents.

The rest of the day dragged by interminably. The bump tingled all the time now, not just when she touched it. It was all she could think about, like a persistent buzz in her head. She didn't talk to anyone at lunchtime and felt bad about that, but she couldn't concentrate on anything while her back was tingling so much.

By the time her last class finally ended, she had given the wrong answer four times when she was called on. The questions had gotten progressively easier—as if Señora Martinez were trying to give her a chance to redeem herself—but her teacher may as well have been speaking Swahili. As soon as the bell sounded, Laurel was out of her seat and heading to the door ahead of everyone else. And definitely before Señora Martinez could corner her about her abysmal performance.

She saw David and Chelsea chatting by Chelsea's locker, so she headed the other way and hurried toward the back doors, hoping neither of them would turn and recognize her from behind. As soon as she'd escaped the school, she headed across the football field, not sure where to go in the still-unfamiliar town. As she walked, she couldn't shake her growing fear. *What if it's cancer? Cancer doesn't just go away. Maybe I should tell Mom.*

"Monday," Laurel whispered under her breath as the cold air whipped at her hair. "If it's not gone by Monday, I'll tell my parents."

She climbed the bleachers, her feet pounding on each metal step, until she reached the top. She stood against the railing, looking out over the tops of the trees at the western skyline. Being so far above her surroundings made her feel separate and apart. It was fitting.

Her head shot up as she heard footsteps behind her. She turned to see David's rather embarrassed face. "Hey," he said.

Laurel said nothing as relief and annoyance warred in her mind. Relief was winning.

He waved his hand at the bench she was standing on. "Can I sit?"

Laurel stood still for a moment, then sat on the bench and patted the spot beside her with a slight smile.

David sat down gingerly as if not trusting her invitation. "I didn't really mean to follow you," he said as he leaned forward with his elbows on his knees. "I was going to wait for you at the bottom, but . . ." He shrugged. "What can I say? I'm impatient."

Laurel said nothing.

They sat in silence for a long time. "Are you okay?" David asked, his voice unnaturally loud as it bounced off the empty metal benches.

Laurel felt tears burn her eyes but forced herself to blink them back. "I'll be fine."

"You've just been so quiet all week."

"Sorry."

"Did . . . did I do something?"

Laurel's head lifted sharply. "You? No, David. You . . . you're great." Guilt settled over her. She forced a smile. "I just had an off day, that's all. Give me the weekend to get over it. I'll feel better on Monday. I promise."

David nodded and the silence returned, heavy and awkward. Then he cleared his throat. "Can I walk you home?"

She shook her head. "I'm going to stay here awhile. I'll be all right," she added.

"But . . ." He didn't continue. He just nodded, then stood and started to walk away. Then he turned. "If you need anything, you know my number, right?"

Laurel nodded. She had it memorized.

"Okay." He shifted his weight from foot to foot. "I'm leaving now."

Just before he passed out of sight, Laurel called to him. "David?"

But when he turned to her, his face so frank and open, she lost her nerve. "Have fun tomorrow," she said lamely.

His face fell a little, but he nodded and continued walking away.

That night Laurel sat on the vanity in her bathroom staring at her back. Tears slid down her cheeks as she again smeared salve all over it. It hadn't done anything before, and logic told her it wouldn't do anything this time—but she had to try something.

FIVE

SATURDAY MORNING DAWNED COOL, WITH ONLY A light mist that the sun would probably burn off by noon. Laurel predicted a 100 percent chance of everyone at the bonfire diving or being pushed into the chilly Pacific water, and was doubly grateful she had bowed out. She lay in bed for several minutes watching the sunrise with its blended hues of pink, orange, and a soft, hazy blue. Most people enjoyed the beauty of a sunset on a regular basis, but to Laurel, it was sunrise that was truly breathtaking. She stretched and sat up, still facing the window. She thought of the percentage of people in her small town who were sleeping through this incredible sight. Her father, for one. He was an infamous sleeper and rarely rose before noon on Saturday—or Sleepday, as he called it.

She smiled at that thought, but reality trickled in all too soon. Her fingers walked over her shoulder and her eyes flew open wide. She bit off a shriek as her other hand joined the first, trying to confirm what she was feeling.

The bump was gone.

But something else had replaced it. Something long and cool.

And *much* bigger than the bump had been.

Cursing herself for not being one of those girls with a mirror in her room, Laurel craned her neck, trying to see over her shoulder, but she could only catch rounded edges of something white. She threw back the thin bedsheet and ran to her door. The knob turned silently and Laurel opened the door a tiny crack. She could hear her father snoring, but sometimes her mother got up early and she was very quiet. Laurel let her door swing open—consciously grateful, for the first time in her life, for well-oiled hinges—and slid down the hall toward the bathroom with her back to the wall. As if that was going to help.

Her hands were unsteady as she pushed the bathroom door closed and fumbled with the lock. Only when she heard the bolt click into place did she let herself breathe again. She leaned her head against the rough, unfinished wood and forced her breathing to slow. Her fingers found the light switch and she flipped it on. Taking a deep breath, she blinked away the dark spots and stepped toward the mirror.

She didn't even have to turn to see the new development. Long, bluish-white forms rose over both shoulders. For a moment Laurel was mesmerized, staring at the pale things with wide eyes. They were terrifyingly beautiful— almost too beautiful for words.

She turned slowly so she could see them better. Petal-like strips sprouted from where the bump had been, making a gently curved four-pointed star on her back. The longest petals—fanning out over each shoulder and peeking around her waist—were more than a foot long and as wide as her hand. Smaller petals—about eight or nine inches long—spiraled around the center, filling in the leftover space. There were even a few small green leaves where the enormous flower connected to her skin.

All of the petals were tinged a dark blue at the center that faded to the softest sky blue in the middle and white at the ends. The edges were ruffled and looked eerily like the African violets her mother painstakingly grew in their kitchen. There must have been twenty of the soft, petal-like strips. Maybe more.

Laurel turned her front to the mirror again, her eyes on the hovering petals that floated beside her head. They looked almost like wings.

A loud rap on the door snapped Laurel out of her trance. "Done yet?" her mother asked sleepily. Laurel's fingernails bit into her palm as she stared in horror at the huge white things. They were pretty, sure, but who in the world grew an enormous flower out of their back? This was ten—no—a *hundred* times worse than the bump. How was she going to hide it?

Maybe the petals would just pluck off. She grabbed one of the oblong strips and yanked on it. Pain radiated down her spine and she had to bite her cheek hard to stifle a scream. But she couldn't stop the whimper that escaped from between her teeth.

Her mother knocked again. "Laurel, are you okay?"

Laurel took several deep breaths as the pain faded to a dull throb and she regained her power of speech. "I'm fine," she said, her voice shaking a little. "Just a minute." Her eyes swept the room looking for something useful. The thin, strappy nightgown she was wearing would be no help at all. She grabbed her oversized towel and threw it over her shoulders, pulling it close around her. After a quick check in the mirror to make sure there were no gigantic petals in sight, Laurel opened the door and forced a smile at her mother. "Sorry I took so long."

Her mom blinked. "Did you take a shower? I didn't hear the water running."

"It was short." Laurel hesitated. "And I didn't get my hair wet," she added.

But her mother wasn't paying much attention. "Come on down when you're dressed and I'll make you some breakfast," she said with a yawn. "It looks like it's going to be a beautiful day."

Laurel skirted past her mother into the safety of her own room. She didn't have a lock on her door, but she wedged a chair under the doorknob like she'd seen people do in movies. She looked at the setup dubiously. It didn't look like it would keep much out, but it was the best she could do.

She let the towel fall from her shoulders and examined the crushed petals. They were a tad rumpled, but they didn't hurt. She pulled one long piece over her shoulder and examined it. The huge bump was one thing, but what was she going to do about *this*?

She sniffed at the white thing, paused, and sniffed again. It smelled like a fruit blossom but stronger. A *lot* stronger. The intoxicating scent was starting to fill the room. At least the huge thing didn't stink. She'd have to tell her mom she got a new perfume or something. Laurel inhaled again and wished she *could* find something that smelled this good at the perfume counter.

As the enormity of the situation crashed over Laurel, the room seemed to spin beneath her. Her chest felt tight as she tried to consider what to do.

The most important thing first; she had to hide it.

Laurel opened her closet and stood in front of it, looking for something to help her hide an enormous flower growing out of her back, but that hadn't exactly been her first priority when she'd gone clothes shopping in August. Laurel groaned at the closet full of light, thin blouses and sundresses. Hardly made for hiding *anything*.

She sifted through her clothes and grabbed a few tops. After checking to make sure the coast was clear, Laurel ran to the bathroom, swearing she would get to a store today and buy a mirror for her room. The door closed a little harder than she intended, but though she stood next to it with her ear pressed against the cool wood for several seconds, she didn't hear any response from her mother.

The first top wouldn't even fit over the enormous flower thing. She stared at it in the mirror. There had to be another way.

She grabbed as many of the long, white petals as she could and tried wrapping them around her shoulders. That didn't work very well. Besides, she didn't really want to wear sleeves for the rest of her life—however long that might be.

She pulled them around under her arms and wrapped them around her waist instead. That worked better. *Much* better. She grabbed a long silk scarf off one of the hangers and wrapped it around her waist, securing the petals to her skin. Then she buttoned her shorts up over part of the scarf. It still didn't hurt, but she felt confined and smothered.

Still, it was better than nothing. She picked a lightweight, peasant-style blouse and threw it over the whole thing. Then, with trepidation, she turned to look in the mirror.

Pretty impressive, if she did say so herself. The fabric of the blouse was bunchy anyway, so you couldn't tell anything was underneath. Even from the side the bulge down her back was only barely noticeable and if she brushed her hair down over it, no one would be able to tell. One small problem solved.

A hundred big ones left.

This was way more than some strange manifestation of puberty. Mood swings, disfiguring acne, even periods that went on for months were at least semi-normal. But growing oversized flower petals out of your back from a zit the size of a softball? This was something else entirely.

But what? This was the kind of stuff you saw in cheap horror movies. Even if she did decide to tell someone, who would believe her? Never, even in her worst nightmares, had she imagined something like this could happen to her.

This was going to ruin everything. Her life, her future. It was like everything was washed away in an instant.

The bathroom suddenly felt too warm. Too small, too dark, too . . . too *everything*. Desperate to get away from the house,

Laurel scooted through the kitchen, grabbed a can of soda, and opened the back door.

"Going for a walk?"

"Yeah, Mom," she said without turning around.

"Have fun."

Laurel made a noncommittal sound under her breath.

She stomped down the path toward the woods, paying no attention to the dew-speckled greenery around her. There was still a touch of fog on the western horizon where it rolled off the ocean, but the peak of the sky was blue and clear and the sun was making its way steadily to the top of the sky. It would indeed be a beautiful day. *Figures*. She felt like Mother Nature was mocking her. Her life was unraveling, yet everything around her was beautiful, as if to spite her.

She ducked behind a large cluster of trees, out of sight of both the road and her house; it wasn't enough, though. She kept going.

After a few more minutes, she stopped and listened for the sound of anyone—or anything—around her. Once she felt safe, she pushed the back of her shirt up and untied the confining scarf. A sigh escaped her lips as the petals whipped back into their original position on her back. It felt like being released from a tiny, cramped box.

A beam of sunlight shone down from a break in the trees above, making her silhouette stretch out on the grass in front of her. The outline of her shadow looked like an enormous butterfly with gauzy wings. And in the same strange way balloons cast shadows, the blackness had just a tinge of blue in it. She tried to make the wing-things move, but although she could feel them—feel every inch of them now, soaking in the rays of sunlight—she had no control over them. Something so life-shattering shouldn't be this beautiful.

She stared at the image on the ground for a long time, wondering what to do. Should she tell her parents? She had promised herself she'd tell them Monday if the bump wasn't gone.

Well, it *was* gone.

Pulling one of the long strips over her shoulder, Laurel ran her fingers down it. It was so soft. And it didn't hurt. *Maybe it will just go away*, she thought optimistically. That was what her mom always said. Eventually most things go away on their own. Maybe . . . maybe it would be okay.

Okay? The word seemed to fill her head, reverberating in her skull. *I have a humongous flower growing out of my spine. How is this supposed to be okay!*

As her emotions tumbled around like a hurricane, her thoughts suddenly centered on David. Maybe David could help her make sense of this. There had to be a scientific explanation. He had a microscope—a really good one, from what he said. Maybe he could look at a piece of this weird flower. He might be able to tell her what it was. And even if he told her he had no idea, she'd be no worse off than she was now.

She wrapped her scarf around the flower again and hurried into the house, almost running into her dad as he lumbered into the kitchen.

"Dad!" she said in surprise. Her nerves—already at the breaking point—stretched farther.

He leaned down and kissed the top of her head. "Morning, beautiful." He laid an arm across her shoulders, and Laurel sucked in a nervous breath and hoped he couldn't feel the petals through her shirt.

But then, her father rarely noticed anything before his second cup of coffee.

"Why are you up?" she asked, a slight quaver in her voice.

He groaned. "I have to go open the store. Maddie needed the day off."

"Sure," Laurel said absently, trying not to see this change in the normal routine as some kind of bad omen.

He started to pull his arm away, then stopped and sniffed the air by her shoulder. Laurel froze. "You smell nice. You should wear that perfume more often."

Laurel nodded, praying her eyes weren't popping out of her head, and unwound herself from her dad's embrace. She hurried to pick up the cordless phone and then headed up the stairs.

In her room, she stared at the phone for a long time before her fingers managed to dial David's number. He picked up after the first ring. "Hello?"

"Hey," she said quickly, forcing herself not to hang up.

"Laurel. Hey! What's up?"

The seconds stretched into silence.

"Laurel?"

"Yeah?"

"You did call *me*."

More silence.

"Can I come over?" she blurted.

"Um, sure. When?"

"Right now?"

SIX

A FEW MINUTES LATER, LAUREL HAD HER CHAIR WEDGED under the doorknob again. She lifted the front of her shirt and pulled the end of one of the long white-and-blue strips free from the pink scarf. It looked so harmless, sitting there in her hand. She could almost forget it was attached to her back. She picked up her mother's nail scissors and studied the end of the petal. She probably didn't need too big of a piece. She eyed it again and selected a small curve at the ruffled tip.

She braced herself as she moved the shiny scissors into position. She wanted to close her eyes, but she was afraid she'd do even more damage that way. She counted silently. *One, two, three! . . . I meant to count to five.* After mentally calling herself a wimp, she positioned the scissors again. *One, two, three, four, five!* She pressed down and the scissors cut cleanly, flipping a small piece of white onto her bedspread. Laurel gasped and hopped up and down for a few seconds until the sting eased and she looked down at the cut edge. It wasn't bleeding, but it oozed a little bit of clear liquid. Laurel blotted the liquid away with a towel before smoothing the end back into the scarf. Then she wrapped the small white piece in a tissue and tucked it carefully into her pocket.

She bounced down the stairs trying to look as casual as possible. As she breezed by her mom and dad sitting at the table eating breakfast she said, "I'm going to David's."

"Hold it," her dad said.

Laurel stopped walking, but she didn't turn around.

"How about, 'May I go to David's?' "

Laurel turned with a forced smile on her face. "*May* I go to David's?"

His eyes didn't even leave the paper as he lifted his coffee to his mouth. "Sure. Have fun."

Laurel made her feet walk at a normal pace to the door, but as soon as it shut behind her, she ran to her bike and kicked off on her way. It was only a few blocks to David's, and soon Laurel was leaning her bike up against his garage. She stood on his doormat, focused on the bright red front door, and rang the doorbell before she could convince herself to turn tail and run home. She held her breath as she heard footsteps and the door opened.

It was David's mother. Laurel tried to hide the surprise on her face—after all, it was Saturday, and Laurel should have expected her to be home. But it was only the second time Laurel had met her. She was wearing a cute red tank top and jeans and her long, almost-black hair was loose and tumbling down her back in waves. She was the most unmotherly mom Laurel had ever met. In a good way.

"Laurel, how nice to see you."

"Hi," Laurel said nervously, then just stood there.

Luckily David came around the corner. "Hey," he said with a broad smile. "Come on back." He gestured Laurel down the hall. "Laurel needs a little help with some biology homework," he explained to his mother. "We'll just be in my room."

David's mom smiled at them both. "Do you need anything? A snack or something?"

He shook his head. "Just some quiet. It's a pretty intense assignment."

"I'll leave you alone, then."

The forest-green door to David's bedroom stood ajar; with a sweep of his arm, David ushered Laurel in. He bent down to pull out his biology binder and, after glancing down the hall to make sure his mom wasn't near, swung the door closed.

Laurel stared at the closed door. She'd been in his bedroom before, but he'd never closed the door. She noticed for the first time that his doorknob didn't have a lock. "Your mom wouldn't, like, listen at the door, would she?" Laurel asked, feeling silly even as the question escaped her mouth.

David snorted. "Never. I've earned a lot of privacy by not asking why a lot of my mom's dates don't leave until morning. I stay out of Mom's personal business; she stays out of mine."

Laurel laughed, a bit of her nervousness melting away now that she was actually here.

David pointed her to the bed and pulled up a chair for himself. "So?" he said after a few seconds.

It was now or never. "Actually, I was hoping you might look at something under your microscope for me."

Confusion flashed across David's face. "My microscope?"

"You said you had a really good one."

He recovered quickly. "Uh, okay. Yeah, sure."

Laurel dug in her pocket and pulled out the tissue. "Could you tell me what this is?"

He took the tissue, unwrapped it carefully, and looked down at the small white fragment. "It looks like a piece of a flower petal."

Laurel forced herself not to roll her eyes. "Could you look at it under your microscope?"

"Sure." He turned to a long table covered with various pieces of equipment—a few of which Laurel recognized from the bio lab. A very few. He pulled a gray cover off a shiny black microscope and grabbed a slide from a box of the small glass panes separated by sheets of thin tissue paper. "Can I cut this?" he asked, looking over at her.

Laurel shuddered, remembering cutting it off of herself less than half an hour earlier, and nodded. "It's all yours."

David cut a tiny piece and laid it on a slide, added a yellow solution, and dropped a cover slip over the top. He clipped the slide under the lens and fiddled with the dials as he peered into the eyepiece. The minutes passed slowly as he adjusted more dials and moved the slide around, looking at it from different angles. Finally he leaned back. "All I can really tell you for certain is that it's a piece of a plant and the cells are very active, which means it's growing. Flowering, I assume from the color."

"A piece of a plant? Are you sure?"

"Pretty sure," he said, looking back through the eyepiece.

"It's not part of an . . . animal?"

"Uh-uh. No way."

"How can you tell?"

He flipped through a few preprepared and labeled slides in another box. He selected one with a pinkish blob on it and went back through the process of focusing the microscope. "Come here," he said, standing and gesturing to his chair.

She took his place and leaned tentatively forward over the microscope.

"It's not going to bite you," he said with laugh. "Lean in close."

She did and opened her eyes to a pink world shot through with maroon lines and dots. "What am I supposed to be seeing?"

"I want you to look at the cells. They look pretty much like the pictures in our bio book. See how they're round or irregularly shaped? They look like blobs all connected together."

"Okay."

He slid the microscope back in front of him and switched in the yellowed slide he had prepared a few minutes before. After turning more dials, he scooted the microscope back to her. "Now look at this one."

Laurel put her forehead back down toward the eyepiece, far more afraid of this slide than the other. She hoped David wouldn't notice her hands shaking.

"Look at the cells now. They're all pretty square and very uniform. Plant cells are orderly, not like animal cells. And they have thick cell walls that are square like the ones you see here. That's not to say you never see squarish animal cells, but they wouldn't be nearly this uniform, and the cell walls would be much thinner."

Laurel sat back very slowly. This didn't make sense at all.

She had an actual plant growing out of her back! A mutant, parasite flower! She was the freak of all freaks, and if anyone ever found out, she'd be poked and prodded for the rest of her life. Her head started to spin and she felt like all the air had suddenly been sucked out of the room. Her chest constricted and she couldn't seem to draw in a big enough breath. "I gotta go," she mumbled.

"Wait," David said, holding on to her arm. "Don't go. Not when you're all freaked out like this." He tried to meet her eyes, but she refused to look at him. "I'm really worried about you. Can't you just tell me?"

She stared into his blue eyes. They were soft and earnest. It wasn't that she didn't think he could keep a secret; she was sure he would. She trusted him, she realized. She had to tell someone. Trying to muddle through on her own hadn't worked. *Really* hadn't worked.

Maybe he could understand. What did she have to lose?

She hesitated. "You won't tell *anyone*? Ever?"

"Never."

"Do you *swear*?"

He nodded solemnly.

"I need to hear you say it, David."

"I swear."

"There's no expiration date on this promise. *If* I tell you"— her emphasis on the *if* was unmistakable—"you can't ever tell anyone. *Ever.* Not in ten years or twenty or fifty—"

"Laurel, stop! I promise I won't tell anyone. Not unless you tell me to."

She stared at him. "It's not a piece of a flower, David. It's a piece of *me*."

David looked at her for a long time. "What do you mean, it's a piece of you?"

She'd passed the point of no return. "I got this lump on my back. That's why I've been so weird. I thought I had cancer or a tumor or something. But this morning this . . . this flower-thing bloomed out of my back. I have a *flower* growing out of my spine." She sat back with her arms folded over her chest, daring him to accept her now.

David stared with his mouth slightly open. He stood, hands at his waist, lips pressed together. He turned and walked to his bed and sat down with his elbows on his knees. "I'm going to ask this once, because I have to—but I won't ever ask again because I'll believe your answer, okay?"

She nodded.

"Is this a joke, or do you really believe what you just said?"

She shot to her feet and headed toward the door. It had been a mistake to come to him. A *huge* mistake. But before she could turn the doorknob, David stepped in front of her, blocking her way.

"Wait. I said I had to ask once. And I meant it. You swear to me that this isn't a joke, and I'll believe you."

She met his eyes and studied them carefully. What she saw there surprised her. It wasn't disbelief; it was uncertainty. He just didn't want to be the victim of a stupid prank. She wanted to prove she wouldn't do that—not to him.

"I'll show you," she said, but it sounded more like a question.

"Okay." His voice was tentative too.

She turned her back and fiddled with the knot in the scarf. As she released the enormous petals, she pushed her shirt up in the back so they could slowly rise to their normal position.

David gaped, his eyes wide and his mouth hanging open. "But how—you can't—they're—what the hell?"

Laurel gave him a tight-lipped grimace. "Yeah."

"Can I . . . can I look closer?" Laurel nodded and David stepped forward hesitantly.

"I won't bite," she said, but her tone was humorless.

"I know, it's just . . ." His face reddened. "Never mind." He stepped close behind her and stroked his fingers along the long, smooth surfaces. "Is this okay?" he asked.

Laurel nodded.

David prodded very gently all around the base where her skin melded into the small, green leaves. "There's not even a seam here. They flow right into your skin. It's the most incredible thing I've ever seen."

Laurel looked down at the floor, unsure of what to say.

"I can understand why you've been a little weird this week."

"You have no idea," Laurel said as she sat down on his bed and turned her back to the window so the sun could shine on the petals. The sunlight was strangely comforting.

David stared at her, his eyes full of questions. But he said nothing. He sat across the room from her, his eyes darting from her face to the tips of the petals sticking up over her shoulders, and back again. "Do you . . . ?" But he stopped.

After a minute he stood and paced a few times. "Could it . . . ?" He stopped speaking again and continued pacing.

Laurel rubbed her temples. "Please don't pace—it drives me nuts."

David immediately dropped into a chair. "Sorry." He studied her again. "You know this is impossible, right?"

"Trust me, I'm aware."

"I just . . . I know, seeing is believing, but I feel like if I blink a couple of times, I'll wake up . . . or my vision will suddenly clear or something."

"It's okay," Laurel said, focusing on her hands in her lap. "I'm still waiting to wake up too." She reached over her shoulder, grabbed a long petal, and studied it for a few seconds before letting it go. It bounced right back up to float beside her face.

"You're not going to tie them up again?" David asked.

"They feel better if I leave them loose."

"They *feel* better? You can feel them?"

Laurel nodded.

He looked over at the remaining bit she had cut off. "Did that hurt?"

"It stung pretty good."

"Can you . . . move them?"

"I don't think so. Why?"

"Well, if you can feel them, they might be more a part of you than just a . . . growth. Maybe it's not really flower petals, maybe they're more like—well, wings." He laughed. "Sounds really weird, huh?"

Laurel giggled. "Weirder than the fact that they're growing out of my back in the first place?"

"You've got a point." He let out a sigh as his eyes drifted back to the petals shimmering in the sun. "So . . . do you have to water it . . . them?"

"I don't know." Laurel snorted. "Wouldn't that be nice? Then I'd have an easy way to make it die."

David muttered something under his breath.

"What?"

David shrugged. "I think it's pretty, that's all."

Laurel glanced over her shoulders at the blue-tinged ruffly edges that spanned out on each side of her. "Do you?"

"Sure. If you went to school like that, I bet half the girls there would be insanely jealous."

"And the other half would be staring at me like I was a freak of nature. No, thank you."

"So what are you going to do?"

She shook her head. "I don't know what I *can* do. Nothing, I guess." She laughed humorlessly. "Wait for it to take over my body and kill me?"

"Maybe it will go away."

"Right, that's what I kept telling myself about the bump."

David hesitated. "Have you . . . told your parents?"

Laurel shook her head.

"Are you going to?"

She shook her head again.

"I think you should."

Laurel swallowed hard. "I've been thinking about that since

I woke up." She turned to look at him. "If you were a parent and your kid told you she had a giant flower growing out of her back, what would you do?"

David started to say something, then looked down at the ground.

"You would do the responsible thing. You'd take her to the hospital; she'd get poked and prodded and become a medical freak. That's what would happen to me. I don't want to be that kid, David."

"Maybe your mom could make something to help," David suggested halfheartedly.

"We both know this is way bigger than anything my mom could fix." She clasped her fingers in front of her. "Honestly, if this thing is going to kill me, I'd rather it did it in private. And if it goes away," she said with a shrug, spreading her hands out in front of her, "then it's better that no one else knew."

"Okay," David finally said. "But I think you need to reconsider if anything else happens."

"What *else* could happen?" Laurel asked.

"It could get bigger. Or spread."

"Spread?" She hadn't considered that.

"Yeah, like if leaves started growing across your back—or you got flowers . . . some other place."

She was quiet for a long time. "I'll think about it."

He chuckled dryly. "I guess I see now why you can't come to the beach today."

"Oh, shoot. I'm so sorry. I completely forgot."

"It's okay. It's not for another couple of hours." He was quiet for a while. "I'd invite you again, but . . ." He gestured at the petals, and Laurel nodded ruefully.

"Wouldn't exactly work."

"Can I come see you afterward, though? Just to make sure you're okay?"

Tears built up in Laurel's eyes. "Do you think I will be okay?"

David joined her on the bed and draped one arm around her shoulders. "I hope so."

"You don't know that though, do you?"

"No," David replied honestly. "But I certainly hope so."

She rubbed her arm across her face. "Thanks."

"So can I come?"

She smiled up at him and nodded.

SEVEN

LAUREL WAS LOUNGING ON THE COUCH WHEN THE doorbell rang. "I'll get it," she called. She opened the door and smiled at David in his black tee over bright yellow board shorts. "Hey," she said, stepping out onto the porch and pulling the door shut behind her. "How was the party?"

David shrugged. "Would've been more fun with you there." He hesitated. "How are you?"

Laurel looked down at the ground. "I'm okay. Same as this morning."

"Does it hurt or anything?"

She shook her head.

She felt his hand trace down her arm. "It'll be okay," he said softly.

"How's it supposed to be okay, David? I have a flower growing on my back. That is *not* okay."

"I meant, we'll figure something out."

She smiled sadly. "I'm sorry. You came over to be nice, and

I'm just—" Her voice cut off as bright headlights flashed across her face. She held a hand up to block the glare and watched a car pull into the driveway. A tall, broad-shouldered man stepped out and began walking toward them.

"This the Sewell residence?" His voice was low and gravelly.

"Yeah," Laurel said as he stepped into the light on the porch. Laurel wrinkled her nose involuntarily. His face didn't look quite right. The facial bones were sharp and rugged and his left eye drooped. His long nose looked like it had been broken a few times without being set correctly, and even though he wasn't sneering, his mouth was set in a permanent look of disappointment. His shoulders were enormously broad and the suit he was wearing looked out of place on his bulky form.

"Are your parents home?" the man asked.

"Yeah, just a sec." She turned slowly. "Um, come on in."

She held the door open and both the man and David stepped through. As the three of them stood in the entryway, the man sniffed, then cleared his throat. "You have a bonfire or something today?" he asked, looking critically at David.

"Yeah," David said. "Down at the beach. I was in charge of lighting it, and let's just say there was a lot of smoke before there was any fire." He laughed for a second, but when the man did not even smile, he fell silent.

"I'll go get them," Laurel said hurriedly.

"I'll help," David said, following her.

They walked into the kitchen, where Laurel's parents were having tea.

"There's a guy here to see you," Laurel said.

"Oh." Her dad set his teacup down and marked his place in his book. "Excuse me."

Laurel lingered in the doorway, watching her dad. David's hand was at the small of her back, and she hoped he wouldn't move it. It wasn't precisely that she was afraid, but she couldn't shake a hovering sense that something wasn't quite right.

"Sarah," her dad called. "Jeremiah Barnes is here."

Laurel's mom put her teacup down with a loud clatter and hurried past David and Laurel to the front door.

"Who's Jeremiah Barnes?" David asked under his breath.

"Realtor," Laurel answered. She looked around. "Come here," she said, grabbing David's hand. She pulled him to the stairs behind the couch where Mr. Barnes was taking a seat. She tiptoed up a few steps, just out of sight. She let go of David's hand, but as they sat, he laid his arm across the stair behind her. She leaned in a little, enjoying the feel of him beside her. It chased away a little of the unease that had been building since Mr. Barnes drove up.

"I hope you don't mind me just dropping by," Barnes said.

"Not at all," Laurel's mom said. "Could I get you a cup of coffee? Tea? Water?"

"I'm fine, thank you," Barnes said.

His deep voice set Laurel's whole body on edge.

"I had a few questions about the origins of the property before we submit our official offer," Barnes said. "I understand it is family land. How long has it been in your family?"

"Since the gold-rush days," Laurel's mom said. "My great-some-odd-grandfather claimed the land and built the first cabin there. Never found gold, though. Everyone in my family has lived there at one time or another ever since."

"No one ever tried to sell it?"

She shook her head. "Nope, just me. I imagine my mother's turning in her grave, but . . ." She shrugged. "As much as we hate to see it go, there are more important things."

"Indeed. Is there anything . . . unusual about the property?"

Laurel's parents looked at each other then shook their heads. "I don't think so," her dad said.

Barnes nodded. "Have you had any trouble with trespassers? Strangers trying to squat there? Anything like that?"

"Not really," Laurel's dad said. "We occasionally have people take walks across the land, and we see people here and there. But then, we're right up against Redwood National Park; we don't have a fence and we don't post any warning of property lines. I'm sure that if you did, you wouldn't have any trouble."

"I wasn't able to find out what your asking price is." Barnes left the unspoken question hanging in the air.

Laurel's dad cleared his throat. "It's been difficult to get a good appraisal on the land. We've had two appraisers out and both have managed to lose our file. It's been very frustrating. We'd prefer that you name your price and we'll go from there."

"Understandable." Barnes stood. "I hope to have my written offer to you within a week."

He shook hands with her parents, then left.

Laurel held her breath until she heard the car roar to life and back out of the driveway. David's arm loosened from around her and Laurel made her way down the stairs.

"Finally, Sarah," her dad said excitedly. "It's been almost six months since he first approached me. I was beginning to think I'd gotten all worked up over nothing."

"It would make things so much easier," Laurel's mom agreed. "It's not a done deal, though."

"I know, but it's so close."

"We've been close before. There was that one woman last summer who was so excited about the house."

"Yeah, real excited," Laurel's dad argued. "When we called her to check up on things she said, and I quote, 'What house?' She'd completely forgotten about it."

"You're right," her mom agreed. "Guess she wasn't *that* impressed."

"You're not seriously thinking of selling our land to him?" Laurel said vehemently.

Her parents turned to her with questioning eyes. "Laurel?" her mom said. "What's the matter?"

"Oh, come on. He was totally creepy."

Laurel's mom sighed. "You don't refuse a life-changing sale to someone just because they're not very charismatic."

"I didn't like him. He scared me."

"Scared you?" her dad asked. "What was scary about him?"

"I don't know," Laurel said, feeling a little cowed now that Mr. Barnes was gone. "He . . . he looked funny."

Her dad laughed. "Yeah. Probably a football player who took one too many hard hits. But you can't base your opinion on the way someone looks. Remember that whole book-and-cover thing?"

"Yeah, I guess," Laurel relented, but she wasn't convinced. There was something odd about him, something strange in his eyes. And she didn't like it.

Finally David cleared his throat. "I gotta head home," he said. "I just stopped by for a minute."

"I'll walk you out," Laurel said quickly, leading the way to the door.

Laurel took just a second to double-check that the driveway was empty before she stepped out onto the porch.

"Did he seem weird to you?" Laurel asked as soon as David closed the front door.

"The Barnes guy?" He waited a long moment, then shrugged. "Not really," he admitted. "He was kind of weird-looking, but I think it's mostly that nose. It's like Owen Wilson's. Probably got smashed playing football like your dad said."

Laurel sighed. "Maybe it's just me. I'm probably just being oversensitive because . . ." She gestured at her back. "You know."

"Yeah, that's what I wanted to talk to you about." David pushed his hands into his pockets, then withdrew them and crossed them over his chest. After a few seconds he changed his mind and shoved them back in his pockets. "I have to tell you, Laurel, this is the weirdest thing I've ever heard of. I can't pretend it's not."

Laurel nodded. "I know. I'm a total freak."

"No, you're not. Well . . . you know, kinda. But it's not you," he added hurriedly. "You just have this weird thing. And I . . .

I'll do what I can to help. Okay?"

"Really?" Laurel whispered.

David nodded. "I promise."

Grateful tears threatened, but Laurel forced them back. "Thanks."

"I have church with my mom tomorrow and then we're going out to eat in Eureka with my grandparents, but I'll be back in the evening and I'll give you a call."

"Great. And have fun."

"I'll try." He hesitated for a minute and looked like he was about to turn and leave. But at the last second, he stepped forward and hugged her.

Surprised, Laurel hugged him back.

She watched as David's bike disappeared into the murky dusk and stood looking after him for a long time after he was out of sight. She had been so frightened when she went to his house that morning. But she knew now that he had been the right person to tell. She smiled, then turned to head back inside.

Monday was Laurel's first day of school with the huge bloom on her back. She considered faking sick, but who knew how long the flower would stay? *Forever, maybe*, she thought with a shiver. She couldn't fake being sick every day. She met David in the front atrium before school and he assured her several times that he couldn't tell there was anything under her shirt. She took a deep breath and headed off to her first class.

At lunch, Laurel sat and watched David. The clouds broke for just a few moments, releasing a bright beam of sunlight, and Laurel noticed the way the sun shone on him—it glinted off the subtle highlights in his sandy brown hair and caught the tips of his eyelashes. She hadn't thought much before about how handsome he was, but the last few days, she'd found herself looking at him more and more, and twice already during lunch he'd turned and caught her. He was starting to provoke the butterflies-in-the-stomach feeling she'd always read about in books.

When no one was looking, Laurel held her own hand up to the sun. It didn't look quite the same. David's body had blocked out the sun entirely, and it came snaking around the sides. Her hand appeared to only block out part of the sun, and the light seemed to glow as if it had found some route through her skin. She shoved her hand in her pocket. She was getting paranoid now.

The petals around her waist were rather uncomfortable, and she longed to free them—especially with the bright sunlight that she knew would be so scarce in the coming months. But it was a discomfort she could—and would—deal with. She hoped the sun would reappear later this afternoon when she could sneak off for a walk.

Chelsea was home sick, so David walked with Laurel to her English class by himself.

"Hey, David?" she said.

"Yeah?"

"You want to take a little trip with me this afternoon? Me and my parents," she added.

David's face fell. "I can't."

"Why not?"

"I'm getting my driver's license in a few weeks and Mom's decided I need to work enough to pay for gas and insurance. She got me a job at the drugstore and I have to start today."

"Oh. You didn't tell me."

"I only found out yesterday. Besides"—he leaned in close—"your problems are a little bigger than mine at the moment."

"Well, good luck," Laurel said.

David sighed. "Yeah, nothing like a little nepotism to make all your coworkers like you." He laughed shortly. "Where are you going?"

"Down to my old house. My mom's been talking about nothing but the sale for the last two days. She's excited about it, but she's kind of having second thoughts too."

"Why? I thought they really wanted to sell."

"I thought so too. But Mom's getting sad about it. She grew up there. And her mom before that. And back and back. You know?"

"I think that's awesome. I wish you didn't have to sell."

"Me too," Laurel said. "Not that it's not great here," she said quickly. "I'm glad we moved. But I kinda like the idea of being able to go back and visit."

"Have you been back since you moved?"

"No. We've all been so busy getting the store going and moving in and, well, we just haven't had time. So Mom wants to visit and make sure she's really certain about selling and rake the leaves while we're at it. And wash the windows.

And Dad'll probably want to trim the hedges." She smiled with fake excitement. "It's gonna be fun, fun, fun," she said sarcastically.

David nodded, then looked at her more seriously. "I wish I could go," he said. "I really do."

Laurel looked down; his eyes were so intense. "Another time," she said earnestly, trying not to sound too disappointed.

"I hope so."

EIGHT

LAUREL'S HAIR WAS WILD AND TANGLED WHEN THEY arrived. It would take ages to brush out later, but it was worth the forty-five-minute drive in the old convertible with the wind whipping across her face. They pulled into the long driveway, and Laurel held her breath as it curved around a clump of trees and the cabin came into view.

The appearance of her old house was accompanied by a wave of nostalgia Laurel hadn't expected. The log cabin was small but quaint, nestled in a large circle of thick green grass surrounded by a rickety fence. Laurel had often missed her old home since moving but never as intensely as the moment it came into view for the first time in four months. For twelve years she'd lived in this house and on this land. She knew all the twisty paths through the vast forest behind the house and had spent hours wandering them. It wasn't precisely that she wished she lived there again, but she didn't want to let it go.

Her parents began unloading rakes and buckets and cleaning supplies. Laurel pulled her guitar from the backseat, and her mom laughed. "I love that you play that old thing."

"Why?"

"It just reminds me of when I used to play it back at Berkeley." She grinned at Laurel's dad. "When we first met. We were such hippies back then."

Laurel eyed her mom's long braid and her dad's Birkenstock sandals and gave a snort. "You're hippies *now*."

"Nah, this is nothing. We were *really* hippies back then." Her mom slipped one hand into her dad's, entwining their fingers. "I used to take that guitar to sit-ins. I'd play 'We Shall Not Be Moved' terribly off-key and everyone would bellow along. Remember that?"

Her dad smiled and shook his head. "The good ol' days," he said sarcastically.

"Aw, it was fun."

"If you say so," her dad relented, leaning in for a kiss.

"Do you mind if I wander a bit?" Laurel asked, slipping the strap of the guitar over her shoulder. "I'll come back in a while to help."

"Sure," her mom said as she dug through the trunk.

"See ya soon," Laurel said, already walking toward the back of the house.

The forest was filled with both broad-leaf and pine trees that shaded the soft green foliage carpeting the ground. Most of the tree trunks were covered with dark green moss that hid the rough bark. Everywhere you looked was green. It had rained lightly that morning and the sun was out, turning the millions of droplets of water into sparkling orbs that made every surface twinkle like sheets of emeralds. Paths twisted into the darkness between the trees, and Laurel slowly headed down one.

It was easy to imagine she was walking through hallowed ground—the ruins of some great cathedral from ages before memory. She smiled when she saw a moss-clad branch illuminated by a thin beam of sunshine and rubbed her hand across it so the glistening drops of water dripped from her fingers and caught the light as they fell to the ground.

When she had been out of her parents' sight for several minutes, Laurel slipped her guitar to the front and untied the scarf. With a sigh of relief, she lifted her shirt a bit to let the flower petals spring free. After being tied down most of the day, they ached to be released. The petals stretched out slowly like sore, cramped muscles as Laurel continued down the thin, leaf-strewn path. She heard the distant gurgle of a large stream and picked her way through the vegetation in its direction, finding it in just a few minutes and plopping down on a rock at its edge. She kicked off her flip-flops and let her toes dangle into the chilly water.

She'd always loved this stream. The water was so clear in the still current that you could see to the bottom and watch fish flit back and forth. Where it splashed over rocks in small waterfalls, it churned into a perfect white foam that looked like thick, frothy soap bubbles. The whole scene belonged on a postcard.

Laurel began picking out chords from her favorite Sarah McLachlan song. She hummed along quietly as the scent from the flower enveloped her.

After the first verse, a rustle off to her left made her head jerk up. She listened carefully and thought she heard soft whispers. "Mom?" she called tentatively. "Dad?"

She leaned the guitar against a tree and worked at the knot in the scarf where she'd tied it around her wrist. She'd better get the petals out of sight before her parents saw.

The long silk scarf refused to come loose from her wrist and she heard another rustle, louder than the first. Her eyes shot to the spot the sound had come from, just over her left shoulder. "Hello?"

Carefully, Laurel folded the soft petals down and wrapped them around her waist. She was about to secure them with the scarf when a figure stumbled out from behind a tree as though he had been pushed. He shot a nasty look at the tree for just a second before his face turned to Laurel. His agitation melted away and an unexpected warmth filled his eyes. "Hi," he said with a smile.

Laurel gasped and tried to back away, but her heel caught on a root and she fell, letting go of the petals to catch herself.

It was too late to conceal anything; they sprang up in full view.

"No, don't . . . ! Oh, dear. I'm sorry. Can I help you?" the stranger said.

Laurel looked up into deep-green eyes almost too vibrant to be real. A young man's face peered down at her as she lay splayed on the ground.

He extended his hand. "I really am sorry. We . . . I did make some noise. I thought you'd heard me." He smiled sheepishly. "I guess I was wrong." His face looked like a classic painting—cheekbones clearly defined under smooth, tanned skin that looked like it would fit in better on an L.A. beach than in a chilly, moss-covered forest. His hair was thick and black, matching the eyebrows and lashes framing his concerned eyes. It was rather long and damp—as though he hadn't gone inside when it started raining—and somehow he'd managed to dye just the roots the same brilliant green as his eyes. He had a soft, gentle smile that made Laurel's breath catch in her throat. It took her a few seconds to find her voice.

"Who are you?"

He paused and studied her with a strange, unflinching look in his eyes.

"Well?" Laurel prompted.

"You don't know me, do you?" he asked.

She was slow to answer. She felt like she *did* know him. There was a memory there, at the edge of her mind, but the harder she reached for it, the faster it slipped away. "Should I?" Her voice was guarded.

The probing gaze disappeared as abruptly as it had come. The stranger laughed softly—almost sadly—and his voice bounced off the trees, sounding more like a bird than a human. "I'm Tamani," he said, still holding a hand out to help her up. "You can call me Tam, if you like."

Suddenly aware that she was still lying on the damp ground where she had fallen, Laurel felt embarrassment flood over her. She ignored his hand and pushed herself to her feet, forgetting to hold onto her petals. With a sharp gasp she yanked her shirt down, wincing as the bloom crushed against her skin.

"Don't worry," he said. "I'll keep my distance from your blossom." He grinned and she felt like she was missing some in-joke. "I know whose petals I'm allowed to get into and whose I'm not." He inhaled deeply. "Mmmm. And fabulous as you smell, your petals are off-limits to me." He raised an eyebrow. "At least for now."

He lifted a hand to her face and Laurel couldn't move. He brushed some leaves out of her hair and glanced quickly up and down her frame. "You seem to be intact. No broken petals or stems."

"What are you talking about?" she asked, trying to conceal the petals peeking out from the bottom of her shirt.

"It's a little late for that, don't you think?"

She glared at him. "What are you doing here?"

"I live here."

"You don't live here," she said, confused. "This is *my* land."

"Really?"

Now she was flustered all over again. "Well, it's my parents' land." She held tight to the tail of her shirt. "And you're . . . you're not welcome here." How had his eyes gotten so intensely, impossibly green? *Contacts,* she told herself firmly.

"Aren't I?"

Her eyes widened as he took a step closer. His face was so confident, his smile so contagious, she couldn't step away. She was sure she'd never met anyone like him before in her life, but a sense of familiarity overwhelmed her.

"Who *are* you?" Laurel repeated.

"I told you; I'm Tamani."

She shook her head. "Who are you really?"

Tamani pressed a finger to her lips. "Shh, all in good time. Come with me." He took her hand and she didn't pull away as he led her deeper into the forest. Her other hand gradually forgot what it was doing and she let go of her shirt. The petals slowly rose until they were spread out behind her in all their beautiful glory. Tamani looked back. "There, that feels better, doesn't it?"

Laurel could only nod. Her mind felt fuzzy, and although somewhere in the back of her consciousness she suspected she should be bothered by all of this, it somehow didn't seem important. The only thing that mattered was following this guy with the alluring smile.

He brought her to a small clearing where the leaves above them parted, allowing a circle of sunlight to filter down through the branches onto a patch of grass dotted with spots of spongy green moss. Tamani sprawled in the grass and gestured for her to sit in the spot across from him.

Enraptured, Laurel just stared. His green-and-black hair hung in long strands that fell across his forehead, just shy of his eyes. He was dressed in a loose white shirt that looked homemade and similarly styled brown baggy pants that tied just below the knees. They were decidedly old-fashioned, but he made them seem as trendy as the rest of him. His feet were bare, but even the sharp pine needles and broken sticks along the path hadn't seemed to bother him. He was maybe six inches taller than her and moved with a catlike grace she'd never seen in another boy.

Laurel folded down into a cross-legged perch and looked over at him expectantly. The strange desire to follow him was slowly starting to fade, and confusion was working its way in.

"You gave us quite a scare, running off like that." His voice had a soft lilt—not quite British, not quite Irish.

"Like what?" Laurel asked, trying to clear her head.

"Here one day, gone the next. Where have you been? I was starting to panic."

"Panic?" She was too bewildered to argue or demand more information.

"Have you told anyone about that?" he asked, pointing over her shoulder.

She shook her head. "No—oh, yes. I told my friend David."

Tamani's face snapped into an unreadable slate. "Just a friend?"

Laurel's wits slowly began to trickle back in. "Yes . . . no . . . I don't think that's any of your business." But she said it quietly.

Small lines showed at the corner of Tamani's eyes, and for just an instant, Laurel thought she saw a flash of fear. Then he leaned back and his soft smile returned; she must have imagined it. "Perhaps not." He fiddled with a blade of grass. "But your parents don't know?"

Laurel started to shake her head, but the absurdity of the situation finally managed to get through. "No . . . yes . . . maybe—I shouldn't be here," she said sharply, rising to her feet. "Don't follow me."

"Wait," Tamani said, his voice panicked.

She pushed past a low-hanging branch. "Go away!"

"I have answers!" Tamani called.

Laurel paused and looked back. Tamani had risen up on one knee, his expression imploring her to stay.

"I have answers to all of your questions. About the blossom and . . . anything else."

She turned slowly, not sure if she should trust him.

"I'll tell you whatever you want to know," he said, his voice more quiet now.

Laurel took two steps forward and Tamani instantly relaxed. "You stay over there," Laurel said, pointing to the far side of the clearing. "And I'm going to sit over here. I don't want you to touch me again."

Tamani sighed. "Fair enough."

She settled into the grass again but stayed tense and alert, ready to run. "Okay. What is it?"

"It's a blossom."

"Will it go away?"

"My turn now; where did you go?"

"Crescent City. Will it go away?" she repeated, her voice sharper.

"Sadly, yes." He sighed forlornly. "And more's the pity."

"You're sure it goes away?" Laurel's hesitation disappeared as she clung to the good news he offered.

"Of course. You'll blossom again next year, but like all blossoms, they don't last forever."

"How do you know that?"

"My turn again. How far is this Crescent City?"

She shrugged. "Forty, fifty miles. Something like that."

"Which direction?"

"Nope, my turn. How do you know about this thing?"

"I'm just like you. We're the same kind."

"Then where is yours?"

Tamani laughed. "*I* don't blossom."

"You said you were my kind. If that's true, you should have one too."

Tamani leaned on one elbow. "I'm also a guy, in case you didn't notice."

Laurel felt her breath quicken. She was *very* aware that he was a guy.

"What direction?" he repeated.

"North. Don't you have a map?"

He grinned. "Is that your question?"

"No!" Laurel said, then glared at Tamani when he laughed. She felt her real question itching to be asked, but she was afraid of the answer. Finally she swallowed and asked quietly, "Am I turning into a flower?"

An amused smile ticked at the corner of Tamani's mouth, but he didn't laugh. "No," he said softly.

Laurel felt her whole body relax with relief.

"You've *always* been a flower."

"Excuse me?" she said. "Just what do you mean by that?"

"You're a plant. You're not human, never have been. Blossoming is only the most obvious manifestation," Tamani explained, more calm than Laurel thought he had any right to be.

"A plant?" Laurel said, not bothering to hide the disbelief in her voice.

"Yes. Not just any kind of plant, of course. The most highly evolved form of nature in the world." He leaned forward, his green eyes sparkling. "Laurel, you're a faerie."

Laurel's jaw clenched as she realized how stupid she'd been. Taken in by a handsome face, conned into letting him lead her far into the forest, and even half-believing his outrageous claims. She stood, her eyes flashing with anger.

"Wait," Tamani said, lunging forward to grab on to her wrist. "Don't go yet. I need to know what your parents are going to do with this land."

Laurel yanked her wrist away. "I want you to leave," she hissed. "If I ever see you here again, I *will* call the police." She turned and ran, tugging her shirt back down over the petals.

He called after her, "Laurel, I have to know. Laurel!"

She pushed herself to go faster. Nothing seemed more important than putting as much distance as possible between herself and Tamani, this strange person who stirred up so many confusing emotions within her.

When she reached the clearing where she'd been before following Tamani, Laurel paused for a few moments to wrap the petals back around her waist and secure them with the scarf. She picked up her guitar and lifted the strap over her back. As she did, her hand crossed a beam of sunlight. She paused and stuck her hand out again. Her wrist glittered with tiny specks of shimmering powder. *Great. He left some sort of residue on me. That's a stupid trick.*

When she got within sight of the cabin, she paused, her chest heaving. She looked at her wrist again and anger bubbled up inside of her as she rubbed at the glittery powder till all traces of it were gone.

NINE

THE NEXT DAY, LAUREL FELT LIKE A ZOMBIE. SHE didn't want to believe anything Tamani had said. But she couldn't help but think about it and wonder. Was it possible? Then she would get angry with herself for being ridiculous, and the whole cycle would start again.

David tried to catch her several times in the hallway, but she managed to duck into her classes ahead of him.

But she couldn't avoid him in biology.

He hurried to claim his usual seat beside her. "What's wrong?" he asked. "Is it spreading?" he whispered before she could turn away.

She shook her head and her hair fell around her face like a wall between them.

David scooted his chair a little closer as the rest of the class noisily took their seats. "Laurel, you've got to talk to me. You're going to drive yourself crazy holding everything in like this."

"I can't—" Her voice choked off as tears welled up in her eyes. "I can't talk right now."

David nodded. "Can we talk after school?" he whispered as Mr. James started the class.

Laurel nodded and tried to subtly wipe away her tears without attracting attention.

David patted her leg under her desk, then started doodling in his notebook. Laurel wished he'd take a few more notes for her to copy.

The day dragged by as Laurel went back and forth in her mind, berating herself for promising to tell David, then being relieved that she had someone to tell. She wasn't sure how to even start. How does one just come out and say, "Oh, hey, I might be a mythological creature"?

"I'm not," Laurel whispered under her breath. "It's stupid."

But she couldn't quite convince herself.

After school, she and David walked toward his house. David seemed to sense she wasn't quite ready to talk, so they walked in silence.

He was especially gentle as he helped her over his back fence, his hand studiously avoiding her back. He held onto her arms when she jumped down from the fence, and once she'd landed and was steady, he still didn't pull his hands away.

Laurel felt the urge to curl herself up against his chest and just forget about all this nonsense. But she knew that was impossible. He stared at her unblinkingly until she shoved her hands into her pockets and forced herself to turn away.

"This way," David said, taking the lead as they walked out to the twisted tree.

Laurel looked up at the dense canopy of foliage above her. It was October now and the leaves were in a perfect state of half-transformation. The edges were orange and red—with some branches boasting yellows and pale browns, the centers still fighting to remain green. It made the forest beautiful with the blends of colors, but Laurel was a little sad to see the green lose its battle to the more flamboyant hues.

It made her think of her own blossom. Would it slowly die like the leaves? *Would it hurt?* she thought suddenly with a clench of fear. Even if it did, it would be worth it just to have it gone. But Tamani had also said she would grow another one next year. She hoped most of what he said was true. The rest of it . . . she didn't even want to think about it.

But her thoughts kept wandering back anyway. And although she hated to admit it, it wasn't just because the information was so bizarre; it was because of Tamani himself. He had shaken her—introduced emotions she'd never experienced. That sharp sense of wanting someone without even knowing them—she'd never felt that way before. Not with anyone. It was exciting and exhilarating but also a little scary. A part of her that seemed totally out of her control. She wasn't sure she liked it.

He was so . . . was beautiful the right word? It seemed like the right word. Whatever he was, she could hardly pull her eyes away from him. That's the part that really made her wonder if he had been some sort of mirage. A super-realistic dream.

She glanced down at her wrist where she'd rubbed the glittering powder away. That had been real. She'd found a small streak of it on her jeans when she got home. He had to be real.

And then there was the nagging suspicion that she'd seen him before. She couldn't shake it. And he'd certainly acted as if he knew her. Why would he know her? *How* could he know her? The whole situation was making her head spin.

"So, what happened yesterday?" David finally asked as they came into sight of the tree.

Laurel groaned, thinking how silly this had all started to seem *after* she'd agreed to talk to David. "It's so ridiculous, David, I don't know why I'm so worked up over it. Probably because it makes me feel stupid."

"Does it have to do with the, uh, flower?"

"Sort of, maybe. I don't know," Laurel said. Her words spilled out as she started to pace. "Only if it's true, and I can't believe that. I'm starting to think I made the whole thing up, like a dream I don't remember falling asleep for or something."

"You're not making any sense."

"Sense," Laurel said with a snort. "When I tell you what he said, I'll be making even less sense."

"Who?"

Laurel stopped pacing and leaned against a tree. "I met someone. Up at the land. A guy, sort of." *A man almost,* but she didn't say it out loud. "He said he lives there."

"On *your* land?"

"That's what *I* said."

"What did your parents say?"

Laurel shook her head. "They didn't see him."

"You met him alone?"

Laurel nodded.

"Some strange guy all by yourself? You're lucky you didn't get hurt!" He paused for a second, then asked quietly, "Did you get hurt?"

But Laurel was already shaking her head. "It wasn't like that." For a moment, she remembered the feeling she'd had while sitting in the small glade. "I felt safe; I *was* safe. He . . . he knew me. I don't know how. He saw the flower and wasn't surprised at all. He told me it's a blossom."

"A blossom?"

"He also said it'll go away. That's the only part of the conversation I'm hoping and praying was true."

"Who was he? Did he say?"

"He said his name was Tamani." As soon as she said his name she wished she hadn't. The name seemed somehow magical and saying it aloud brought back that out-of-control feeling that made her feel strangely impulsive. His face invaded her mind, blocking her view of anything else. His intense eyes, that half-grin, the way she'd been overwhelmed by a sense of comfort and familiarity when he touched her hand.

"Tamani?" David said, bringing her back to reality. "Weird name."

Laurel just nodded, forcing her thoughts back to the present.

"What else did he say?"

"He told me he was my kind; that's why he knew about the blossom."

"Your *kind*? What does that mean?"

Laurel laughed, trying to break the tension. It didn't work. "It's just so dumb. He said . . . he said I'm a flower, a plant."

"A plant?"

"Exactly. It's ridiculous."

David paused to contemplate this. "Anything else?" he asked.

"Anything else? Isn't that bad enough? He said I'm a freaking plant. I'm not a plant. I'm not," she added for good measure.

David slid his back down the tree trunk and sat on the ground, his fingers drumming on his knees. "It *would* explain a lot, you know," he said hesitantly.

"Oh, please, David, not you too."

"Did he say anything else?" David asked, ignoring her comment.

Laurel turned away and began picking small pieces of bark off the tree she'd been leaning against. "He just said some other crazy stuff, that's all."

David stood and walked over to the tree she was assaulting and waited until she looked up at him. "If it was just crazy talk, why are you so upset?"

"Because—because it was so stupid."

"Laurel."

Her eyes darted up to his.

"What did he say?"

"It's dumb. He said I'm a—you're just going to laugh."

"I won't laugh. What did he say you are?"

She blew out a long breath and her shoulders slumped forward. "He said I'm a faerie," she whispered.

David was quiet for a moment before he held up his hand, thumb and finger about three inches apart. "A faerie?" he said dubiously.

"Well, obviously I'm a little bigger than that," Laurel scoffed.

David just smiled.

"What?" Her voice was sharper than she intended, but she didn't apologize.

"It just . . . well, it kinda makes sense."

Laurel's hand went to her hip. "Some crazy guy claims I'm a mythical creature, and that makes *sense* to you?"

David blushed now and shrugged. "If I had to pick one person who I thought reminded me of a faerie, it would be you."

Laurel had expected David to laugh and tell her it was silly. She had been depending on that. But he kind of believed it. And even though she knew it was irrational, it made her angry. "Can we go now?" She turned and started back down the path.

"Wait." David ran to catch her. "Doesn't it make you curious?"

"No, David," she snapped. "It doesn't. It makes me want to go home and go to sleep and wake up to find that all of this is a dream. That the flower, the bump, even public school never happened. That's what it makes me want!" She turned without letting him answer and jogged down a random trail. She didn't care where it led. She just had to get away.

"What scares you more, Laurel," David yelled after her, "that he's right, or that he's wrong?"

★ ★ ★

Laurel ran all the way home and stood panting in her driveway for several minutes before she made her way up the curving walk to her front door. The days were getting shorter, and already the sun was beginning to set. She collapsed onto the front porch with her arms wrapped around her knees. It was that magical time when the clouds were purple, tinged with a fluorescent orange. Laurel loved this time of day. Their new house had a big, west-facing picture window where she and her mother would often watch the clouds flush bright purple, then fade slowly to lilac as the orange of the dying sun overcame them.

Tonight it held no beauty for her.

Laurel looked out into her yard at the white dogwoods that lined the front walk. If Tamani could be believed, she had more in common with the trees than with her living, breathing parents waiting just on the other side of the door.

She looked down at her feet. Without thinking, she had slipped out of her flip-flops and pushed her toes into the crumbly dirt of the front flower beds. She took quick, shallow breaths to stave off her panic as she dusted the dirt from her feet and returned them to her shoes. What if she went into the backyard, buried her feet in the rich dirt, and lifted her arms to the heavens? Would her skin slowly harden into tree bark? Would she bloom with more petals, maybe from her stomach or the top of her head?

It was a terrifying thought.

But Tamani had looked normal. If he was really the same as her, did that mean she wouldn't change? She still wasn't sure she could trust anything he'd said.

The front door rattled, and Laurel shot to her feet and turned as her father's head poked out. "I thought I heard someone," her dad said with a smile. "What are you doing?"

Laurel paused, trying to remember what had made her stop and sit in the first place. "I was just watching the sunset," she said with a forced smile.

He sighed and leaned against the door frame. "It is beautiful, isn't it?"

Laurel nodded and tried to swallow the lump in her throat.

"You've been very quiet the last few weeks, Laurel. Are you all right?" he asked softly.

"Just stressed about school," Laurel lied. "It's harder than I thought."

He joined her on the porch step. "Are you handling it okay?"

"Yeah, it just takes a lot out of me."

He smiled and laid his arm across Laurel's shoulders. Laurel stiffened, but her dad didn't seem to notice that or the thin petals separated from discovery by a mere millimeter or so of fabric. "Well, we've got a lot of peaches to keep your energy up," he said with a grin.

"Thanks, Dad."

"Come in when you're ready," he said. "It's almost dinnertime."

"Dad?"

"Yeah?"

"Was I . . . different from other kids when I was little?"

He stopped, saw Laurel's face, then joined her on the front step again. "What do you mean?"

She considered confiding in him but quickly changed her mind. She wanted to find out what he knew first. "Like the way I eat. Other kids don't eat like me. Everyone thinks it's weird."

"It is a little different. But I don't know anyone who eats more fruits and vegetables than you do. I think that's healthy. And you haven't had any problems, have you?"

Laurel shook her head. "Have I *ever* been to a doctor?"

"Sure. When we were finalizing the adoption, a pediatrician came over to the cabin to make sure you were in good health." He paused. "Actually, this is a funny story. He checked you over and everything looked good." Her dad laughed. "Except that your knee wouldn't do that kick thing when he hit it with his little mallet. He was concerned, but I didn't think it really mattered. Then he pulled out his stethoscope. That's when things got weird. He kept moving his stethoscope all over your back and chest. I asked him what the problem was, and he told me that I should go get your mom. He wanted to talk to both of us. So I went to get her, and by the time we got back, he was packing his things up. He smiled and said you were in perfect health."

"Then what was up?"

"That's what I asked him. He said he didn't know what I was talking about. Let's just say that didn't help your mom's view of doctors. She railed about what a nut he was for weeks."

"And you never did find out?"

Her dad shrugged. "I don't think there was anything wrong with you. I think his stethoscope was broken, or he used it wrong or something. Then he realized his mistake, didn't want to look incompetent, and tried to brush it all off. Doctors never like to admit they're wrong." He looked over at Laurel. "What is this about? Do you want us to take you to the doctor? We got you exempted from your school physical, but if it would make you feel better, we can take you now."

Laurel shook her head. That was the last thing she wanted. "No. I really don't."

"Are you okay?"

Laurel smiled. "Yeah, I think I am."

"You sure?" her dad pressed, his eyes soft but concerned.

She nodded. "I'm fine."

"Good." He stood and turned the knob on the door. "Oh, by the way, we got the offer from Barnes this morning."

"That's awesome," Laurel said as she stared out at the darkening horizon. "I hope he buys it fast." *I don't ever want to go back,* she added in her head.

TEN

LAUREL WAS SITTING ON DAVID'S PORCH WHEN HE walked out for school the next morning. He stared down at her for a few seconds, then took a deep breath and locked the door.

"I'm sorry," Laurel said before David could turn back around. "I had no reason to yell at you. You were so great and tried to help and I slapped you in the face for it."

"It's fine," David mumbled, pocketing his key.

"No, it's not," Laurel said, falling into step beside him. "I was awful—I yelled at you. I never yell. I've just been so stressed."

David shrugged. "I kinda deserved it. I pushed too hard. I should have backed off."

"But I need that sometimes. I don't like to face hard things. You're way better at that than me."

"That's just because it's not so personal for me. I'm not the one with a blossom."

Laurel stopped and grabbed David's hand to turn him around. When he did, she didn't let go. It felt nice to have her hand in his. "I can't do this without a friend. I'm really sorry."

David shook his head, then lifted a hand slowly to her face and brushed some hair behind her ear, his thumb lightly caressing her cheek as he did. She held very still, loving the feeling of his hand against her face. "You're impossible to stay mad at."

"Good." Standing so close, the warmth of his chest almost touching her, she had the sudden urge to kiss him. Without stopping to question it, she shifted her weight to the front of her toes and leaned forward. But a car flew by just at that moment and Laurel lost her nerve. She turned abruptly and started walking. "Don't want to be late," she said, laughing tensely.

David quickly caught up. "So, did you want to talk about it?" he asked.

"I don't know what there is to talk about," Laurel replied.

"What if he's right?" David didn't have to specify who *he* was.

Laurel shook her head. "It doesn't make sense. I admit I'm a little different, and this flower on my back is seriously weird, but to actually be a plant? How could I even be alive?"

"Well, *plant* could mean a lot of things. There are plants with more capabilities than you could possibly imagine—and those are only the ones scientists have discovered. They suspect there are millions of species in the rain forests that no one has ever been able to study."

"Sure, but have you ever seen a plant step out of the dirt and walk up the street?"

"No." He shrugged. "But there are a lot of things I've never seen before. That doesn't mean they don't exist." He rolled his eyes. "I'm learning that every day."

"It doesn't make sense," she repeated.

"I thought about this a lot last night, actually. You know, on the odd chance that you were ever going to talk to me again. There's actually a fairly easy way to prove or disprove it."

"How?"

"Tissue samples."

"What?"

"You give me various samples of cells from your body and we look at them under my microscope and see if they're plant or animal cells. That should be pretty conclusive."

Laurel wrinkled her nose. "How do I give you tissue samples?"

"We could get epithelial cells from your cheek like they do on *CSI.*"

Laurel laughed. "*CSI?* You're going to *investigate* me now?"

"Not if you don't want me to. But I figure you should at least test out what this guy—what was his name?"

"Tamani." A small shiver traveled up her spine.

"Yeah. You should check out what Tamani said and find out if there's any truth to it."

"What if it *is* true?" Laurel had stopped walking.

He looked back at her, and her face was etched with fear. "Then you'd know."

"But it would mean that my whole life would be this terrible lie. Where would I go? What would I do?"

"You wouldn't have to leave. Everything could stay the same."

"No, it couldn't. People would find out and they'd want to . . . I don't know, do stuff to me."

"No one has to find out. You won't tell; I won't tell. You'll have this amazing secret that sets you apart from everyone else. You would know that you were this . . . incredible thing, and no one else would ever suspect."

Laurel kicked at the asphalt. "You make it sound exciting and glamorous."

"Maybe it is."

Laurel hesitated, and David stepped a little closer. "It's your call," he said softly, "but whatever you decide, I'll help you." He placed a soft, warm hand at the back of her neck and Laurel's breath caught in her chest. "Whatever you need, I'll be. If you need the science geek to give you answers from a textbook, I'm your guy; if you just want a friend to sit by you in bio and help you feel better when you're sad, I'm still your guy." His thumb slowly stroked across her earlobe and down her cheek. "And if you need someone to hold you and protect you from anyone in the world who might want to hurt you, then I am definitely your guy." His pale-blue eyes bore into hers, and for a second she couldn't breathe. "But it's all up to you," he whispered.

It was so tempting. Everything about his presence was so comforting. But Laurel knew it wouldn't be fair. She liked him—a lot—but she wasn't sure if her feelings were romantic or just needy. And until she was sure, she couldn't commit to anything. "David, I think you're right—I should get some answers. But right now all I need, all I can handle, is a friend."

David's smile was a little forced, but he squeezed her shoulder gently and said, "Then that's what you'll get." He turned and started walking again, but he stayed close enough to her side that their shoulders brushed.

She liked that.

"These are definitely plant cells, Laurel," David said, squinting at his microscope.

"Are you sure?" Laurel asked, taking her turn looking at the cells she had swabbed from the inside of her cheek. But even she recognized the thick-walled, square cells that dotted the brightly lit slide.

"Ninety-nine percent certain," David said, stretching his arms above his head. "I think this Tamani guy's on to something."

Laurel sighed and rolled her eyes. "You weren't there; he was seriously weird." *Yeah, keep telling yourself that; maybe you'll believe it.* She pushed the little voice away.

"All the more reason for him to be related to you."

Laurel scrunched up her eyebrows and kicked David's chair as he laughed. "I am incredibly offended," she said, widening her eyes dramatically.

"Still," David said, "it looks like he's right. At least about this."

Laurel shook her head. "There's got to be something else."

David paused. "There is one thing, but—no, it's dumb."

"What?"

David studied her for a minute. "I—I could look at a blood sample."

"Oh." Laurel's heart sank.

"What's the matter?"

"How would you get the blood?"

David shrugged. "A finger prick should do it easy."

Laurel shook her head. "I can't do needles. They terrify me."

"Really?"

Laurel nodded, her face pinched. "I've never been stuck with a needle."

"Never?"

Laurel shook her head. "No doctors. Remember?"

"What about shots?"

"I didn't have any. My mom had to fill out a special form to get me into school."

"No stitches?"

"Oh, gosh," she said, covering her mouth. "I don't even want to think about that."

"Okay, forget it then."

They sat in silence for quite a while.

"I wouldn't have to look?" Laurel asked.

"I promise. And it doesn't really hurt."

Laurel's breath caught in her throat, but this seemed important. "Okay. I'll try."

"My mom's diabetic, so she's got lancets in her room for testing her blood. That's probably the easiest way. I'll be right back."

Laurel forced her breathing to even out while David was out of the room. He walked back in, hands empty.

"Where is it?" she asked.

"I'm not telling you. I'm not even going to let you see it. Scoot over. I have an idea." He sat on the bed just in front of her. "Okay, sit behind me and put your arms around my waist. You can keep your head down against my back and squeeze me if you get scared."

Laurel scooted behind him. She pressed her face against his back and squeezed his waist as hard as she could.

"I do need one hand," David said, his voice a little strained.

Laurel forced herself to loosen her hold and relinquished one hand. David rubbed her palm softly as she started to squeeze him again. "Ready?" he asked.

"Surprise me," she said, her voice breathless.

He rubbed her hand a little longer, then she let out a squeak as a sensation like a static shock erupted on her finger. "Okay, it's over," David said calmly.

"Did you put it away?" Laurel asked without lifting her head.

"Yeah," David said, his voice strangely flat. "Laurel, you need to see this."

Curiosity helped dissipate her fear as Laurel peeked over David's shoulder. "What?"

David was gently applying pressure to the end of her middle finger. A bead of clear liquid pooled out.

"What is that?" Laurel asked.

"I'm more concerned with what it's not," David replied. "It's not red."

Laurel just stared.

"Um, can I . . . ?" David gestured at the box of slides.

"Of course," Laurel said numbly.

David took a thin glass slide and dabbed Laurel's finger against it. "Can I get a couple?"

Laurel just nodded.

Three slides later, David wrapped Laurel's finger in a tissue and Laurel tucked her hands into her lap.

David sat beside her, his thigh touching hers. "Laurel, is this what always comes out when you cut yourself?"

"I haven't cut myself in ages."

"You have at least had a scraped knee at some point, haven't you?"

"I'm sure I have, but . . ." Her voice trailed off as she realized she couldn't pinpoint a single instance. "I don't know," she whispered. "I can't remember."

David ran his fingers through his hair. "Laurel, have you *ever* bled . . . from anywhere in your whole life?"

She hated everything he was implying, but she couldn't deny the truth. "I don't know. I honestly can't remember *ever* bleeding."

David slid his chair back over to the microscope and put the new slide under the lighted scope, then studied it through the lens for a long time. He switched the slides and looked again. Then he pulled out a few red-stained slides from another box and worked them into the rotation.

Laurel didn't move the whole time.

He turned to her. "Laurel," he said, "what if you don't

have blood? What if this clear fluid is all that flows through your veins?"

Laurel shook her head. "That's not possible. Everybody has blood, David."

"*Everybody's* epithelia are animal cells as well, Laurel—but not yours," he responded. "You said your parents don't believe in doctors. Have you ever been to see one?"

"When I was really little. My dad told me about it the other night." Her eyes widened. "Oh, my gosh." She related the story to David. "He knew, he must have."

"Why wouldn't he tell your parents?"

"I don't know." She shook her head.

David was quiet, his brow knitted. When he spoke, it was hesitantly. "Do you mind if I try something?"

"As long as it doesn't include cutting me open to look at my guts."

He laughed.

Laurel didn't.

"Can I take your pulse?"

Laurel was caught off-guard by the wave of relief and humor that washed over her. She started to laugh and couldn't stop. David looked at her silently while she laughed out her hysteria, until she finally got herself back under control. "Sorry," she said, breathing heavily as she warded off yet another wave of giggles. "It's just . . . this is so much better than cutting me open."

David smiled halfway and rolled his eyes. "Let me have your hand," he said.

She held out her arm and he laid two fingers on her wrist.

"Your skin is really cool," he said. "I'm kinda surprised I haven't noticed that before." Then he was quiet, concentrating. After a while, he shifted from the chair to the bed beside her. "Let me try it up here on your neck."

He held the back of her neck with one hand and placed his fingers firmly against the right side. She could feel his breath on her cheek, and even though he was looking studiously away from her face, she couldn't look anywhere else. She saw things she'd never noticed before. A light smattering of freckles along his hairline, a scar almost hidden by his eyebrow, and the graceful curve of his eyelashes. She vaguely felt his fingers push a little harder. When her breath caught, he drew back. "Did that hurt?"

She shook her head and tried not to notice how close he was.

A few seconds later, his hands drew away. She didn't like the look in his eyes—the worried crease between his eyebrows. "What?" she asked.

But he just shook his head. "I have to be sure. I'm not going to scare you for nothing. Can I . . . can I listen to your chest?"

"Like with a stethoscope?"

"I don't have a stethoscope. But if I . . ." He hesitated. "If I put my ear right over your heart, I should be able to hear it loud and clear."

Laurel sat up a little straighter. "Okay," she said quietly.

David put one hand on each side of her ribs and slowly lowered his head. Laurel tried to breathe evenly, but she was sure her heart must be racing. His cheek was warm against her skin, pressing against the neckline of her shirt.

After a long moment he lifted his face away.

"So—"

"Sshh," he said, turning his head and putting his other cheek against the opposite side of her chest. He didn't stay there very long before he raised his head again. "There's nothing," he said, his voice very soft. "Not on your wrist or at your neck. And I can't hear anything in your chest. It sounds . . . empty."

"What does that mean, David?"

"You don't have a heartbeat, Laurel. You probably don't even have a heart."

ELEVEN

LAUREL'S WHOLE BODY WAS SHAKING NOW. SHE FELT David's arms, warm and heavy around her, and it seemed like she couldn't feel anything else. He was a lifeline, and she wasn't sure she could survive the next few seconds if he let go. "What am I supposed to do, David?"

"You don't need to do anything."

"You're right," she said in a despondent tone. "I just need to wait for the rest of my body to realize it's dead."

David pulled her close and stroked her hair. She clung to his shirt as tears overwhelmed her, and she struggled to draw breath.

"No," David murmured close to her ear. "You're not going to die." His cheek rubbed against hers, rough with a sparse growth of stubble. The tip of his nose traveled the length of her face, and her tears halted as she focused on the feeling of his face touching hers. He was so warm against her skin, which was always cool. His lips brushed her forehead, and a tiny shiver went up her spine. His brow rested on hers, and her eyelids opened of their own accord, her thoughts lost in the ocean of blue in his eyes. He brushed his lips ever so softly against hers, and a wave of heat unlike anything she'd ever felt spread from her lips across her face.

When she didn't move, he kissed her again, a little more confidently this time. In an instant, he became part of the storm that raged within her and her arms twined up around his neck, pulling him in closer, tighter, trying to draw that incredible warmth inside her. It could have been seconds, minutes, hours—time was meaningless as his warm body pressed against hers and that slow heat enveloped her.

When David pulled back almost violently and gasped for breath, reality invaded Laurel's mind. *What have I done?*

"I'm so sorry," he whispered. "I didn't mean to—"

"Ssshh." Laurel pressed her fingers against his lips. "It's okay." She didn't let go of him, and when she didn't seem to protest, David hesitantly leaned in again.

At the last second, Laurel stopped him with a hand on his chest and shook her head. She took a deep breath then said, "I don't know if what I feel is real or just me panicking or . . ." She paused. "I can't do this, David. Not with everything else going on."

He pulled away slowly and was quiet for a long time. "Then I'll wait," he said, barely audible.

Laurel picked up her backpack. "I should go," she said uselessly.

David's eyes followed her as she crossed the room.

She paused to look back once more before stepping through the doorway and pulling the door shut behind her.

In biology, Laurel selected her usual spot but didn't get her books out. She sat with her back totally straight and strained her ears for the sound of David's familiar step. Even so, she was startled when he plunked his backpack down on the table beside her. She made herself look up at him, but instead of the tense, wary face she was expecting, she found a broad smile and cheeks flushed with excitement. "I did some reading last night," he said without greeting, "and I have some theories."

Theories? She wasn't sure she wanted to know. In fact, something about the expression on his face made her fairly certain she *didn't* want to know.

He flipped a book open and slid it in front of her.

"A Venus flytrap? You sure know how to sweet-talk a girl." She tried to shove the book back over to him, but he put both hands on it and held it there.

"Just listen for a second. I'm not saying you're a Venus flytrap. But read a little about its eating habits."

"It's carnivorous, David."

"Technically yes, but read why." His fingers flew over the paragraphs he had highlighted in bright green. "Flytraps grow best in poor soil—generally soil that has very little nitrogen. They eat flies because flies' bodies carry a lot of nitrogen but no fat or cholesterol. It's not about the meat; it's about the kind of nutrients they need." He turned to the next page. "Look here, it talks about what to feed a household Venus flytrap. It says a lot of people feed it little pieces of hamburger and steak because, like you said, they just think, 'Hey, it's carnivorous.' But actually you can kill a flytrap by feeding it hamburger, because hamburger has a lot of fat and cholesterol and the plant can't digest that."

Laurel just stared in horror at the picture of the monstrous-looking plant and wondered how in the world David could think she was like it. "I'm not following," she said flatly.

"The nutrients, Laurel. You don't drink milk, do you?"

"No."

"Why not?"

"It makes me sick."

"I bet it makes you sick because there's fat and cholesterol in it. What *do* you drink?"

"Water, soda." She paused, thinking. "The syrup in my mom's canned peaches. That's pretty much it."

"Water and sugar. You ever put sugar in a vase of flowers to keep them alive? The flowers love it; they suck it right up."

David's explanation made way too much sense. Laurel's head began to ache. "So why don't I eat flies?" Laurel asked sarcastically as she rubbed her temples.

"Too small to do you any good, I imagine. But think about the things you *do* eat. Plain fruits and vegetables. Plants that have grown in the ground and sucked up all those nutrients through their roots. You eat them and get the same nutrients as if you had roots and could get them yourself."

Laurel was quiet for several seconds as Mr. James began calling the class to order. "So you still think I'm a plant?" Laurel asked in a whisper.

"An incredibly evolved, highly advanced plant," David replied. "But yes, a plant."

"That sucks."

"I don't know," David said with a grin. "I think it's kind of cool."

"You would; you're the science geek. I'm the girl who just wants to get through gym class without being stared at."

"Fine," David persisted. "I'll think it's cool for the both of us."

Laurel snorted and caught Mr. James's attention.

"Laurel, David? Would you like to share the joke with the rest of the class?" he asked, one hand on his skinny hip.

"No, sir," David said. "But thank you for asking." The students around them laughed, but Mr. James didn't look pleased. Laurel leaned back and grinned. *David, one. Teacher who wishes he was as smart as David? Zero.*

On Saturday, Laurel and David met at David's house to "study." David showed her an article he had found online about how plants absorb carbon dioxide through their leaves. "What about you?" he asked. She was sitting on his bed with her petals unwrapped and turned toward his western window where they could absorb the sunlight. It was just one of the many advantages of "studying" in David's empty house after school nearly every day. David even made a valiant effort not to stare—though Laurel wasn't sure whether he was stealing glances at her petals or her bare midriff.

Either way, she didn't mind.

"Well, I don't have leaves—except the little tiny ones under the petals. *Yet*," she added cryptically.

"Not technically, but I think your skin probably counts."

"Why? Is it looking a little green these days?" she asked, then clamped her mouth shut. The thought of turning green made her think of Tamani and his green hair. She didn't want to think about him. It was too confusing. And it seemed unfair to think about him while she was with David. Disloyal, in a strange way. She saved those thoughts for nighttime, just as she was about to fall asleep.

"Not all leaves are green," David rattled on, without noticing. "In most plants, the leaves are the largest outer surface, and on you that would be your skin. So maybe you absorb carbon dioxide through your skin." He blushed. "You do like wearing tank tops even when it's cold."

Laurel stirred her Sprite with her straw. "Then why do I breathe? I *do* breathe, you know," she said pointedly.

"But do you *have* to?"

"What do you mean do I have to? Of course I have to."

"I don't think you do. Not the way I have to, anyway. Or at least not as frequently. How long can you hold your breath?"

She shrugged. "Long enough."

"Come on, you've been swimming—you must have some idea. A rough estimate," he pressed, when she shook her head.

"I just come up when I'm done being underwater. I don't go under a lot, anyway. Just to get my hair wet, so I don't know."

David grinned and pointed to his watch. "Shall we find out?"

Laurel eyed him for a few seconds, then pushed her soda away and leaned forward, poking David in the chest with a grin. "I'm tired of being experimented on. Let's see how long *you* can hold your breath."

"Fair enough, but you go next."

"Deal."

David took several deep breaths and when Laurel said go, he sucked in a lungful of air and leaned back in his chair. He lasted fifty-two red-faced seconds before the air whooshed out of him and it was Laurel's turn.

"No laughing," she warned. "You're probably going to blow me away."

"I highly doubt it." He smirked with the same confidence he always had when he was sure he was right.

Laurel took a deep breath and leaned back on David's pillows. He started the timer with a soft beep.

It unnerved her to look at his self-assured smile as the seconds ticked by, so she turned to the window instead. She watched a bird fly against the pale blue sky till it soared out of sight over a hill.

With nothing else interesting to look at, she began paying attention to her chest. It was starting to get uncomfortable. She waited a little while longer, decided she didn't like the sensation, and let her air out. "There. What's the verdict?"

David looked at his watch. "Did you hold your breath as long as you could?"

"As long as I wanted to."

"That's not the same thing. Could you have gone longer?"

"Probably, but it was getting uncomfortable."

"How much longer?"

"I don't know," she said, flustered now. "How long did I last?"

"Three minutes and twenty-eight seconds."

It took a moment for the numbers to sink in. She sat up. "Did you let me win?"

"Nope. You just proved my theory."

Laurel looked at her arm. "A leaf? Really?"

David took her arm and put his up beside it. "Check it out—if you look closely, our arms don't look quite the same. See?" he said, pointing to veins that spidered along his arms. "Granted, veins usually stick out more on guys anyway, but with your light skin, you should at least be able to see pale streaks of blue. You don't have any."

Laurel studied her arm, then asked, "When did you notice that?"

He shrugged guiltily. "When I checked for your pulse, but you were so freaked out that I decided it could wait a while. Besides, I wanted to do some research first."

"Thanks...I think." She was quiet for a long time as thoughts rushed through her head. But she came back to the same conclusion again and again. "I really am a plant, aren't I?"

David looked up at her, then nodded solemnly. "I think so."

Laurel wasn't sure why the tears came. It wasn't exactly a surprise. But she'd never truly accepted it before. Now that she had, she felt an overwhelming combination of fear, relief, amazement, and a strange sadness.

David climbed up on the bed beside her. Without a word, he leaned back on his headboard and pulled her against his chest. She joined him easily, enjoying the safety she felt in his arms. His hands occasionally moved up and down her arms and back, carefully avoiding her petals.

She could hear his heart beating a regular rhythm that reminded her some things were still normal. Dependable.

The warmth from his body spread into her, warming her in a way that was strikingly similar to how the sun did. She smiled and snuggled a little closer.

"What are you doing next Saturday?" David asked, and his voice reverberated in his chest where her ear was pressed.

"I don't know. What're you doing?"

"That depends on you. I was thinking about what Tamani told you."

She raised her head from his chest. "I don't want to talk about that."

"Why not? He was right about you being a plant. Maybe he was right about . . . about you being a faerie."

"How can you even say that where your microscope can hear you, David?" Laurel asked with a laugh, trying to keep the subject light. "It might stop working if it realizes its owner is so unscientific."

"It's pretty unscientific to have a friend who's a plant," David said, refusing to adopt her humorous tone.

Laurel sighed but let her head sink back down onto his chest. "Every little girl wishes she was actually a princess or a faerie or a mermaid or something. Especially girls who don't know who their real mothers are. But you lose that dream when you're, like, six. No one still thinks that when they're fifteen." She set her jaw stubbornly. "There's no such thing as faeries."

"Maybe not, but you don't necessarily have to be one for real."

"What do you mean?"

David was staring at her blossom. "There's a costume dance at school next Saturday. I thought maybe you could go as a faerie and try out the role. You know, get used to the idea as a costume before you try to tackle the idea that it's real. Get comfortable with it."

"What? Strap wings on and wear some funky dress?"

"Seems to me you already have wings," David said, his voice serious.

His meaning slowly dawned on Laurel and she looked at him in disbelief. "You want me to go like this? With my blossom out for everyone to see? You must be crazy! No!"

"Just listen," David said, sitting up. "I've thought about this. You know that tinsel garland stuff? If we wrapped that around the base of the flower and then looped it over your shoulders no one would know it wasn't fake. They'd just think it was an awesome costume."

"I couldn't pass this off as a costume, David. It's too good."

David shrugged. "People generally believe what you tell them." He grinned. "And do you really think someone's going to look at you and say, 'Hmm, I think that girl's a plant'?"

It really did sound absurd. Laurel's mind drifted to the shimmery sky-blue formal she'd worn to her mother's cousin's wedding last summer. "I'll think about it," she promised.

After school on Wednesday David had to work, so Laurel decided to go to the public library. She stepped up to the reference desk where the librarian was trying to explain the Dewey decimal system to a kid who clearly neither understood nor wanted to. After a couple of minutes, he shrugged and walked away.

With a frustrated sigh, the librarian turned to Laurel. "Yes?"

"Can I use the internet?" Laurel asked.

The librarian smiled, probably glad for a rational question. "That computer over there," she said, pointing. "Log in with your library card number and you'll have one hour."

"Just one?"

The librarian leaned forward conspiratorially. "It's a rule we had to make a couple of months back. Had a retired lady who would come in and play Internet Hearts *all day*." She shrugged as she straightened again. "You know how it is; a couple of crazies ruin it for the rest of us. It's high-speed though," she added as she turned back to a stack of books she was scanning in.

Laurel headed over to the carrel that held the only internet-enabled computer. Unlike the sprawling library Laurel and her dad had often visited in Eureka, the Crescent City library was hardly bigger than a regular house. It had one shelf of picture books and one shelf of adult fiction, and other than that, it was all old reference books. And not even very many of those.

She sat at the computer and logged in. After a quick glance at her watch, she started Googling.

Forty-five minutes later, she had found pictures of faeries living in flowers, wearing clothes made of flowers, and sipping tea out of tiny flower cups. But no mention of faeries actually being flowers. Or plants. Or whatever. *Lame,* she thought peevishly.

She started reading through a long Wikipedia article, but every two or three sentences, she had to look up a reference she didn't understand. So far she was only a few paragraphs into the article.

With a deep breath, she squinted and started reading the article again.

"I *love* faeries!"

Laurel almost fell out of her chair as Chelsea's voice sounded right in her ear.

Chelsea dropped into a seat next to Laurel. "I went through this phase about a year ago where everything I did had something to do with faeries. I have like, ten books all about faeries and pictures on my ceiling. I even found a pamphlet on some guy's conspiracy theory about how Ireland is controlled by the Seelie Court. And even though his ideas were a little farfetched, he did make some valid points."

Laurel closed her browser as quickly as she could, although the phrase *too little, too late* came to mind.

"Back in the Dark Ages, people used to think anything bad that happened was caused by faeries," Chelsea continued, not seeming to notice that Laurel still hadn't said a word. "Of course, they also blamed anything good that happened on faeries too, so I guess it evens out. Still." She grinned. "So why were you looking up faeries?"

Laurel's mouth went dry. She tried to think up some kind of excuse, but after trying to wrap her mind around dozens of conflicting faerie legends, she had nothing. "Um, I just wanted to find out for—" She barely managed to remember that Chelsea was in her English class before using it as an excuse.

Then she remembered David's proposition.

"I'm going to the dance as a faerie this Saturday," she blurted. "I thought I'd try to learn a little more about them."

Chelsea's face lit up. "That is so cool. I totally want to be a faerie. We should try to match."

Oh, great. "Actually, David's making me some kind of wings. He says it's a surprise."

"Oh." Chelsea hesitated for just a second. "That's okay. I should probably collaborate with Ryan anyway." Her cheeks colored a little. "He asked me on Friday."

"That's great."

"Yeah. He's cute. Isn't he cute?"

"Sure."

"Good." She looked lost in thought for a moment. "So you're going with David?"

Laurel nodded.

Chelsea smiled, though it looked a little pained. "Well, you'll be a gorgeous faerie. You practically look like a faerie anyway, so it'll be perfect."

"Do I?"

Chelsea shrugged. "I think so. Especially with your hair and skin being so light. People used to think angels were faeries, so faeries must be very light and fragile-looking."

Fragile? Laurel thought, a little taken aback.

"You'll look perfect," Chelsea said. "I'll wait for you by the door. I want to see your costume first thing."

"Deal," Laurel said with a forced smile. She didn't like how she'd suddenly gotten herself locked into David's idea. But it was better than telling Chelsea the truth.

"Why are you surfing here, anyway?" Chelsea asked. "Don't you have internet at home?"

"Dial-up," Laurel said, rolling her eyes.

"Really? Do they still have that? My dad's a computer tech and he set up this whole wireless network in our house. We have high-speed internet on six computers. He'd just die if I told him you were still using dial-up. You should come to my house next time. Lots of bandwidth and I'll lend you some books, okay?"

Laurel said okay instinctually, but there was no way she could go to Chelsea's to research. Chelsea was too smart—she'd put the pieces together.

Assuming there were any pieces to be had. Laurel hadn't found a single source that talked about faeries being anything like she was. The closest she'd found were dryads—wood spirits—and they were just the spirits of trees.

She was pretty sure she wasn't a spirit.

"Well, I gotta go," Chelsea said. "I have to do some *real* research." She held up her history book. "I'm supposed to find at least three sources not including the net. I swear, Mrs. Mitchell is *so* behind the times. Anyway, see you tomorrow?"

"Yeah," Laurel said, waving. "Tomorrow." She turned back to the computer to run one more search. But when she opened her Web browser, her time had expired.

Laurel sighed and collected her sparse notes. If she wanted more, she'd have to come back another day. She glanced over toward the bookshelves where she could just see Chelsea's bouncing curls.

Chelsea's house *would* be more convenient.

Too bad convenience was way down on her list of priorities these days.

TWELVE

"STILL NOTHING?" DAVID ASKED WHEN LAUREL CALLED him Saturday afternoon, a few hours before the dance.

"Nothing. I've been to the library three days in a row and there's *nothing*."

"Not even hints?"

"Well, you can read any explanation into something if you really want to, but no descriptions of . . ." She lowered her voice. ". . . faeries that sound anything like me."

"What about Shakespeare? *A Midsummer Night's Dream*?"

"Actually, those are about as close as it comes. But they still have wings and seem very magical. Not to mention mischievous. I'm not like that . . . am I?"

David laughed. "No, you're not." He was quiet for a few moments. "Maybe the stories are wrong."

"All of them?"

"How true are most legends?"

"I don't know. It just seems like there would be *some* documentation if it were true."

"Well, we'll keep looking. Anyway, are you ready for tonight?"

"Of course."

"I'll see you at eight, then?"

"I'll be ready."

David showed up a few hours later with a large box that supposedly held the "wings." Laurel answered the door in her blue dress with a shawl tightly wrapped around her shoulders.

"Wow," David said. "You look great."

Laurel looked down, half wishing she'd chosen something less attention-drawing; everyone would be looking at her in this. The dress was a shimmering light-blue satin with silver beading, cut on a diagonal that fell in a perfect drape across every one of her curves. The front had a soft sweetheart neckline and it was backless. She was bared almost to her waist by a round edge and more of the sparkling silver beading. A mini-train provided the finishing touch.

David was wearing black pants with a white tuxedo jacket complete with tails. A red silk cummerbund encircled his waist, and he'd managed to find a cravat to fasten around his neck. White gloves poked out of his breast pocket and he'd gelled his hair.

"What are you supposed to be?" Laurel asked appreciatively.

David blushed. "Prince Charming?" When Laurel laughed, he shrugged. "I figured we could both be mythical creatures from a fairy tale."

"My mom knows you're coming," Laurel whispered, leading David quickly upstairs, "but I think it's best if we try to get the preparations all done before she knows you're here. She might insist I keep the door open or something."

"No problem."

She swept him into her room and, after a cautious glance down the hallway, closed the door. Laurel untied the knot of her white shawl and let her blossom flutter free. She helped the petals back into their upright position; they'd seemed a little limp the last couple of days and didn't stand quite so high. She turned when she heard David's sharp intake of breath.

"What?"

"They're just so beautiful—especially with that dress. I'm amazed every time I see them."

"Sure," Laurel said sarcastically. "They're fabulous when they're not yours."

It took only about two minutes for David to secure the garland around the base of the flower and over her shoulders. Laurel turned to the new mirror hanging on the back of her door and laughed. "David, you're a genius. It totally looks like a costume."

David stood beside her, smiling at their reflection. "I'm not quite done yet." He turned back to the box. "Sit," he said, pointing to the chair. "And close your eyes."

She did, starting to enjoy this now. His hands touched her face and then she felt something cold brush along her eyelids and cheeks. "What are you doing?"

"No questions. And keep your eyes closed."

She heard something shake and then a cool mist covered the length of her hair. "Just a sec," he said. Then she felt his warm breath, making the still-wet spots on her eyelids even colder but warming the rest of her face. "Okay, you're done."

She opened her eyes and stood to look in the mirror. She gasped and laughed as she turned her face to one side, then the other, letting the fading sunlight catch the glitter on her cheekbones and around her eyes. And her hair was full of glitter that sparkled and fell to decorate her dress when she shook her head. She almost didn't recognize herself amid the glitter and glimmer of the face paint and the tinsel on her shoulders.

"Now you look like a faerie," David said approvingly.

Laurel sighed. "I *feel* like a faerie. I never thought I'd say that." She turned to David. "You're amazing."

"Nope," David said with a grin. "We've proved it scientifically—*you're* amazing." He ran his fingers through his glossy hair with a lopsided grin. "I'm just human."

Laurel smiled and squeezed his hand. "Maybe, but you're the best human."

"Speaking of humans," David said, gesturing toward the door, "we should go show your parents. My mom will be here to pick us up in about ten minutes."

All the tension of the evening rushed back. "You don't think my mom will see right through this?" she asked.

"She won't have a clue," David said. "I'm sure." He took both of her hands. "You ready?"

She wasn't, but she nodded stiffly anyway.

David opened the door, then offered his arm with a flourish. "Shall we?"

Laurel's mom caught them as they were headed down the stairs. "There you are," she said, brandishing her camera. "I was afraid you'd try to sneak out on me." She studied Laurel with a smile. "You look gorgeous," she said. "You look handsome too," she added to David.

"Where's Dad?" Laurel asked, surveying the living room.

"He had to work late tonight. But I promised him tons of pictures. So come on, smile!"

She took about fifty pictures before David's mom finally honked for them.

Laurel pulled David along behind her as her mom called out to them to have a good time. David's mom gushed over them too, but she'd already gotten pictures of David, so they got off the hook with only five or six more of the two of them together.

By the time they were done, Laurel had almost changed her mind. "It's too attention-getting," she whispered to David in the back of his mom's car. "Someone's going to figure it out."

David laughed. "No one's going to figure it out," he assured her. "I promise."

"You better be right," Laurel grumbled as they pulled into the high school parking lot.

"Look at you!" Chelsea squealed when she and David walked into the decorated gymnasium. "David said the wings were going to be awesome, but I had no idea they would be *this* good." She made Laurel turn a full circle. "You know, it kind of looks more like a flower than wings, don't you think?"

"They're like, flower-wings, I guess," Laurel responded nervously.

But Chelsea just shrugged. "They're totally gorgeous. David, you're a genius," she said, touching his shoulder.

Laurel stifled a grin. David would get most of the credit for her flower tonight, but that was fine with her. Especially when the other option was everyone finding out she'd grown it!

Chelsea sniffed at her shoulder and Laurel stiffened. "Wow," Chelsea said, sniffing openly now. "What did you spray on these? I'd totally pay for whatever you used."

Laurel was stuck for just a second, then she said "Actually, it's just this old perfume I've had forever. I don't even remember what it's called."

"If you ever don't want it, I do. Mmmm."

Laurel smiled and looked meaningfully at David as she inclined her head toward the other side of the room. Away from Chelsea's nose.

"We're going to go get something to drink," David said, taking Laurel's hand. Luckily, Ryan walked up and Chelsea was distracted enough that she didn't follow them.

Laurel left her hand in David's. He hadn't exactly said this was a date, but he hadn't said it wasn't, either. She preferred to think it was. Despite her hesitance to call him her boyfriend, she wasn't completely sure that wasn't what she wanted. What else could she want in a guy? He was sweet, patient, smart, fun, and he made no secret that he adored her. She smiled as she followed him. Walking hand in hand might start a few rumors, but she didn't mind.

As she walked, everyone made way for her "wings." People who'd never spoken to her before sought her out to tell her how cool her costume was. Everywhere she looked people were watching her. But it didn't make her nervous tonight. She knew what they were seeing—she'd seen it herself in the mirror earlier. She looked magical; there was no other word for it.

A slow song started at about eleven thirty and David finally claimed her for his first dance of the night. He'd hung back, chatting with his friends and watching her most of the evening as several other guys had asked her for dances.

"So tell me," he said, drawing her close, "was it all that bad?"

She smiled up at him as she placed her arms around his neck. "Not at all. You were totally right."

David laughed. "About what?"

The smile remained on her face, but her words were serious. "Everyone can see me for what I am, and no one's afraid or freaked out. No one's calling wacko scientists or anything. They just think it's cool." She hesitated then added, "*I* think it's kind of cool."

"It is cool. It's awesome." He grinned. "*You're* awesome."

Laurel's gaze dropped to his shoulder, but a tingly warmth spread through her.

"So how does it feel to be a faerie?"

Laurel shrugged. "Not so bad. Of course, it wouldn't be like this every day."

"No, but if you can just get used to the idea, then maybe you can start thinking about whether it's true."

Laurel stared at him in amusement. "You *want* it to be true!"

"What if I do?"

"Why?"

"Because being mythical by association is as close as *I'm* ever going to come."

"What do you mean? You're Prince Charming."

"Yeah, but—you know—not really. But you? Laurel, I think it's true. And it's awesome. Who else is best friends with a faerie? No one!"

Laurel smiled. "Am I really your best friend?"

He looked down at her with serious eyes. "For now."

She stepped in closer, laying her head against David's shoulder for the last half of the song. When it was over, she pulled him in closer for a hug. "Thanks," she whispered in his ear.

He grinned and offered her his arm dramatically. "Shall we?"

He led her back to the table where most of their friends were sitting and Laurel dropped into a seat. "I have to say, I'm totally exhausted."

David leaned close to her ear. "What do you expect? The sun's been down for hours. All good faeries should be home tucked into their flower beds."

Laurel laughed, then started when someone tapped her shoulder. A senior she recognized from school was standing just behind her. "Hey, this fell off when you stopped dancing. I figured you'd want it back." He handed her a long white-blue petal.

Laurel stared wide-eyed at David. After a few seconds, David took the petal from him. "Thanks, man."

"No problem. What did you make that out of? It feels like an actual flower petal."

"That is a trade secret," David said with a grin.

"Well, it's seriously awesome."

"Thanks."

The senior ambled back into the crowd as David laid the petal on the table. Laurel was strangely embarrassed to have it sitting there where everyone could see it. It felt intimate—as if David had laid out a pair of her underwear. "Did it just fall out?" David asked, leaning close again. "Did you feel it?"

Laurel shook her head.

"It couldn't have been yanked out without you noticing, could it?"

Laurel remembered the excruciating pain when she tried to pluck one of the petals a few weeks ago. "No way."

"Laurel," David began, so quietly she could barely hear him, "isn't this what Tamani said would happen?"

Laurel nodded quickly. "I didn't believe it; I couldn't. It was too good to be true." Her mouth said the words automatically, but her mind fixated on the obvious question. *If he was right about this, was he right about me being a faerie?*

David looked at the floor behind her for a second, then ducked down and sat back up holding two more petals. He grinned at the group and shrugged. "Looks like my creation is falling apart."

"That's all right," Chelsea said. "Dance'll be over in a few minutes anyway." She smiled at Laurel. "It was gorgeous while it lasted."

"David, can we go wait for your mom?" Laurel asked desperately.

"Of course. Come on."

Laurel frantically picked up petals all the way to the door as David led her through the crowd. But every time someone bumped her, more petals fell out. By the time they'd made it through the front doors, only a few petals still clung to her back, and her arms were full of them. "Did I get them all?" she asked, searching the ground around her.

"I think so."

Laurel sighed and rubbed at her face. A shower of glitter sprinkled to the ground. "Shoot, I forgot."

David laughed and looked at his watch. "It's twelve o'clock. You gonna lose a shoe too?"

Laurel rolled her eyes. "*So* not funny."

David just pushed his hands into his pockets and grinned.

"How does it look?" Laurel asked, turning her back to him.

"Can't tell with the tinsel on."

"Good."

She paused for a long time and looked down at the armful of petals. Her throat felt dry as she looked up at David. "It's true, isn't it?"

"What?"

She shrugged but forced herself to say it. "I really am a faerie, aren't I?"

David just smiled and nodded.

And for some reason, Laurel felt better. She chuckled. "Whoa," she said.

His mom pulled up a few minutes later and they scooted into the backseat. "Oh, the wings fell apart," she said. "It's a good thing I already took pictures."

Laurel didn't say anything as she turned and picked up two more petals and added them to the pile.

They pulled into Laurel's driveway and David got out to help Laurel to the door with her armful of petals. "There's only five left," David said, looking at her back. "And those will probably fall out while you're sleeping."

"Ha! If they make it that far."

David paused. "Are you relieved?"

Laurel thought about that for a minute. "Kind of. I'm glad I won't have to hide anything anymore—except maybe a mark where the bump used to be. I'll be glad to wear tank tops again. But . . ." She hesitated, gathering her thoughts. "Something changed tonight, David. For a few hours I liked the flower. Really, really liked it. It felt special and magical." She smiled. "You did that for me. And . . . I'm really glad."

"Remember, you'll get it again next year. That's what Tamani said, right?"

Her brow wrinkled at the sound of his name.

"We could make it a tradition. You can come out of hiding and be a faerie for everyone to see once a year."

She nodded. She liked the idea more than she could have predicted before tonight. "The other girls will be jealous," she warned. "They'll all want you to make wings for them too."

"I'll have to tell them that only Laurel gets wings. They won't know just how true that is."

"You don't think anyone will catch on?"

"Maybe. There's always someone who secretly believes in myths and legends; or at least parts of them. Those are the people who will look beyond the obvious and see things in this world that are truly wonderful." He shrugged. "But they won't say anything, even if they do. Because the rest of us who view the world as logical and scientific wouldn't see the truth if it was posted up on a billboard. I'm lucky you hit me over the head with it—I'd have never seen you for what you really are."

"I'm just me, David."

"That's the best part."

Before she could say anything, he leaned forward and pressed a soft kiss to her forehead, then turned with a murmured good night and headed to the car.

THIRTEEN

LAUREL STARED INTO THE MIRROR OVER HER SHOULDER at her bare back. There was a tiny white line down the middle—like a long-forgotten scar—but it was scarcely noticeable.

She sighed as she pulled a tank top over her head. This was *so* much better.

The idea of being a faerie had seemed so real last night. Today, it was a million miles away. She scrutinized the angles of her face, half-expecting them to have changed.

"I'm a faerie," she whispered. But her reflection didn't respond.

It felt silly to say it. She didn't feel like a faerie—she didn't feel any different than she ever had. She felt normal. But no matter what, she knew the truth now—and normal was not a word that would ever describe her life again.

She needed to talk to Tamani.

She tiptoed downstairs and picked up the phone, dialing David's cell phone number. Only when he answered with a gravelly voice did she think of the time. "What?"

There was no point in hanging up now—she'd already woken him. "Hi. Sorry. I didn't think."

"What are *you* doing up at six o'clock in the morning?" he asked sleepily.

"Um, the sun's up."

David snorted. "Of course."

Laurel looked up at her parents' room with its door slightly ajar and slid around the corner into the pantry. "Will you cover for me today?" she asked in a half-whisper.

"Cover?"

"Can I tell my parents I'm at your house?"

David sounded more alert now. "Where are you actually going?"

"I have to see Tamani, David. Or at least, I have to try."

"You're going to the land? How're you going to get there?"

"The bus? They'll have something going down the 101 on a Sunday, don't you think?"

"That's how you'll get to Orick, but how far is it to your old house?"

"I can put my bike on the front of the bus. It's only a mile or so from the bus station; it won't even take me ten minutes."

David sighed. "I wish I had my license."

Laurel laughed. He whined about it frequently. "Two more weeks, David. You'll make it."

"It's not that. I'd like to go with you."

"You can't. If he knows you're there he might not come out. He wasn't real keen on the idea that I'd told you about the blossom in the first place."

"You told him that?"

Laurel wrapped the phone cord around her wrist. "He asked if I'd told anyone and I just blurted it out. He's kind of different—persuasive. It's like you can't lie to him."

"I don't like this, Laurel. He could be dangerous."

"You're the one who's been saying he was right all week. He says he's like me. If he told the truth about everything else, why would he lie about that?"

"What about Barnes? What if he's there?"

"Papers aren't signed yet. We still own it."

"Are you sure?"

"Yeah. Mom mentioned it just yesterday."

David sighed and the line was silent.

"Please? I have to go. I *have* to find out more."

"All right. One condition—when you get back you tell me what he said."

"Everything I can."

"What's that supposed to mean?"

"I don't know what he's going to tell me. What if there's some big faerie secret I'm not supposed to tell anyone about?"

"Fine, everything except the big secret of the world if there is one. Deal?"

"Deal."

"Laurel?"

"Yeah?"

"Be careful. Be very, very careful."

After chaining her bike to a small tree, Laurel hefted her backpack onto one shoulder. She passed the empty house, then hesitated at the edge of the tree line where several paths snaked into the thick bushes and forest. She decided to take the path to the place he found her last time. That seemed as good a plan as any.

When she reached the large rock by the creek, Laurel looked around. Sitting by the beautiful stream made her feel calm and happy; for a moment she considered just sitting there for an hour, then returning home without speaking to Tamani at all. It was just so nerve-racking to talk to him.

But she forced herself not to wimp out, took a deep breath, and yelled, "Tamani?" Rather than echoing off the rocks, her voice seemed to absorb into the trees, making her feel very small. "Tamani?" she called again, a little softer this time. "Are you still here? I want to talk." She turned in a circle, trying to look everywhere at once. "Tam—"

"Hey." The voice was welcoming but strangely hesitant.

Laurel turned and nearly ran into Tamani's chest. She threw her hands up over her mouth to silence a scream. It was Tamani, but he looked different than before. His arms were bare, but his shoulders and chest were covered in what looked like armor made from bark and leaves. A long spear stuck up over his shoulder, its stone tip sharpened to a razor edge. He was as stunning as before, but an air of intimidation hung around him like a thick fog.

Tamani looked at her for a long time, and though she tried, Laurel couldn't look away. The side of his mouth tugged up into a half grin and he pulled the strange armor over his head, shedding it along with his intimidating air. "Sorry about the getup," he said, stowing the armor behind a tree. "We're on high alert today." He straightened and smiled hesitantly. "I'm glad you came back. I wasn't sure you would." Under the armor, he was dressed all in dark green—a tight shirt with three-quarter-length sleeves and the same style of baggy pants he'd been wearing last time. "And you came alone." It wasn't a question.

"How'd you know?"

Tamani laughed, his eyes sparkling. "What kind of sentry would I be if I didn't know how many people invaded my turf?"

"A sentry?"

"That's right." He was leading her down the path now, toward the clearing they'd talked in last time.

"What do you guard?" she asked.

He turned with a grin and touched the tip of her nose. "Something very, very special."

Laurel tried to catch her breath and only just succeeded. "I came to . . . um . . . to apologize," she stammered.

"For what?" Tamani asked, not slowing his pace.

Is he teasing, or did it really not bother him? "I overreacted last time," she said, falling into step beside him. "I was already freaked out about everything that was happening, and the things you told me just put me over the edge. But I shouldn't have blown up at you like that. So I'm sorry."

They walked a few more steps. "And . . . ?" Tamani prompted.

"And what?" Laurel asked, her chest growing tight as his green eyes studied her.

"And everything I said was true, and now you're here to learn more." He stopped abruptly. "That *is* why you're here, right?" He leaned against a tree and looked at her playfully.

She nodded, unable to speak. She'd never felt so awkward. Why was he so utterly tongue-tying? She couldn't think or talk around him. He, on the other hand, seemed perfectly comfortable with her.

Tamani sank gracefully to the ground, and Laurel realized they'd reached the clearing. He gestured to a spot a few feet away. "Have a seat." He grinned lopsidedly and patted the grass beside him. "Of course, you can sit by me if you prefer."

Laurel cleared her throat and sat down across from him.

"I'm not that lucky yet?" He laced his fingers behind his head. "There's still time. So," he said as she settled in, "your petals wilted."

Laurel nodded. "Last night."

"Relieved?"

"Mostly."

"And you're here to find out more about being a faerie, right?"

Laurel was embarrassed at being so transparent, but he was right and there was nothing to do but admit it.

"I don't know that I really have a lot to tell you—you've survived for twelve years on your own; you don't need me to warn you not to eat salt."

"I've been doing some research," Laurel said.

Tamani snickered. "This should be good."

"What?"

"It's just that humans never get it right."

"I've noticed." After a moment's hesitation she asked, "You don't have any wings hidden under that shirt somewhere, do you?"

"You want to check?" His hand went to the bottom of his shirt.

"That's okay," Laurel said quickly.

Tamani turned serious now. "There are no wings, Laurel. Not on anyone. Some blossoms resemble wings, the way some flowers resemble butterflies—your blossom was pretty wingish, actually. But they're just flowers—as you've discovered."

"Why are the stories so wrong?"

"I suppose humans are just good at misinterpreting what they see."

"I've never read *anything* about faeries being plants. And trust me, I looked," she said.

"Humans like to tell stories about other humans, but ones with wings or hooves or magic wands. Not about plants. Not about something they aren't and could never hope to be." He shrugged. "And humans look so much like us, I guess it's a reasonable assumption."

"But still. They're *really* off. I don't have wings. And I certainly don't have magic."

"Don't you?" Tamani said with a grin.

Laurel's eyes widened. "Do I?"

"Of course."

"Really?!"

Tamani laughed at Laurel's excitement.

"So there's magic? Real magic? It's not just all scientific like David says?"

Tamani rolled his eyes. "David again?"

Laurel bristled. "He's my friend. My best friend."

"Not your boyfriend?"

"No. I mean . . . no."

Tamani stared at her for several seconds. "So the position's open?"

Laurel rolled her eyes. "We are *so* not having this conversation."

He stared pointedly at her for a few seconds, but she refused to meet his eyes. He looked at her so possessively, as if she were a lover he had already won and he was just waiting for her to realize it.

"Tell me about the magic," she said, changing the subject. "Can you fly?"

"No, like the wings, that's just folklore."

"What can you do?"

"Aren't you curious about what *you* can do?"

"I can do magic?"

"Absolutely. You can do very powerful magic. You're a Fall faerie."

"What does that mean?"

"There are four kinds of faeries; Spring, Summer—"

"Fall, and Winter?"

"Yep."

"Why am I a Fall faerie?"

"Because you were born in the fall. That's why your blossom grows in the fall."

"That doesn't sound very magical," Laurel said, a little disappointed. "It sounds like science."

"It is. Not everything in our lives is magical. Actually, faeries are pretty normal, for the most part."

"Then what about the magic?"

"Well, each kind of faerie has its own kind of magic." His face took on an air of reverence. "Winter faeries are the most powerful of all faeries, and the most rare. Only two or three are produced in an entire generation, often less. Our rulers are always Winter faeries. They have dominion over the plants. All of them. A mature redwood would bend itself in half if a Winter faerie asked it to."

"It sounds like they can do almost anything."

"Sometimes I think they can. But Winter faeries mostly keep their abilities—and their limitations—to themselves, passing them down through the generations. Some say the greatest gift of the Winter faeries is their ability to keep a secret."

"So what do Fall faeries do?" Laurel asked impatiently.

"Fall faeries are the next most powerful, and like Winter faeries, more rare. Fall faeries make things."

"What kind of things?"

"Things from other plants. Elixirs, potions, poultices. That sort of thing."

That didn't sound very magical at all. "So, I'm like a cook? I mix stuff together?"

Tamani shook his head. "You don't understand. It's not a matter of simply mixing things together—otherwise everyone could do it. Fall faeries have a magical sense for plants and can use them for the realm's benefit. Give me every book ever written on tonics and I still couldn't even make a mixture to stop mold. It's magic, even if it seems sensible."

"It just doesn't *sound* like magic, that's all."

"But it is. Different Fall faeries have different specialties. They make potions and elixirs to do all sorts of things—like creating a mist to confound intruders or making a toxin to put them to sleep. Fall faeries are crucial to the survival of the fae as a species. They're very, very important."

"I guess that's cool." But Laurel wasn't entirely convinced. It sounded like chemistry to her, and if her biology class was any kind of indicator, she wouldn't be very good at it.

"What do Summer faeries do?"

Tamani smiled. "Summer faeries are flashy," he said, resuming his conversational tone. "Like summer flowers. They create illusions and the most incredible fireworks. The sorts of things humans typically think of as magic."

Laurel couldn't help but think that being a Summer faerie sounded a lot more fun than being a Fall faerie. "Are you a Summer faerie?"

"No." Tamani hesitated. "I'm just a Spring faerie."

"Why 'just'?"

Tamani shrugged. "Spring faeries are the least powerful of all the faeries. That's why I'm a sentry. Manual labor. I don't need much magic for that."

"What can you do?"

Tamani looked away. "If I tell you, you have to promise not to be angry."

"Why would I be angry?"

"Because I did it to you last time you were here."

FOURTEEN

"DID WHAT?" LAUREL'S VOICE ROSE.

"You have to promise not to get upset."

"You cast some kind of spell on me and now you expect me to just smile and tell you that's okay? Well it's not!"

"Look, it didn't even work very well . . . never does on other faeries."

Laurel crossed her arms. "Just tell me."

Tamani leaned back against his tree. "I enticed you."

"Enticed me?"

"I got you to follow me here."

"Why would you do that?"

"You had to listen long enough to hear the truth."

"So . . . what? You threw faerie dust in my eyes?"

"No, that's ridiculous," Tamani said. "I told you—real faerie magic isn't quite what you're thinking. There's no pixie dust to make you fly, no waving magic wands, no puffs of smoke. It's just things we can do that help us in our roles in life."

"How does *enticing* help you be a sentry?" Laurel's voice dripped with sarcasm, but Tamani continued explaining as though he hadn't noticed.

"Think about it. I can chase an intruder away with my spear, but what good does that do? He'll just run and tell his friends what happened, and they'll come back looking for us." Tamani spread his hands in front of him. "Instead, I entice him away, give him a memory elixir, and then send him off. Ever heard of a will-o'-the-wisp?"

"Sure."

"That's us. After a human drinks the elixir, all they remember of the whole incident is following a flash of light. It's peaceful that way. No one gets hurt."

"But *I* remembered you."

"I didn't give you an elixir, did I?"

"You still used your magic on me." She refused to give up so easily.

"I had to. Would you have followed me if I didn't?"

Laurel shook her head, but in her mind she knew that wasn't quite true. She might have followed Tamani anywhere.

"Besides, like I said, it doesn't work very well on other faeries—and it doesn't work at all if they know what's coming. You broke it pretty easily when you thought about it." The half-grin was back.

"What about today?" Laurel asked before the smile could hypnotize her.

"Are you afraid I used it on you again?" he asked with a grin.

"Kind of."

"Nope. All this charm and charisma comes naturally." His smile was confident now. Arrogant.

"Promise me you'll never try it on me again."

"That's an easy one. Now that you know, it wouldn't work if I did try. And I won't," he added. "I like it better when I can bewitch you *without* my magic."

Laurel hid her grin and sat back waiting for the comforting feeling around her to melt away.

It didn't.

She furrowed her eyebrows. "Stop it. You promised."

Tamani's eyes widened in confusion. "Stop what?"

"That enticing thing. You're still doing it."

Tamani's confused expression shifted to a warm smile. Satisfaction hovered around his eyes. "That's not me."

Laurel glared at him.

"It's the magic of the realm. It seeps in from the world of the faeries. Helps the sentries feel at home when we can't be." His smile was calm and serene now, and a trace of satisfaction hovered around his eyes. "You felt it before—I know you did. It's why you love this bit of land so much. But now that you know what you are and you've blossomed for the first time, it will be stronger." He leaned forward, his nose mere inches from hers. Her breath caught in her chest as his nearness made her whole body feel limp. "It's the realm calling you home, Laurel."

Laurel tore her eyes from the endless depths of Tamani's gaze and concentrated on what she was feeling. She looked into the foliage around her and the feeling intensified. The pleasant sensation seemed to emanate from the trees, and the air reverberated with it. "Is it really magic?" she asked breathlessly, knowing it couldn't be anything else.

"Of course."

"It's not you?"

Tamani laughed softly but not mockingly. "It's far greater magic than a lowly Spring faerie could even attempt."

She met his eyes and for a moment couldn't look away. His bright green eyes held on to hers. He looked mostly human, but there was something—she couldn't quite put her finger on it—that seemed to indicate he was much more than what he appeared to be. "Are most faeries like you?" she asked quietly.

He blinked, and she managed to look away. "That depends on what you mean," he said. "If you're referring to my charm and wit, no—I'm as charming as they come. If you mean my appearance . . ." He paused to look down and take stock of himself. "I guess I'm fairly normal. Nothing real special."

Laurel would have to argue with that. He had the kind of face even movie stars only got with airbrushing. But if he was right, maybe all faeries looked like him.

With a start Laurel wondered if she looked that way to her peers. Her face seemed normal to her, but then, she'd seen it in the mirror every day for her whole life.

She wondered briefly if what she saw when she looked at Tamani was what David saw when he looked at her.

The thought made her a little uncomfortable. She cleared her throat and began digging in her backpack to cover it. She pulled a can of soda from her bag. "Want one?" she asked absently as she popped the top.

"What is it?"

"Sprite."

Tamani laughed. "Sprite? You're kidding me."

Laurel rolled her eyes. "Do you want one or not?"

"Sure."

She showed him how to pop the tab and he tried it tentatively. "Huh, isn't that something." He scrutinized her for a few seconds. "Is this what you usually drink?"

"It's one of the few things I like."

"No wonder your hair and eyes are almost colorless."

"So?"

"You never wondered why mine aren't?"

"I . . . guess I wondered about your hair." *That was an understatement.*

"I eat a lot of dark-green stuff. The moss down by the river, mostly."

"Eww."

"Nah, it's good. You were just raised with human ideals. I bet you'd like it if you tasted it."

"No, thanks."

"Suit yourself. You're pretty enough as you are."

She smiled shyly as he raised his can in her direction before sipping.

"I eat peaches," she said suddenly.

Tamani nodded. "They're good, I guess. I don't have much of a sweet tooth, personally."

"That's not the point. Why don't I turn orange?"

"What else do you eat?"

"Strawberries, lettuce, and spinach. Apples sometimes. Basic fruits and vegetables."

"You eat a variety, so your hair and eyes don't pick up on any certain color; they just stay light." He smirked. "Try eating nothing but strawberries for a week—that'll give your mother a shock."

"Would I turn red?" Laurel asked in horror.

"Not *all* of you," Tamani said. "Just your eyes and the roots of your hair. Like mine. Back home it's a fashion thing. Blue, pink, purple. It's fun."

"That's so weird."

"Why? Don't half the humans' stories say we have green *skin*? That's a lot weirder."

"Maybe." Laurel remembered something from the last time she'd met Tamani. "You said there's no faerie dust, right?"

Tamani inclined his chin somewhat, apparently in agreement, but his face was unreadable.

"Last time I was here, you grabbed my wrist and later there was this sparkly powder on it. What was that, if not faerie dust?"

Now Tamani grimaced. "Sorry about that; I should have been more careful."

"Why, was it dangerous?"

Tamani laughed. "Hardly. It was just pollen."

"Pollen?"

"Yeah, you know." He studied his hands as if they had suddenly become very interesting. "For . . . pollinating."

"Pollinating?" Laurel started to laugh, but Tamani didn't look like he was telling a joke.

"Why do you think you grew a flower? It's not just for looks. Although yours was very attractive."

"Oh." Laurel was quiet for a few moments. "Pollinating is how flowers reproduce."

"It's how we reproduce, too."

"So you could have . . . pollinated me?"

"I would never do that, Laurel." His face was deadly serious.

"But you could have?" Laurel pressed.

Tamani spoke slowly, choosing his words with great care. "Technically, yes."

"Then what? I would have a baby?"

"A seedling, yes."

"Would it grow on my back?"

"No, no. Faeries grow in flowers. That's one thing the human stories generally get right. The . . . female . . . is pollinated by a male and when her petals fall off she's left with a seed. She plants it and when the flower blooms, you have a seedling."

"How do you . . . we . . . you know, *faeries* pollinate?"

"The male produces pollen on his hands and when two faeries decide to pollinate, the male reaches into the female's blossom and lets the pollen mix. It's a somewhat delicate process."

"Doesn't sound very romantic."

"There's nothing romantic about it at all," Tamani replied, a confident smile spreading across his face. "That's what sex is for."

"You still . . . ?" She let the question hang.

"Sure."

"But faeries don't get pregnant?"

"Never." Tamani winked. "Pollination is for reproduction—sex is just for fun."

"Can I see the pollen?" Laurel asked, holding her hands out for his.

Tamani pulled his hands back instinctively. "I don't have any right now—you're not in bloom anymore. We only produce pollen when we're around a female who's in bloom. That's why I forgot and left some on your wrist. I haven't been around a female with a blossom in a long time."

"Why not?"

"I'm a sentry. There are always other sentries, but the ones here are all male. And I don't go home too often."

"Sounds lonely."

"Sometimes." He looked at her again and something changed about his eyes. His guard was down and she saw deep, mournful sadness. It almost hurt to keep looking, but she couldn't turn away.

Then as quickly as it had come, it was gone—replaced with a careless grin. "It was more fun when you were here. You got me into big trouble, by the way."

"What did I do?"

"You disappeared." Tamani laughed and shook his head. "Boy, we're glad you came back. When you—"

"Who's 'we'?"

"You didn't think I was the only faerie here, did you?"

Laurel played with a strand of hair that had come loose from her ponytail. "Kind of, yeah."

"You won't see us unless we let you."

Despite what Tamani had just said, Laurel glanced around at the trees. "How many?" she asked, wondering if she was surrounded by legions of unseen fae.

"Depends. Shar and I are almost always here. Ten or fifteen others usually rotate through for six months or a year at a time."

"How long have you been here?"

He looked at her for several silent seconds with an unreadable expression. "A long time," he finally said.

"Why are you here?"

He smiled. "To watch you. Well, till your disappearing act."

"You were here to watch *me*? Why?"

"To help protect you. Make sure no one found out what you are."

Laurel remembered something from her research. "Am I a . . . a changeling?"

Tamani hesitated for a second. "In the loosest sense of the word, yes. Except that we didn't steal someone and replace them with you. I prefer to think of you as a scion."

"What's a scion?"

"It's a plant that's taken from one plant and grafted into another. You were taken from our world and put in the human world. A scion."

"But why? Are there lots of . . . scions?"

"Nope. At the moment, there's just you."

"Why me?"

He leaned forward a little. "I can't tell you everything, and you have to respect that, but I'll tell you what I can, okay?"

Laurel nodded.

"You were placed here twelve years ago to integrate into the human world."

Laurel rolled her eyes. "I should have known. Who else would put me in a basket on someone's porch?" Her eyes widened when Tamani laughed. "Did *you* do that?"

He laughed harder now, throwing his head backward in his amusement. "No, no. I was too young. But when I joined the sentries here, I pretty much got briefed on your whole life."

Laurel wasn't sure she liked that idea. "My whole life?"

"Yep."

She narrowed her eyes. "Did you spy on me?"

"It's not exactly spying. We were helping."

"Helping . . . right." She folded her arms across her chest.

"Really. We had to keep your parents from finding out what you are."

"That sounds like a really seamless plan." Her tone turned sarcastic. "Hmm, how should we keep these two humans from finding out about faeries? Oh, I know, let's plop one on their doorstep."

"It wasn't like that. We needed them to have a faerie child."

"Why?"

Tamani hesitated, then pursed his lips.

"Fine, Mr. I'd-tell-you-but-then-I'd-have-to-kill-you. Why didn't you send me out here as a baby?" She chuckled a little awkwardly. "Trust me, I'd have fit in the basket better if I wasn't three."

Tamani didn't smile this time. "Actually, you were quite a bit older than that."

"What do you mean?"

"Fairies don't age the same way humans do. They're never really babies. I mean, they look like human babies when they first blossom, but faerie babies are never helpless the way humans are. They're born knowing how to walk and talk, and mentally they are about the equivalent of . . ." He considered for a moment. "Maybe a five-year-old."

"Really?"

"Yeah. Then they age a bit slower physically, so by the time a faerie looks like a three- or four-year-old, they're actually seven or eight . . . and mentally they act like they are about eleven or twelve."

"That's weird."

"You need to remember that we're plants. Nurturing helpless young is what animals do. Not plants. Plants produce seedlings and those seedlings grow on their own. They don't need help."

"So what, faeries don't even have parents? *I* don't have faerie parents somewhere?"

Tamani bit his lip and looked at the ground. "Things are very different in the faerie realm. There's not much time to be a child and not enough adult faeries to just sit around and watch kids play. Everyone has a role and a purpose, and they take on those roles very early. We grow up quickly. I've been a sentry since I was fourteen. I was a mite young but only by a year or two. Most faeries are practicing their profession and living on their own by fifteen or sixteen."

"That doesn't sound very fun."

"Fun isn't really the point."

"If you say so. So, I couldn't come as a baby because I could walk and talk, right?"

"Yep."

"So how old was I when I did come?"

He sighed, and for a moment Laurel didn't think he would tell her. Then he seemed to change his mind. "You were seven."

"Seven?" The idea was a little shocking. "Why don't I remember anything?"

Tamani leaned forward, his elbows on his thighs. "You have to understand before I answer that, even though you don't remember, you agreed to all this."

"All what?"

"Everything. Coming here, fulfilling your role, living with the humans, all of it. You were selected for this a long time ago, and you agreed to come."

"Why don't I remember?"

"I told you I can make humans forget they saw me, right?"

She nodded.

"That's what they did to you. Once you were at the age that you could pass for a human child, they made you forget your faerie life."

"Like, with a potion or something?"

"Yes."

Laurel sat stunned. "They made me forget seven years of my life?"

Tamani nodded solemnly.

"I . . . I don't know what to say."

They sat in silence for several minutes as Laurel tried to comprehend what this meant for her. She began adding up the years Tamani claimed she had lost. "I'm nineteen?" she asked in amazement.

"Technically, yes. But you're still just like a fifteen-year-old human."

"How old are you?" she asked, anger heavy in her voice. "Fifty?"

"Twenty-one," Tamani said quietly. "We're almost the same age."

"So they just made me forget everything?"

Tamani shrugged, his face tense.

Laurel's tight clutch on her temper came loose. "Did you guys even think this through? A million things could have gone wrong. What if my parents didn't want me? What if they found out I don't have a heart, or blood, or that I don't hardly have to breathe? Do you know what most people feed three-year-olds? Milk, cookies, hot dogs! I could have died!"

Tamani shook his head. "What do you take us for? Amateurs? There has rarely been a time in your life when you didn't have at least five faeries watching you, making sure everything was going smoothly. And it wasn't like the eating thing was a problem. That's why you were selected in the first place."

"Didn't I forget what I was supposed to eat?"

"That's the cool thing about Fall faeries. Part of their magic is knowing intrinsically what is good and bad for themselves as well as other faeries. They have to, in order to make their elixirs. We knew you wouldn't eat something bad for you of your own free will. The only thing we had to watch for was that your parents didn't force-feed you. Which they never did," he said before she could ask. "We had everything completely under control. Well," he added reluctantly, "till you left."

"Till I left? If you were watching me so closely, you should have known we were moving."

"We stopped watching you as closely a few years ago. I insisted. I'm . . . kind of in charge of you right now. You weren't a child anymore. In terms of faerie age, you were more than an adult. The signs of you being a faerie weren't as obvious. You didn't fall down very often, and your parents were used to your eating habits. I felt you deserved a little more privacy. I thought you would appreciate it," he added morosely.

"I probably would have if I had known," Laurel conceded.

Tamani sighed. "But I pulled back too far and we totally missed you moving until the movers showed up. I wanted to go extreme and stop everything right then. Dope the movers, take you back to the realm, call the whole damn project a wash. But . . . let's just say I was outvoted. So you and your parents took off in the car and then you were just . . . gone." He laughed humorlessly. "Boy, did I get in trouble."

"I'm sorry."

"It's okay. You came back. Everything's all right now."

She looked at him warily. "Are you going to follow me home and move into my backyard since you apparently like to watch me so much?"

He laughed. "No. We're fine right here, thanks. Mostly we were worried about you blossoming and having major problems with that. Luckily, you managed just fine."

"So I'll live there and you'll just keep living out here?"

"For the time being."

"Then what was the point of me being a . . . a scion? Was I just an experiment?"

"No. Not at all." Tamani let out a loud, exasperated breath, then looked around the clearing quickly. "The point of sending you here was to help protect this land. It's . . . an important spot for faeries. It's imperative that someone who understands be in possession of the land. That's the main reason you were placed with them. When your mom's mother died, your mom got really bitter and immediately put this place up for sale. She was nineteen and I guess it just held too many memories."

"She's told me about that."

Tamani nodded. "Things got better when she married your dad, but she never did stop trying to sell. That's when the Seelie Court came up with the idea of adding you to her family. Worked even better than they had hoped. After your mom really bonded with you, she stopped trying to sell. Other than an occasional buyer who comes through now and then, that part of our job has been easy. It seems to be pretty much all downhill now." Tamani leaned back with his hands stretched behind his head. "We just sit back and wait for you to inherit."

Laurel looked down at her hands. "What if I don't inherit? What if—what if my parents sell?"

"They can't sell," he said matter-of-factly.

Her head jerked up. "Why not?"

Tamani smiled slyly. "You can't sell a house if no one remembers it exists."

"Huh?"

"Seeing us isn't the only thing we can make humans forget."

Laurel's eyes widened as she understood. "You've been sabotaging them! You made people forget they'd even seen the house."

"We had to."

"And the appraisers?"

"Trust me, it would be too tempting if your mom found out how much this land is worth."

"So you made them forget too?"

"It was necessary, Laurel. Believe me."

"Um . . . it didn't work," Laurel said quietly.

Tamani's face turned wary. "What do you mean?" he asked in a low, serious tone.

"My mom's selling the land."

"To who? No one's come out to look. We'd have taken care of it."

"I don't know; some guy my dad met in Brookings."

Tamani leaned forward. "Laurel, this is very important. You *can't* let her sell."

"Why not?"

"For starters, because I live here. I wouldn't really appreciate being homeless. But—" He glanced around and growled in frustration. "I can't explain everything right now, but you

162

can't let her sell. Whatever it takes, you need to talk to her when you get home and do anything you can to convince her to tell this guy no."

"Um, that could be a problem."

"Why?"

"The offer's already in. They're drawing up the papers soon."

"Oh, no." Tamani pushed his hair off his forehead. "This is bad, this is *so* bad. Shar's going to kill me." He sighed. "Can you do anything about it?"

"It's not really my decision," Laurel said. "I can't tell them what to do."

"I'm just asking you to try. Say . . . *something.* We'll try to figure it out from over here too. If you knew how important this land is to the realm, you wouldn't sleep until it was safe. I don't know that *I'll* be able to sleep until you come back and tell me it's safe."

"Why?"

He released a breath in an exasperated hiss. "I can't say— it's forbidden."

"Forbidden? I'm a faerie, aren't I?"

"You don't understand, Laurel. You don't get to know everything just because you're one of us—not yet. Even in the realm, young faeries aren't allowed to enter the human world until they've proven their loyalty—if at all. You're asking me to reveal one of the greatest secrets of our species. You can't expect that of me."

Several seconds passed in silence. "I'll do what I can," Laurel finally said.

"That's all I'm asking."

She forced a smile. "My parents are going to think I'm nuts."

"That's okay with me."

Laurel looked at him for a few seconds before reaching out to smack his shoulder.

Tamani just laughed.

Then he sobered and stared at her. Hesitantly, he slid closer and let his fingers run down her bare arm. "I'm glad you came today," he said. "I've missed you."

"I . . . I think maybe I missed you too."

"Really?" Hope shone in his eyes so raw that Laurel had to look away and laugh nervously.

"You know, after I got done thinking you were a crazy homeless guy."

They laughed together and Laurel marveled at the soft, tinkling quality of Tamani's voice. It made a warm tingle shiver up her back. She glanced at her watch. "I . . . need to get going," she said, apology heavy in her voice.

"Come back soon," Tamani said. "We'll talk more."

Laurel smiled. "I'd like that."

"And you promise you'll talk to your parents?"

She nodded. "I will."

"Will you bring me news?"

"As soon as I can. But I don't know when that will be."

"Are you going to tell your parents about all this?" Tamani asked.

"I don't know," Laurel said. "I don't really think they'd believe me. Especially since I don't have the blossom to prove it anymore. That's how I convinced David."

"David," Tamani said with a scoffing tone.

"What's wrong with David?"

"Nothing, I guess. But are you sure he's trustworthy?"

"I'm sure."

Tamani sighed. "I guess you had to tell someone. I don't like it, though."

"Why not?"

"Because he's a human. Everyone knows humans can't be trusted. You should be careful."

"I don't have to be careful with him. He wouldn't tell."

"I hope you're right."

They walked slowly, Laurel leading the way down the familiar path. They stopped at the edge of the tree line. "Are you sure you have to go?" Tamani asked quietly.

Laurel was surprised by the emotion in his voice. She had sensed in their conversation that he liked her . . . a lot. But this seemed like something more. Something more personal. She was a little surprised to realize that she was reluctant to leave as well. "My parents don't even know I'm here. I kind of snuck away."

Tamani nodded. "I'll miss you," he whispered.

Laurel laughed nervously. "You hardly know me."

"I'll miss you anyway." He met her eyes. "If I give you something, will you keep it to remember me by—and maybe think of me just a little more?"

"Maybe." Tamani's dark green eyes seemed to see through her—into her.

He snapped a thin piece of string from around his neck and held out a small, glistening circle. "This is for you."

He laid the tiny sparkle on her hand. It was a shining gold circlet, just bigger than a pea, with a minuscule crystal flower on the top. "What is it?" Laurel asked in awe.

"It's a ring for a seedling," Tamani replied. "You know, a baby faerie. Every seedling gets a ring when they are young. If you wear it, it grows with you. Winter faeries make them. Well, Spring faeries *make* them, but Winter faeries enchant them." He held up his hand to show her a plain silver band. "See, this is mine. It used to be as small as that one. You're not a seedling anymore, so it won't adjust to your finger, but I thought maybe you'd like it."

The tiny ring was exquisite, beautiful in every detail. "Why are you giving this to me?"

"To help you feel more like one of us. You can hang it on a necklace." He hesitated a moment longer. "I just think you should have it."

Laurel looked up at him in question, but he wouldn't meet her eyes. She wished she had more time to draw secrets from him. "I'll wear it always," she said.

"And think of me?" His eyes held her captive, and she knew there was only one answer.

"Yes."

"Good."

She started to turn, but before she could step away, Tamani grabbed her hand. Without breaking eye contact, he raised her hand to his face and brushed his lips over her knuckles. For just a second, his eyes were unguarded. A spark went through Laurel at what she saw there: raw, unbridled desire.

Before she could look any closer, he smiled, and the flash was gone.

Laurel walked toward her bike, her breath shallow as she tried to stop the warm flush that was spreading through her body from the place Tamani's lips had touched. She kept glancing back at him as she rode toward the highway. Every time she turned, his eyes were still locked on her. Even when she pedaled onto the bike path along the road, she could feel them following her long after she could see them.

FIFTEEN

IT WAS FOUR O'CLOCK WHEN LAUREL PARKED HER bike in the garage, way later than any study session could really justify. She braced herself and pushed open the front door.

Her father was napping on the couch, his snores a quiet, familiar rhythm. No threat of trouble from that source. She listened for her mother and heard bottles clinking in the kitchen. "Mom?" she called as she came around the corner.

"There you are. You and David must have gotten that last page done quickly. I only called half an hour ago."

"Uh, yeah. It was easier than I thought," she said quickly.

"Did you have a good time? He's a nice boy."

Laurel nodded, her mind nowhere near David—about forty-two miles away from David, to be precise.

"Are you two . . . ?"

"What?" Laurel tried to focus on what her mom was saying.

"Well, you spend an awful lot of time over at his house; I thought maybe the two of you were . . . becoming an item."

"I don't know," she said honestly. "Maybe."

"It's just—I know David's mom sometimes works long hours, so you and David spend a lot of time alone. It's easy for things to get out of control when you're in an empty house together."

"I'll be careful, Mom," she said wryly.

"I know you will, but I'm the mom, and I have to say it anyway," she said with a smile. "Remember," she added, "just because you haven't started your period doesn't necessarily mean you can't get pregnant."

"Mom!"

"I'm just saying."

Laurel thought of Tamani's words earlier that day. *Pollination is for reproduction—sex is just for fun.* She wondered what her mom would say if Laurel told her she *couldn't* get pregnant— would *never* start her period. That sex for her was just sex, with no strings attached. If there was anything Laurel could say to truly rattle her mother, that would be it. *She* was still trying to wrap her mind around it.

"Mom," Laurel said haltingly, "I wanted to talk to you about the land. It's been in your family for so long. And we lived there for my whole life." She ducked her head when she thought of her real origins—her secret home. "As long as I can remember, anyway." Unexpected tears pricked at her eyes when she looked back up at her mom. "It's the most magical place in the world. I wish you wouldn't sell it."

Her mom looked at her for a long time. "Mr. Barnes is offering us a lot of money, Laurel. All the things you've wanted lately that we couldn't afford would be in our budget again."

"But what if you didn't sell? Would we be okay?"

Her mom sighed and thought about that for a moment. "Your dad is doing good business, but there's no guarantee that will continue." She leaned forward over the counter on her elbows. "We would have this tight budget for a long time, Laurel. I don't like living this frugally. You're not the only one who has to give things up."

Laurel was quiet for a while. It seemed too monumental a task for a fifteen-year-old girl. *But then*, she added mentally, *I am no ordinary girl*. Buoyed up by that thought, she said, "Could you at least think about it? For like, a week?" Laurel added when her mom pursed her lips.

"We're supposed to sign papers on Wednesday."

"A week? Please? Just tell Mr. Barnes you need a week. And if you really think about it for a week, I won't bother you about it ever again."

Her mom studied her with skepticism.

"Please?"

Her face softened. "I guess Mr. Barnes probably wouldn't rescind his offer if I needed one more week."

Laurel bounded around the bar and hugged her mom. "Thanks," she whispered. "It means a lot."

"So he really didn't tell you much." David sat on a stool at the bar in his kitchen. His mom was on a date, so he and Laurel had the house to themselves tonight. David was eating microwaved leftovers and Laurel was doodling on a notebook, trying to distract herself from the smell.

"He told me enough," Laurel said defensively. "It was like he wanted to tell me more, but he wasn't allowed. I could tell it annoyed him."

"He sounds kind of weird."

"He's definitely different—and not just in his looks." She paused in the middle of a spiral and looked up, remembering. "He's so intense. Everything he feels—good or bad—seems enhanced. And contagious." She started scribbling again. "You want to feel like he does, but there's just no way you could keep up, because the way he's feeling changes so quickly. It must be exhausting to be so passionate." Her body shivered as she found just the right word for him. *Passionate*, always.

"So are you two, like, friends now?"

"I don't know." The truth was that she knew he wanted her. And that, despite trying not to, she felt much the same way. It seemed disloyal spending the evening with David after her day with Tamani. Or maybe she felt disloyal having spent the day with Tamani. It was hard to tell for sure.

She reached up to touch the ring he'd given her, strung on a thin, silver chain. She'd done so at least a hundred times already that day. It brought back the feeling of being with him. In their short visit, they had become more than friends—no, not more, *beyond* friends. The word *friend* seemed too paltry to describe the connection they shared. It was more like they had a bond. She couldn't tell David that. It would be hard enough to explain to an unaffected observer—and David was far from unaffected. If he had any idea of the storm of emotions she felt for Tamani, he would be terribly jealous.

But that didn't mean she didn't like David. She considered him her best friend and sometimes more. David was everything Tamani wasn't—calm and centered, logical, soothing. Her feelings for him weren't a storm of chaos but a calm, strong pull. He was a constant in her life in a way Tamani never could be. Two halves that could never be a whole.

David finally finished his dinner and Laurel pushed the notebook aside to face him. "Thanks for covering for me, by the way. I never dreamed my mom would actually call you."

David shrugged. "You'd been gone a long time, and she knows you don't actually like biology."

"I did some reading this afternoon," Laurel said. "You know how plants absorb carbon dioxide from the air and then release oxygen as a by-product, right?"

"Yeah, that's why we're supposed to save the trees and all that stuff."

"I was thinking it wouldn't make sense for me to breathe oxygen."

"So . . . you think you breathe carbon dioxide?"

"And exhale oxygen, yeah."

"I guess that would make sense."

"I was thinking," Laurel began slowly, "that we could try another experiment."

David looked at her, puzzled. "Okay. What kind of experiment?"

"Um, well, air's not something you can look at under a microscope or anything, so the only way to tell if I was exhaling oxygen would be to see if you could inhale it without any problems."

David began to see where this was headed. "And how do you propose we do that?" he asked, with a tiny smile hovering around the corner of his mouth.

"Well, I was kind of thinking it would be sort of like . . . mouth-to-mouth resuscitation. Except you'd breathe into my mouth first and then, without getting another breath of air, I could breathe into yours." She looked at him for a second then blurted, "But there's no reason you have to. It was just an idea I had."

"I'm impressed," David said. "You studied bio all by yourself."

Laurel rolled her eyes but grinned. "Google is my friend."

David snorted, then tried to cover it with a cough.

Laurel glared at him.

"It makes sense," David said. "Let's do it."

David turned toward her till their knees were touching.

"First you take a breath of air and hold it for about ten seconds so your lungs can convert it to carbon dioxide. Then blow it into my mouth, and I'll breathe it in. Then I'll wait about ten seconds and blow it back into your mouth, okay?"

David nodded.

It sounded simple enough. Well, except the mouth-to-mouth part. But she could handle that. Right?

David's chest expanded as he sucked in a lungful of air, and his face flushed red while he held it.

No backing out now.

After about ten seconds he gestured to her and leaned forward, his eyes trained on her mouth. She forced herself to focus as she leaned forward to meet him. Their lips touched gently at first and Laurel almost forgot herself and breathed in a nervous gulp of air. Then David pressed more firmly and blew into her mouth. She let her lungs fill.

He pulled back and Laurel made the mistake of meeting his eyes. She smiled, then had to look away as she counted to ten. Then he was leaning back in, his hand tugging softly on her shoulder.

Laurel met him halfway without any hesitation this time. His mouth pressed to hers and he opened his lips just a little. She blew all the air from her lungs back into his mouth and felt him inhale it. He lingered for just a moment before pulling back and breaking contact.

"Wow." He exhaled and ran his fingers through his hair. "Wow. That was amazing. My head's spinning a little. I think you're exhaling almost pure oxygen, Laurel."

"You're not going to fall off your stool, are you?" She placed her hands on his legs.

"I'm all right," David said, breathing slowly. "Just give me a couple more seconds." He let his hands slide down to cover hers, where they were still braced on his legs. She looked up as he sucked on his bottom lip, then grinned.

"What's so funny?"

"Sorry," David said, reddening again. "You just taste so sweet."

"What do you mean, sweet?"

He licked his bottom lip one more time. "You taste like honey."

"Honey?"

"Yeah. I thought I was going nuts the day . . . well, you know, that one day. But it was the same today. Your mouth is really sweet." He paused for a second, then grinned. "Not like honey—like *nectar*. That makes more sense."

"Great. Now I'm going to have to explain that to everyone I kiss for the rest of my life unless it's you or . . . or another faerie." She'd almost said Tamani's name. Her fingers flew to the ring around her neck.

David shrugged. "Then don't kiss anyone except me."

"David . . ."

"I'm just offering up the obvious solution," he said, hands up in protest.

She laughed and rolled her eyes. "I guess that'll keep me from being one of those girls who kisses everyone."

David shook his head. "You could never be like that. Your feelings are too soft. You'd worry that you were breaking the heart of every guy you kissed."

She wasn't sure if he meant that as a compliment or not, but it felt that way. "Um, thanks. I think."

"So what is that?" he asked, pointing to her necklace. "You keep playing with it."

Laurel dropped the ring down the front of her shirt. It was like a talisman that sent her thoughts straight to Tamani. She wondered if Tamani had known before he gave it to her that it would do that. She was a little surprised when the

175

thought didn't irritate her. "It's a ring," she finally confessed. "Tamani gave it to me."

David looked at her strangely. "Tamani gave you a *ring*?"

"It's not like that." *Guys.* "It's a baby ring. I guess all faeries get them when they're little." Against her impulse to keep the ring her own special secret, she pulled the chain out from under her shirt and showed David the tiny circlet.

"That's really pretty," he said grudgingly. "Why'd he give it to you?"

Laurel tried to shrug his question away. "I don't know. He just wanted me to have it."

David looked at it for a long time before dropping it back onto her chest.

SIXTEEN

"JUST IN TIME," MOM SAID AS LAUREL WALKED IN THE door from school the next day. "The phone's for you."

Laurel took the phone. She'd just left David at the corner. Why would he call her already? "Hello?" she asked questioningly.

"Hey, Laurel. It's Chelsea."

"Hi," Laurel said.

"Are you busy? It's a sunny day, so I thought you might like to go see the Battery Point Lighthouse."

Laurel had heard of the historic landmark but hadn't yet seen it. "Yeah," she said. "I'd love to."

"Pick you up in five?"

"Great."

"Going somewhere with David?" Laurel's mom asked after she hung up.

"Chelsea, actually. She wants to go to the lighthouse. Is that okay?"

"Sure, that's wonderful. I'm glad to see you branching out. You know I like David a lot, but you should have more friends. It's healthier."

Laurel went to the fridge and opened up a soda while she was waiting.

"I got your midterm grades in the mail today," her mom said.

The soda seemed to stick in Laurel's throat. Up until she blossomed, she'd been doing quite well in school, but she wasn't sure how much of that she'd been able to keep up when her life went crazy.

"Three As, two Bs. I'm pretty happy with that," her mom said with a smile. Then she laughed and added, "Honestly, part of me is proud of myself. I must have done an okay job for you to be doing this well."

Laurel rolled her eyes as her mom handed her the grades. The B in bio wasn't surprising, but then neither was the A in English. All she had to do was make it until the end of the semester now. Shouldn't be too hard. The worst was definitely behind her.

"Why's Dad's car here?" Laurel asked.

Her mom sighed. "Dad's sick. He's been sick all day. Missed work, even."

"Wow," Laurel said. "He hasn't missed a day of work in forever."

"Yeah. I made him stay in bed all day. He should be better tomorrow."

She heard a horn honk in the driveway.

"There's Chelsea," Laurel said, grabbing her jacket.

"Have fun," her mom said with a smile.

Laurel slid into the backseat of Chelsea's mom's car and Chelsea turned and beamed at her. "Hey! The lighthouse is awesome; it's totally classic. You'll love it."

Chelsea's mom dropped them off in the parking lot. "I'll be back in about two hours," she said.

"Bye," Chelsea called, waving.

"Where now?" Laurel said, looking out at the ocean.

"We walk," Chelsea said, pointing to an island about five hundred feet out from the shore.

"We're walking to an island?"

"Technically it's an isthmus when the tide is low."

Shading her eyes from the sun, Laurel squinted out at the island. "I don't see a lighthouse."

"It's not like the lighthouses you see in paintings. It's just a house with a light on the roof."

Chelsea led the way as they walked on a small strip of sand that connected the little island to the mainland. It was fun to be so close to the ocean without actually being in it. Laurel liked the tangy smell of the salt water and the fresh breeze that caressed her face and sent Chelsea's curly hair swinging. It was ironic, really, that she enjoyed the smell of the ocean when she hated salty water.

When they reached the island, there was a gravel road that led up a hill. It was only a few minutes before they came around a small bend and the lighthouse came into view.

"It really is just a normal house," Laurel said, surprised.

"Except for the light," Chelsea said, pointing.

Chelsea played tour guide, under the watchful eye of a

security guard, as she showed Laurel through the small house and explained the history of the lighthouse, including its role in the tsunamis that Crescent City fell victim to every few years. "They're awesome," Chelsea said, "at least, when they don't get too big."

Laurel wasn't sure she shared Chelsea's enthusiasm.

Chelsea took her out to a small yard and pointed out the purple flowers that grew up the rocks on all sides of the tiny island. "They're really pretty," Laurel said, bending to touch a small patch of the tiny blossoms.

Chelsea pulled a blanket out of her bag and spread it on the soft grass. They sat together, watching the sea in silence for a few minutes. Laurel felt so at peace in this rugged, beautiful place. Chelsea dug into her bag again and brought out a Snickers bar for herself and handed Laurel a small Tupperware.

"What's this?" Laurel asked.

"Strawberries. They're organic, if that matters," Chelsea added.

Laurel smiled and popped the top. "Thanks. They look great." A million times better than the candy bar Chelsea was enjoying.

"So what's up with you and David?"

Laurel choked on the strawberry she had just started chewing and coughed energetically. "What do you mean?"

"I just wondered if you guys are a couple yet."

"Well, don't beat around the bush about it or anything," Laurel said, more to her strawberries than to Chelsea.

"He really likes you, Laurel." Chelsea sighed. "I wish he liked me half as much."

Laurel poked at her strawberries with her fork.

"I think I've liked him since the day he moved here. He and I used to be on a soccer team together," she added, smiling.

Laurel could see in her mind a ten-year-old Chelsea—opinionated and outspoken just like now, and not really fitting in—meeting David for the first time. Nonjudgmental, accepting David. It was no wonder Chelsea had latched on to him. But still . . . "Chelsea, no offense, but why are you telling me this?"

"I don't know." They were silent for a little while. "I'm not trying to make you feel bad or anything," Chelsea assured her. "David doesn't like me that way, I know that. Honestly, if he's going to have a girlfriend, I'd rather it was someone like you. Someone I'm friends with too."

"That's good, I guess," Laurel said.

"So . . . are you his girlfriend now?" Chelsea pressed.

"I don't know. Maybe?"

"Is that a question?" Chelsea asked with a grin.

"I don't know." She paused, then glanced sidelong at Chelsea. "You really don't mind if I talk about it?"

"Not at all. It's like living vicariously."

"You say the weirdest things sometimes," Laurel said ruefully.

"Yeah, that's what David says too. Personally, I don't think enough people say what they really think."

"You definitely have a point there."

"So, girlfriend or not?" Chelsea asked again, refusing to let it drop.

Laurel shrugged. "I really don't know. Sometimes I think that's what I want, but I've never had a boyfriend before. I've never really even had a guy who was a close friend. I like it a lot . . . I don't want to lose that part."

"Maybe you won't."

"Maybe. I'm just not sure."

"There could be fringe benefits," Chelsea said.

"Like what?"

"If you guys were on kissing terms he might do your bio homework."

"Tempting," Laurel said. "I suck at bio."

Chelsea grinned. "Yeah, that's what he said."

Laurel's eyes widened. "He did not! Really?"

"It's hardly a secret—you moan about it almost every day at lunch. I think he'd be a great boyfriend," Chelsea added.

"Why are you encouraging this? Most people in your position would be trying to break us up."

"I am *not* most people," Chelsea said defensively. "Besides," she continued in a lighter tone, "it would make him really happy. I like it when David's happy."

"I'm home," Laurel yelled as she entered the house, tossed her backpack on the ground, and walked into the pantry in search of a jar of canned pears. Her mom came in a few minutes later as Laurel was nibbling on a pear half straight out of the jar. But instead of the "Mom look" Laurel usually got for not using a bowl, her mom only sighed and smiled wearily.

"Can you fend for yourself for dinner tonight?"

"Sure, what's up?"

"Your dad's just getting worse. His stomach hurts and is a little swollen, and now he's got a fever. It's not too high—around a hundred—but I can't get it to go down. Not with cold compresses or a cool bath or even my hyssop and licorice-root capsules."

"Really?" Laurel asked. Her mom had an herb for everything, and they worked wonders. Her friends often called her up when they were at the end of their ropes and the over-the-counter medications just weren't cutting it. "Did you try giving him some Echinacea tea?" she suggested, since that was what her mom always gave her.

"Made him a whole batch of it, iced. But he's having trouble swallowing, too, so I don't know that he's getting enough to help."

"I bet it was something he ate," Laurel suggested.

"Maybe," her mom said distractedly, but she didn't sound convinced. "He really took a turn for the worse right after you left. Anyway," she added, snapping her head back to her daughter, "I'm going to spend the evening with him, see if I can make him a bit more comfortable."

"No problem. I've got canned pears and a bunch of homework."

"Exciting night for both of us."

"Yep," Laurel said with a sigh, looking over at the stack of books waiting for her on the table.

SEVENTEEN

AFTER SCHOOL ON THURSDAY, LAUREL GRABBED HER blue apron and headed down the street toward Mark's Bookshelf. Jen, Brent, and Maddie—her dad's staff—had been putting in extra shifts, but if things continued the way they'd been, all three would top forty hours by Friday. Laurel wanted to at least give Brent and Jen the day off. She and Maddie could manage. Maddie was the only employee Laurel's dad had inherited from the former bookstore owner. Maddie had been working in that store for almost ten years now and, luckily, could about run the place herself.

But it wasn't the bookstore Laurel worried about as she walked toward Main Street. She'd gone into her parents' room to get some last-minute instructions from her dad and had been shocked by his appearance. Dad had always been on the thin side, but now his face was sunken and gray, with deep shadows under his eyes. His lips were pale and a thin sheen of sweat covered his brow. Laurel's mom had tried everything.

Poultices of lavender and rosemary on his chest, fennel tea for his stomach, loads of vitamin C to strengthen his immune system. Nothing seemed to be working. She gave him brandy at night to help him sleep and dripped peppermint oil in the humidifier. Still no improvement. Not letting pride stand in her way, she had even tried a handful of conventional medications—NyQuil and Extra Strength Tylenol—and still he didn't feel any better. What everyone had hoped was a nasty flu had turned serious far more quickly than her mom could have anticipated.

When Laurel volunteered to go to the bookstore that afternoon so her mom could stay home with her dad, her mom had hugged Laurel tightly and whispered thanks into her ear. He didn't look like himself at all—more like a sickly caricature of the man he'd been only a few days ago. He'd tried to smile and joke the way he always did—always had—but even that was too much for him.

A cheerful chime sounded as Laurel opened the front door of the store.

Maddie looked up and smiled. "Laurel? You get prettier every time I see you." She hugged her, and Laurel lingered in the embrace, feeling a little better. Maddie always smelled like cookies and spices and something else Laurel could never put her finger on.

"How's your dad?" Maddie asked with an arm still around Laurel's shoulders.

Her answer to everyone else had been a simple, "He's okay." But when Maddie asked, Laurel couldn't just brush it off. "He looks awful, Maddie. Like skin sitting loose on a skeleton. My mom can't do anything to help. Nothing is working."

"Even her hyssop and licorice root?"

Laurel smiled painfully. "That's what I asked."

"Well, it's a miracle cure, as far as I'm concerned."

"Not for Dad. Not this time, anyway."

"I light a candle for him every night." What licorice root and hyssop were to Laurel's mom, candles were to Maddie. She was a devout Catholic who had a rack of candles in her front window and lit one for everything from a fellow parishioner dying of cancer to a neighborhood cat gone missing. Still, Laurel was grateful.

"Dad sent in a schedule for the rest of the week."

Maddie laughed. "Sick in bed and still drawing up schedules—he must not be too close to death's door." She held out her hand. "Here, let's have it." Maddie studied the handwritten schedule. "He's got us cutting business hours, I see."

Laurel nodded. "There just aren't enough employees to maintain regular hours."

"That's fine. I've been telling him for months it was silly to open at eight. Who wants to buy a book at eight o'clock in the morning?" She leaned forward as if sharing a secret. "Truth be told, I don't even like to be out of bed at eight o'clock in the morning."

They worked the next few hours together cheerfully enough, both avoiding the subject of Laurel's father. But he was never far from Laurel's mind. She left Maddie finishing up the end-of-day paperwork and taped a sign to the door apologizing for the unscheduled closing of the store that weekend.

Laurel walked home slowly, her whole body tired after two hours of stocking box after box of books. As she rounded the last corner, she saw a large vehicle parked in her driveway. It took a few seconds to register what she was seeing, but her feet began to run the second she recognized the white and red ambulance. She burst through her front door just as the paramedics were coming down the stairs with her father on a stretcher, her mom only a step behind.

"What's wrong with him?" Laurel asked, her eyes pinned to her father.

Tears were tracing lines down her mom's face. "He started throwing up blood. I had to call."

The stairs finally cleared enough for Laurel to reach her mom. She wrapped her arms around her waist. "It's fine, Mom. He'll be glad you did."

"He doesn't trust doctors," her mom said distractedly.

"That doesn't matter. He needs this."

Her mom nodded, but Laurel wasn't sure she'd even heard her. "I have to go with him," she said. "Only one person is allowed to ride in the ambulance. I think it'll be better if I call you when he's settled."

"Yeah, go. I can take care of myself."

She managed to get her mom's purse hooked over her arm as she continued walking toward the ambulance, unaware of Laurel's presence. She didn't look back as the doors slammed shut.

Laurel watched the ambulance drive away and a sickening, squeezing sensation enveloped her stomach. Neither of her parents had ever been to the hospital in Laurel's memory except to visit someone. Laurel hadn't wanted to believe this was more than an acute virus that would eventually pass on its own. But that didn't seem to be the case.

She walked back into the house and pushed the door shut with both hands. The sound of it clicking into place seemed to echo through the front hallway. The house felt enormous and empty without her parents. She'd been home alone many times in the five months since they'd moved in, but tonight felt different. Frightening. Her hands shook as she turned the key to the deadbolt. She slid down the door and sat on the floor for a long time as the last bits of light left over from the sunset faded, leaving Laurel in murky blackness.

With the arrival of darkness came an unspoken permission to think dark thoughts as well. Laurel pushed herself to her feet and hurried to the kitchen, where she turned on every light before settling down at the dining room table. She pulled out her English assignment and tried to work through it, but after reading the first sentence, the letters swam before her eyes—meaningless gibberish.

She laid her head down on her book. Her thoughts wandered from the bookstore to Tamani to David, then back to her parents at the hospital and around and around until her eyes slowly closed.

A loud ringing jerked her from confusing, senseless dreams. She focused on the sound and managed to press the Talk button on the phone and rasp out a sleepy, "Hello?"

"Hey, sweetie, it's Mom."

Laurel snapped all the way awake and squinted at her rumpled textbook. "What did they say?"

"They're going to keep him overnight and give him anti-biotics. We'll have to wait and see what happens tomorrow." She hesitated. "He's not even in a room yet, and by the time he is, it will be late. Can you stay on your own tonight and come to see him tomorrow?"

Laurel wavered for a few seconds. She had the irrational feeling that if she went to the hospital, she could do something. But that was silly. Tomorrow would be soon enough. She forced a cheery tone into her voice. "Don't worry about me, Mom. I'll be fine."

"I love you."

"I love you too."

Once again, Laurel was by herself in the empty house. Almost of their own accord, her fingers found David's number. He said hello before she consciously realized she'd called him. "David?" she said, blinking. "Hi." She looked over at the kitchen window where the moon was rising. She had no idea what time it was. "Can you come over?"

When the doorbell rang, Laurel ran to let David in. "I'm so sorry I called. I didn't know how late it was," she said.

"It's okay," David said, his hands firm on her shoulders. "It's only ten, and my mom said I could be home whenever. Emergencies happen. What can I do?"

Laurel shrugged. "My mom's gone and . . . I don't want to be alone."

David put his arms around her shoulders as she leaned into him. He held her in the foyer for several minutes while she curled against his chest, holding him for comfort. He felt so solid and warm against her and she tightened her arms till they started to ache. For a little while, it seemed like maybe everything would be okay.

Finally she pulled away. She felt awkward after letting David hold her for so long. But he just smiled and walked over to the couch and picked up her guitar. "Who plays?" he asked, strumming a random chord. "Your dad?"

"No. Um . . . I do. I've never taken lessons or anything. Mostly I've just kind of figured things out on my own."

"How is it that I didn't know this?"

Laurel shook her head. "I'm not that good, really."

"How long have you been playing?"

"About three years." She took the guitar from him and balanced it on her knee. "I found it in the attic. It used to be my mom's. She showed me the basic fingerings and I just kind of play by ear now."

"Will you play something for me?"

"Oh, no," Laurel said, pulling her fingers away from the strings.

"Please? I bet it would make you feel better."

"Why do you think that?"

He shrugged. "You're holding it so naturally. Like you really love it."

Laurel's hands stroked the neck. "I do. It's really old. I like old things. They have . . . history, and stories."

"So play." David leaned back, his hands behind his head.

Laurel hesitated, then strummed the guitar softly, making small adjustments. Slowly her hands transitioned from tuning chords to the soft melody of John Lennon's "Imagine." After the first verse, Laurel started singing the words slowly, softly. It seemed like an appropriate song tonight. As her fingers finished the final chord she sighed.

"Wow," David said. "That was really beautiful."

Laurel shrugged and laid the guitar back in its case.

"You didn't tell me you sing, either." He paused. "I've never heard anything like that before. It wasn't like the way a pop star sings; it was just beautiful and calming." He took her hand. "Feel better?"

She smiled. "I do. Thanks."

David cleared his throat as he squeezed her hand. "So what now?"

Laurel looked around. There wasn't much here for entertainment. "Want to watch a movie?"

David nodded. "Sure."

Laurel chose an old musical where no one was sick and no one died.

"Singin' in the Rain?" David asked, wrinkling his nose a little.

Laurel shrugged. "It's fun."

"Your call."

Fifteen minutes into the movie, David was laughing while Laurel just watched him—his silhouette brightened by the television screen. His face was in an almost-smile, and every once in a while he would tilt his head back and laugh. It was easy to forget about everything else when she was with him. Without stopping to think about her actions, Laurel scooted closer. Almost instinctively, David lifted his arm and draped it around her shoulders. Laurel snuggled up against his ribs and laid her head on his chest. His arm tightened around her, and he leaned his head so his cheek rested against the crown of her head.

"Thanks for coming," Laurel whispered with a smile.

"Anytime," David said, his lips brushing her hair.

Laurel looked up when the chime sounded on the front door of the bookstore. She wasn't sure she had it in her to smile at one more customer. But a smile of relief crossed her face when her eyes found David's. "Hi," she said, and set the stack of books she'd been sorting back on the table beside the shelf.

"Hey," David said quietly. "How are you doing?"

Laurel forced herself to smile. "I'm alive."

"Barely." He hesitated. "How's your dad?"

Laurel turned back to the shelf, trying to blink away her tears for about the fiftieth time that day. She felt David's hands rubbing her shoulders and she leaned on him, letting herself relax, feeling better—safer. "They're transferring him to Brookings Medical Center," she whispered after a few minutes.

"Is he worse?"

"It's hard to tell."

David let his cheek rest against the top of her head.

The chime at the front door sounded again, and even though Jen hurried to help the customer, Laurel stepped away and took a deep, shuddering breath to regain composure. "I need to get this done," she said, picking up the small stack of books from the table. "The store closes in an hour, and I've got four more boxes to unload."

"Let me help," David said. "Just tell me where they go." He grinned. "You can be the supervisor." He took the stack of books from her and rubbed the shiny cover of the top one for a few seconds. "Maybe I could come in and help tomorrow too."

"You have your own job. You have to pay for car insurance, you told me."

"I don't care about my stupid insurance, Laurel." His voice was sharp and he paused before continuing in a soft, calm tone. "This is the first time all week I've seen you for more than lunch or during class. I miss you," he said with a shrug.

Laurel hesitated.

"Please?"

Laurel relented. "Fine, but only till my dad's better."

"That'll be soon, Laurel. They have great specialists in Brookings; they'll figure out what's wrong." He grinned. "You'll be lucky if you get a whole week's worth of labor out of me."

EIGHTEEN

DESPITE DAVID'S OPTIMISTIC WORDS, ONE WEEK turned into two, and still Laurel's dad didn't improve. Laurel moved through her life like a ghost, hardly speaking to anyone except Maddie and David and Chelsea, who often stopped by the bookstore to chat. They hadn't gotten Chelsea to help much yet—she was a natural supervisor, she joked—but the company of Laurel's two friends was comforting.

True to his word, David was determined to work at the bookstore until Laurel's dad came home. Laurel felt guilty as time passed and he kept working for free, but it was an argument she always lost.

Some days they spent the afternoons chatting as they sorted books and dusted shelves, and for just a few minutes Laurel would forget about her dad. It never lasted long, though. Now that he had been transferred, she didn't get to see him every day. But the minute David got his license, he volunteered to play chauffeur every two or three days.

He drove her and Chelsea out to Brookings the first day after getting his license, and though Laurel held on to her seatbelt with white knuckles and Chelsea lectured him every time he went over the speed limit, they made it in one piece.

Laurel brought flowers—just wild ones from their yard. She hoped the reminder of home would make her father more anxious to return. He'd been very weak and only managed to keep his eyes open for a few minutes to say hello and accept a gentle hug. Then he slipped back into the oblivion of the morphine.

That was the last time Laurel had seen her father awake. Shortly afterward, the hospital staff started sedating him full-time to keep him from the continual pain that even morphine couldn't completely take away. Laurel was secretly glad. It was easier to see him there asleep. He looked peaceful and content. When he was awake, she could see the pain he tried to hide and it was horribly obvious how weak he had become. Sleep was better.

The lab tech had been able to isolate a toxin in her dad's blood, but it was one the doctors had never seen before and, so far, were helpless to treat. They tried everything, filling his body with any chemical they thought might help—turning him into a human guinea pig as they attempted to reverse the effects of the toxin. But nothing worked. His body was getting weaker, and two days earlier one of the doctors pulled Laurel's mom out of the room and informed her that, though they would keep trying, if they couldn't cleanse the toxin from his blood, it was only a matter of time before his organs would shut down, one by one.

And it didn't help that Mr. Barnes had started calling every night. For over a week, Laurel had been able to just say that her mom wasn't home, but after a while, he wouldn't accept that answer. After being interrogated twice, Laurel had started letting the answering machine pick up all the calls, snatching it off the hook only if it was David or Chelsea.

She didn't tell her mom about Mr. Barnes at all.

She felt guilty every night as she erased the daily message—sometimes two—but she had promised Tamani she would do what she could.

It was strange to think of Tamani now. He seemed almost like a dream. A bigger-than-life person who belonged with the glitz and excitement that had come with her acceptance that she really was a faerie. None of that seemed very important now. She considered going to see him, but even if she had transportation, what could he do? Enticing certainly wasn't going to help her father.

She'd promised that she would warn him if the property was in trouble, but since she was erasing all of Mr. Barnes's messages, it wasn't. Lately, she just tried not to think about Tamani at all.

Laurel heard the high-pitched ring of the telephone from inside the door as she was coming home from the bookstore, and she hurried to turn her key in the lock. She reached the phone on the sixth ring and heard her mother's voice. "Hey, Mom. How's Dad today?"

The line was silent.

"Mom?"

She heard her mother take a ragged breath and find her voice again. "I just spoke to Dr. Hansen," she said, her voice quivering. "Your dad is showing signs of heart failure. They've given him less than a week."

David was silent as he drove down the darkened highway. Laurel had managed to catch him on his cell phone just as he was reaching his house, and he'd insisted on driving her down to Brookings that night instead of waiting for morning. Laurel had the window down, and even though David must have been freezing with the cold autumn wind rushing through the car, he didn't protest. She felt his eyes flit continually to her, and once in a while he would reach over and run his hand down her arm. But he said nothing.

They pulled into the parking lot of Brookings Medical Center and David took Laurel's hand as they followed the familiar route to Laurel's dad's room. Laurel knocked lightly on the open door and poked her head through the curtain that surrounded the doorway. Her mom sat at the small table with a man whose back was toward them—but she waved Laurel and David in.

Laurel recognized the man immediately. His shoulders were broad and hulking in a shirt that didn't seem to fit quite right. And something about his presence put her nerves on edge. It was Mr. Barnes.

Laurel leaned against the wall with her arms crossed over her chest as her mother continued talking to Barnes. She smiled and nodded several times and, though Laurel couldn't hear what the man was saying, her mother kept repeating, "Oh, yes," and "Of course," and nodding enthusiastically. Laurel narrowed her eyes as she continued to watch her mother smile and nod—signing papers without a single glance at what they said. It was too weird.

Her mom didn't like contracts, didn't trust "legalese," as she called it. She always pored over forms and agreements, often crossing lines out before she would sign. But now Laurel watched her sign about eight pieces of paper without reading a single word.

Barnes hadn't even glanced in their direction the whole time.

Laurel's skin began to tingle and she squeezed David's hand as Barnes obtained a few more signatures, handed a stapled stack of papers to Laurel's mom, and swept the rest into his briefcase. He shook her hand and turned, his eyes meeting Laurel's almost instantly. His eyes snapped from Laurel to David, then back to Laurel. His features broke into a devious grin that made Laurel take a step back.

"Laurel," he said in a voice that sounded so fake to her, "I was just asking about you. It seems that none of my messages made it through." He finished the sentence with the slightest bit of a growl, and Laurel clenched her teeth as terror suddenly filled her chest.

Then Barnes shrugged and his expression turned smug. "Luckily I managed to find your mom, so everything worked out okay."

Laurel said nothing as she glared at him, wishing she and David had arrived just an hour sooner. Then they could have . . . what? She didn't even know, but she wished she could have found out.

"It was a pleasure to see you again, Laurel." He glanced briefly at Laurel's mom, who was still smiling. "Your daughter is . . ." He paused and reached out one hand toward Laurel. She tried to back away, but she was already against the wall. She turned her face, but his rough fingers trailed down her cheek. "Lovely," he finished.

When he threw back the curtain and left, Laurel let out a breath and realized that she had been clutching David's hand so tightly that his fingers were white.

Laurel gritted her teeth. "What was he doing here?" she asked, her voice a little shaky.

Her mom was staring at the curtain still swinging from the man's exit. "What?" she asked, turning toward Laurel and David. "Oh, um . . ." She walked over to the table and began shuffling the papers into a pile. "He came to finalize the papers for the sale of the property in Orick."

"Mom, you promised you'd think about it."

"I did. And apparently you decided to do some of my thinking for me," she said, looking meaningfully at Laurel. "You will pass on my messages from now on, understand?"

Laurel stared at the ground. "Yes, Mom," she said quietly.

Her mom looked down at the papers on the small table and ran her finger along the edge of them, straightening the already orderly sheets. "Actually, I'd decided that if you wanted to keep the land in the family, we'd make do." Hope flooded through Laurel. Maybe it wasn't too late! "But that's not a possibility anymore." Laurel's mom was quiet for a while, and when she spoke again, her voice was small and strained. "He showed up here and upped his offer." She looked up and met Laurel's eyes. "I had to take it."

Laurel's stomach twisted and her breath suddenly felt labored as she thought of losing the land—losing Tamani. "Mom, you can't sell!" Laurel's voice was loud and high-pitched.

Her mom's eyes hardened and she glanced at Laurel's dad for an instant before taking two steps across the room to Laurel and grabbing her upper arm. She stormed out, pulling Laurel with her. Laurel's arm felt weak in her mother's crushing grasp; she couldn't remember her mom ever treating her so roughly. Her mom ducked into a small alcove and released Laurel's arm. Laurel forced herself not to rub it.

"This is not about you, Laurel. I can't hold on to something this valuable just because you like it. Life doesn't work that way." Her mom's face was tense and sharp.

Laurel stood against the wall and let her mother rail. For weeks she had been a rock—but no one could take all this stress without breaking once in a while.

"I'm sorry," Laurel whispered. "I shouldn't have yelled."

With a deep breath, Laurel's mom stopped pacing and looked at her. Her face slowly relaxed till it crumpled into a mess of tears. She backed against the wall and slowly slid down to the floor as tears streamed down her cheeks. Laurel took a deep breath and crossed the small space to sit beside her mother. She slipped an arm around her mom's waist and leaned her head on her shoulder. It felt strange to be comforting her mom.

"Did I hurt your arm?" her mom asked softly after the torrent of tears subsided.

"No," Laurel lied.

She sighed a deep, heavy sigh. "I really did consider not selling, Laurel. But I don't have a choice anymore. Because of these hospital bills, we're drowning in debt."

"Don't we have insurance?"

Her mom shook her head. "Not much. We never thought we'd need it. But with all the tests and medical care there's just—there's too much to pay for."

"Isn't there another way?"

"I wish there was. I've been racking my brain, but there's nowhere else to get money. It's the land or the store. And to be honest, the land's worth a lot more. We've stretched our credit to the limit just to keep your dad here as long as we have. No one will loan us any more."

She turned to Laurel. "I have to be sensible. The truth is—" She paused as tears filled her eyes again. "Your father may not wake up. Ever. I have to look to the future. The store is our only source of income. And even if he does wake up, there's no way to recover from a financial blow like this without selling *something*. Knowing how much your father loves his store, what would you have me do?"

Laurel wanted to look away from her mother's sad brown eyes, but she couldn't. She pushed Tamani from her mind and tried to think rationally. She set her jaw and nodded slowly. "You have to sell the land."

Her mom's face was haggard and her eyes looked gaunt. She lifted a hand to touch Laurel's cheek. "Thank you for understanding. I wish I had another choice, but I don't. Mr. Barnes will be back in the morning with some more paperwork to finalize the sale. He'll push it through escrow as quickly as possible, and with luck the money will be in our account within a week."

"A week?" It was all so fast.

Her mom nodded.

Laurel hesitated. "You acted funny while he was here. You were all happy and agreed with everything he said."

She shrugged. "I suppose I put on my business face. I just don't want anything to happen to mess up this sale. Mr. Barnes has offered enough to cover all the medical bills, and we'd have some left over too." She sighed. "I don't know what he knows, but I want to sell while the price is high."

"But you signed everything he put in front of you," Laurel continued. "You didn't even *read* it."

Her mom nodded forlornly. "I know. But there's just no time. I want to take advantage of this offer while it's on the table. If I hesitate again, he may decide we're too wishy-washy and yank the offer completely."

"I guess that makes sense," Laurel said. "But—"

"No more, please, Laurel. I cannot argue with you right now." She took Laurel's hand. "You have to trust that I am doing the best I can. Okay?"

Laurel nodded reluctantly.

Her mom rose from the floor and wiped the last trace of tears from her face. She pulled Laurel to her feet and hugged her. "We'll get through this," she promised. "No matter what happens, we'll find a way."

As they entered her dad's room again, Laurel's eyes went to the chair where Barnes had been sitting. It was unlike her to dislike someone so much without knowing him. But even the thought of sitting in the chair where Barnes had sat made her skin crawl. She walked over to the table and picked up his business card.

JEREMIAH BARNES, REALTOR.

Underneath was a local address.

It looked legitimate enough, but Laurel wasn't satisfied. She slipped the card into her back pocket and walked over to stand next to David. "Hungry, David?" Laurel said, eyeing him meaningfully.

He missed it entirely. "Not really."

She stepped closer and grabbed a fistful of the back of his shirt. "Mom, I'm going to take David and buy him some dinner. We'll be back in a couple of hours."

Her mom looked up, a little startled. "It's after nine."

"David's hungry," she said.

"Starving," David agreed, smiling.

"And he did drive me down here on a school night," Laurel added.

Laurel's mom looked at them doubtfully for a few seconds, then turned her attention back to her sleeping husband. "Don't try the cafeteria food," she warned.

★ ★ ★

"Why are we doing this again?" David asked after they'd driven around for almost an hour looking for the right part of town.

"David, there's something wrong with that guy. I can feel it."

"Yeah, but sneaking to his office and peeking in the windows? That's a little much."

"Well, what do you expect me to do? Call up and ask him if he'd like to tell me why he creeped me out so badly? That'll work," Laurel muttered.

"So what are you going to tell the cops when they arrest us?" David asked sarcastically.

"Oh, come on," Laurel said. "It's dark. We're just going to circle the office, peek into a few windows, and make sure everything looks legit." She paused. "And if they happen to have left a window open, well, that's not my fault."

"You are so nuts."

"Maybe, but you're here with me."

David rolled his eyes.

"This is Sea Cliff," Laurel said suddenly. "Turn your lights off."

David sighed but pulled over and killed the lights. In stealth mode, they crept to the end of the cul-de-sac and stopped in front of a dilapidated house that looked like it had been built in the early 1900s.

"That's it," Laurel whispered, squinting at the business card and the numbers on the curb.

David peered up at the imposing structure. "This doesn't look like any real-estate office I've ever seen. It looks abandoned."

"Less chance we'll get caught, then. Come on."

David pulled his jacket tighter as they crept around the side of the house and started peeking in the windows. It was dark and the moon was new, but Laurel still felt exposed in her light blue T-shirt. She wished she hadn't left her black jacket in the car. But if she went back now, she might not have the nerve to return.

The house was an enormous, sprawling structure with slightly newer additions sprouting off from the main building like random appendages. Laurel and David peered into the windows and saw a few bulky, shadowy shapes in the dark rooms—"Old furniture," David assured her—but the house was mostly empty. "There's no way he's actually doing business here," David said. "Why would he put this address on the business card?"

"Because he's hiding something," Laurel whispered back. "I knew it."

"Laurel, don't you think we're in a little over our heads here? We should go back to the hospital and call the police."

"And tell them what? That a realtor has a fake address on his business card? That's no crime."

"Let's tell your mom, then."

Laurel shook her head. "She's desperate to sell. And you saw her with this Barnes guy. It was like he had her in a trance. She just smiled and agreed with everything he said. I've never seen her do that before. And that stuff she signed, who knows what it was!" Laurel peered around the corner of a particularly crooked addition and waved at David. "I see a light."

David hurried to crouch beside her. Sure enough, near the back of the house, light shone through a small window. Laurel shivered.

"Cold?"

She shook her head. "Nervous."

"Have you changed your mind?"

"No way." She crawled forward, trying to avoid the large branches and trash strewn across the yard. The window was short enough to peek into while kneeling on the ground, and Laurel and David positioned themselves on either side of it. Blinds covered the glass, but they were warped and easy to see through. They heard voices and movement from inside, but with the window closed, they couldn't make out any words. Laurel took several calming breaths, then turned her head to look into the window.

She saw Jeremiah Barnes almost immediately, with his imposing figure and strange face. He was sitting at a table working on papers she could only assume he would be bringing for her mother to sign in the morning. There were two other men standing together, throwing darts at the wall. If Barnes was unattractive, these two were downright grotesque. Their skin hung on their faces as though not properly attached and their mouths were twisted into severe grins. One of the men's faces was a mess of scars and discoloration and, even from across the room, she could tell one eye was nearly white and the other almost black. The other had bright red hair that grew in a strange patchy pattern that even his hat couldn't completely hide.

"Laurel." David was waving her over to his side of the window. She ducked under the sill and peered in from the other angle. "What the hell is that?"

Chained at the far side of the room was something that looked half human, half animal. Its face was twisted lumps of flesh patched together almost at random. Large, crooked teeth poked out between its lips from a distended jaw topped by a bulbous monstrosity that might have been a nose. It was vaguely humanoid, and Laurel could see scraps of clothing wrapped around its shoulders and abdomen. But a collar lined its corded neck, giving it the appearance of a bizarre house pet. The hulking form slouched on a dirty mat, apparently sleeping.

Laurel's fingernails dug into the windowsill as she stared at the thing. Her breath came in ragged gasps, and somehow she couldn't look away. Just when she thought she might be able to gather the nerve to turn her head, one blue eye cracked open and met hers.

NINETEEN

LAUREL THREW HERSELF AWAY FROM THE WINDOW. "IT looked at me."

"Do you think it saw you?"

"I don't know. But we have to go. Now!" She heard guttural noises from inside and her knees felt glued to the ground.

The two men yelled at the creature to shut up, but Barnes silenced them with a loud word Laurel didn't recognize. A gentle crooning followed, and within seconds the howling of the strange creature had quieted.

Laurel leaned back toward the window but felt a small tug at the back of her shirt. She turned.

David shook his head at her and pointed to the car.

Laurel paused, but she wasn't quite satisfied. She held up one finger to David and snuck one more peek through the side of the window.

Her eyes met the mismatched gaze of Jeremiah Barnes.

"Go!" she hissed to David, and launched herself toward the front of the house. But before she got more than a step away, she heard the glass shatter and felt a large hand grab her by the neck, yanking her through the window into the filthy room. Rough fingers scraped at her throat as she felt the wooden window frame break against her back.

Then she was flying. She screamed for just an instant before she hit the wall on the opposite side of the room. Her head spun. Distantly she heard a grunt from David as he hit the wall beside her. Laurel tried to focus as the room around her seemed to spin. David reached out and pulled her to him, and she felt a trail of hot blood drip onto her shoulder.

The room finally stopped spinning, and she looked up into Barnes's jeering face. "What have we here?" He smiled cruelly. "Sarah's little girl. I've heard more about you today than I ever wanted to know."

Laurel opened her mouth to retort, but David squeezed her arm. Laurel felt a thick, syrupy liquid trail down from the stinging wound on her back and wondered how much damage the window frame had done.

"Good girl, Bess," Barnes said, patting the strange animal on her half-balding head. Then he dropped to a crouch beside Laurel and David. "Why are you here?" he asked in a soft yet commanding voice. Laurel felt her mouth begin to open of its own accord. "We . . . we had to find out why you . . . why you—" Then she managed to grab hold of her wits, forced her mouth shut, and glared at Barnes.

"We could tell something wasn't right," David said. "We came to see if we could find anything."

Laurel turned with wide eyes and looked at David. He was staring straight ahead with a slightly dazed look on his face that was eerily similar to the look Laurel had seen on her mom just an hour earlier. "David!" she hissed.

"And what were you planning to do if you found anything?" Barnes asked in that same strangely compelling voice.

"Get proof. Take it to the cops."

"David!" Laurel yelled, but he didn't seem to hear her.

"Why are you so worried?" Barnes asked.

Again David opened his mouth, but there were too many secrets that could come spilling out. Laurel closed her eyes, apologized mentally, and slapped David across the face as hard as she could.

"Shit! Ow! Laurel!" David cupped his cheek in his hand, stretching out his jawbone.

A sigh of relief escaped Laurel's lips and she squeezed David's hand. He just looked confused.

"I've heard enough," Barnes said, standing up.

The red-haired man smiled—a sinister caricature of a real smile that made Laurel cringe and shrink back against David's chest. "Let's break their legs. I could use the exercise."

Laurel felt David stiffen, and his breathing turned short and erratic.

Barnes shook his head. "Not here; this address is on my card. I've got enough blood to clean up as it is." He crouched down again and looked back and forth between them for a long minute. "You two like to swim?"

Laurel narrowed her eyes and glared at the man, but David held her back.

"I think you'd find a little dip in the Chetco quite . . . refreshing tonight." Barnes stood and grabbed David's shoulders, yanking him to his feet. "Search him." The other two men grinned and began emptying out David's pockets—wallet, keys, and a tin of Altoids. Barnes picked up the keys and tossed them to Scarface and slid the mints and wallet back into David's pants. "So the cops can ID you when your bodies are found in the spring," he said with a chuckle.

Without David to hold her back, Laurel launched herself at Barnes, her nails seeking his face, his eyes, anything. Barnes tossed David to his partners and grabbed Laurel's arms, twisting them behind her till she whimpered in pain. He set his mouth close to her ear and stroked her face. She couldn't even flinch away. "You just hold still now," he whispered soothingly. "Because if you don't," he continued in the same dulcet tone, "I'll tear your arms off."

David was struggling with his captors, yelling and trying to get to Laurel, but he couldn't fight any better than she could. "Quiet!" Barnes roared in a voice that filled the room and echoed off the walls. David's mouth clamped shut.

"Take the car," Barnes said. "Drive up past Azalea and toss them in the river. And don't forget to weigh them down," he added cynically. "Make sure there's no way this one," he gestured toward Laurel, "shows up before the papers are signed tomorrow." He laughed. "Spring is ideal, but as long as it's not tomorrow, I don't really care when they find them. And leave the car up there. Not in the parking lot—beside some trail. I don't need some missing kid's car hanging out in front of my *office*." He glared sidelong at them. "Walk back. It'll do you two good."

"You're not going to get away with this," Laurel muttered between clenched teeth.

But Barnes only laughed. He released her arm and looked at the red splayed across his hand—David's blood. "What a waste," he said, wiping the blood from his hands with a white handkerchief. "Take them away."

The two men trussed Laurel and David together and tossed them into the backseat of David's Civic. "You can scream all you want now," Red said with a grin. "No one'll hear you."

As they drove, streetlights flickered over the car, just enough light that Laurel could make out David's face. His jaw was flexed and he looked as scared as she was, but he didn't bother to scream either.

"Feels good to be out doing this again, doesn't it?" Scarface said, speaking aloud for the first time. Unlike his companion, Scarface's voice was deep and smooth—the kind of voice you'd expect to hear from the hero in an old black-and-white movie, not from this rough, disfigured face.

"Yeah," said Red with a laugh—a wheezing rheumy laugh that made Laurel's stomach turn. "I've been so sick of sitting around that old dump waiting for something exciting to happen."

"We're some of the best in the whole horde. But Barnes

treats us like we're nothing. Sends us off to take care of kids. Kids!"

"Yeah." A few seconds passed in silence. "We should rip 'em to pieces instead of tossing them in the river. That'd make you feel better."

A soft chuckle from that perfect, movie-star voice filled every inch of the car despite its low volume. A chill shivered up Laurel's spine. "I'd like that." He turned to peer back at Laurel and David with a frighteningly calm smile. Then he sighed and turned his eyes back to the road. "But they can't be found for a few days. Pieces are hard to hide—even in a river." He paused. "We better just follow orders."

"Laurel?"

David's whisper distracted her for one blessed instant. "Yeah?"

"I'm sorry I didn't believe you about Barnes."

"It's okay."

"Yeah, but I should have trusted you. I wish . . ." His voice trailed off for a few seconds. "I wish that we could have—"

"Don't you dare start saying your good-byes, David Lawson," Laurel hissed as quietly as she could. "This is *not* over yet."

"Oh, yeah?" David asked, frustrated. "What do you suggest?"

"We'll think of something," she whispered as the click of the turn signal began to sound and the car slowed. She felt the wheels crunch over a dirt road and leave all lights behind. It was a bumpy ride for several minutes before the men pulled over and opened the doors.

"It's time," Scarface said, his face a flat, unreadable slate.

"You don't have to do this," David said. "We can keep our mouths shut. No one—"

"Shhh," Red said, clapping a hand over David's mouth. "Just listen. Do you hear that?"

Laurel paused. She heard a few birds and crickets, but above everything else, she heard the distant rush of the Chetco River.

"That's the sound of your future, waiting to carry you away. Come on," he said, setting David roughly on his feet. "You have an appointment and we wouldn't want you to be late."

They prodded their captives forward along the dark path as one of the men sang raucously and badly off-tune, "Oh Shenandoah, I long to see you. Away you rolling river." Laurel grimaced as she kicked yet another rock with her bare toes and wished for the first time in her life that she'd worn some real shoes instead of flip-flops.

Then the trees cleared and they stood in front of the Chetco River. Laurel sucked in a breath as she stared out at the foamy white rapids rushing by. Scarface pushed her onto the ground. "You just sit here," he snarled. "We'll be right back."

Laurel had no hands to catch herself with and she'd sprawled on her stomach, her cheek resting in dark, wet mud. David soon sprawled beside her, and the hopelessness of their situation finally sank in. It was all her fault and she knew it, but how do you apologize for getting someone killed?

"This isn't how I thought it would end," David muttered.

"Me neither," Laurel said. "Dead at the hands of . . . what

do you think they are? I don't ... I don't think they're human. Not any of them. Maybe not even Barnes."

David sighed. "I've never been so reluctant to admit that I think you're right."

They were silent for a few moments.

"How long do you think it'll take?" Laurel asked, her eyes fixed on the frothy rapids.

David shook his head. "I don't know. How long can you hold your breath?" He laughed morosely. "I guess you'll last a lot longer than me." But his laughter broke off quickly and he sighed.

It took two seconds for Laurel's mind to put it all together. "David!" A tiny spark of hope quivered to life in her head. "Remember my experiment? At your house, in your kitchen?" She heard the mutters of the two men as they made their way back to the riverbank. "David, take a very, very big breath," she whispered.

The men were carrying huge rocks and singing some song Laurel didn't recognize. More loops of rope wound around her hands and she felt Scarface test the weight of a rock almost as big as a beach ball.

A few more minutes found David in the same position. "You ready?" Scarface asked his partner.

Laurel stared out at the river. It was at least a hundred feet to the middle; what did they expect them to do, walk? As if sensing her question, Scarface picked Laurel up in one hand and the rock in the other as if neither weighed more than a pound or two. Red did the same with David. Before Laurel could wrap her mind around this new anomaly, Scarface tossed her. Cold air rushed against her face, and she screamed as she flew high in the air, just past the middle of the river. She barely managed to gulp in a mouthful of air before the rock sank through the surface and dragged her under.

The water stung like frigid needles as the roaring darkness closed in over her head. She blinked her eyes open and strained her ears for David. His rock rushed past her, barely missing her head as it descended into the murky blackness below. She wrapped her legs around his chest as he slid through the water beside her. Her rock yanked at her arms, and she tightened her legs around David. She hoped he'd managed to take a good breath.

It was only a few seconds before their rocks thunked against the bottom of the river with an eerie clack. Laurel looked up but couldn't see even a pinprick of light. She could make out only the barest outline of David's white skin in front of her eyes and couldn't tell if he was still conscious. Her mouth delved in the darkness searching for his. Relief flooded through her when she felt his face move too. Their mouths met and Laurel concentrated on sealing her lips with his before blowing gently into his mouth. He held his breath for a few seconds and blew some of the air back into hers. Hoping he would understand what she was doing, Laurel pulled her mouth away and began wriggling, testing her bonds.

The water was icy cold and Laurel knew she had to work fast. First she had to get her hands in front of her, or none of this was going to work—she might not even be able to get close enough to David to give him another breath if she couldn't use her hands. She bent forward and tried to slide her arms down her back and under her legs, but her back didn't want to bend that far. She felt the skin on her wrists tear as she pulled harder, knowing David couldn't hold his breath for much longer. Her spine ached as she forced it to bend farther—then even a little farther than that.

Her body rebelled, but finally her hands slipped under her knees and she kicked her legs free, searching frantically for David. She looped her arms over his neck and pressed her mouth to his again. They breathed several breaths in and out as she tried to decide what to do next. She blew a big breath back into David's lungs and separated herself again. She pulled on the rope that connected her to her rock, and when she reached the bottom, her numb fingers searched for something sharp.

But the river was too swift. Anything that might once have been sharp had been ground down to a slick, smooth finish. She let herself float up to David for more breaths before pulling herself back down, following David's rope this time. Her fingers fumbled with the knot around the rock and she slowly began to pull a strand of the rope free.

After a few more tries, she swam back up to give David a breath. He was struggling to get his arms in front like hers were, but he wasn't as limber and hadn't made any progress. After a deep breath, David went back to trying to flip his arms around, but he wasn't even close. Laurel gritted her teeth; she'd have to do this alone. She worked herself slowly back down the rope to the knot around David's rock.

It took three more breaths before the knot came apart in her hands. But the rope was still trapped beneath the huge rock. Bracing her feet against the bottom of the river, Laurel heaved at the rock, trying to free the last loop of rope. Her feet slipped, and she kicked off the one flip-flop that had survived the icy plunge. Her toes searched the crevices of the rocks and found a better hold, and she strained against the rock, trying to roll it just a few inches. She felt it start to move and pushed a little harder. The rock shifted suddenly and Laurel's feet slipped away from it. The river tossed her in its current, her arms lurching back as the rope stretched taut.

David's white form rushed past, a slave to the current and out of reach before Laurel could even try to grasp for him. It was less than a second before he was out of sight, a tiny trail of bubbles the only fading sign of his presence.

David was gone and Laurel felt like an idiot. She should have planned that better. All she could think as she stared frantically into the darkness was that it had been a long time since his last breath.

Panic edged into her thoughts and Laurel tried not to let it overtake her. The lack of air had already begun to sting her chest, but it was far less uncomfortable than any of the other things she was feeling right now. Her feet were raw from pushing David's rock, and her wrists ached where the ropes still dug in as she flopped helplessly in the current.

She closed her eyes and thought of her parents for a few seconds, regaining a semblance of calm. She would *not* let her mother lose her entire family. Hand over hand,

Laurel slowly dragged herself down her rope to the rock. It had worked for David, and it was probably her best hope. Because of the cold, her fingers were even clumsier now, and Scarface had done a better job than his companion. The knots yielded more slowly, and by the time she got them undone, her chest was screaming for air with an agony she'd never felt before.

And the hard part was still in front of her.

She found a decent toehold and pushed her rock, begging it to move easily.

It didn't even budge.

She cursed in her mind and, even in the water, tears found their way to her eyes. She took a few precious seconds to move some of the smaller rocks in front of the one blocking her rope and braced her sore, tingling feet again. She pushed with all her might, and as darkness started to descend on the edges of her sight, the rock began to slide. Laurel shifted her hands and pushed again, expelling the last of the air from her mouth as she forced the rock another inch forward. Another, another, just one more.

Suddenly she was flipping through the water like a rag doll, with no concept of which way was up. She kicked frantically, trying to find some sort of bearing in the murky water. Her toe kicked a rock with agonizing force, and she bent her legs against it and thrust upward with every ounce of her dwindling strength. When she thought she could not last one more second, her face broke the surface and she gasped in a chestful of air.

The current was still dragging her along, and though she

kicked toward the shore, her body had been drained of its strength. Her feet scraped the bottom and she tried to stand, but her legs wouldn't obey. The force of the water threw her down, and her arms and legs clattered against the rocks as she tried to gain control.

Then something looped over her head, pushing her under for a few seconds. Laurel whimpered, knowing she'd been found by the two thugs, now ready to finish the job they'd started. But when the heavy loop reached her waist, it yanked her upward and away from the water. Away from the unmerciful rocks.

"I've got you," David said in her ear over the sound of the current. His still-tied arms were looped around her waist, and he slogged through the shallow water toward the shore. He dragged her a few feet out of the river and onto the reed-strewn bank before collapsing on the ground. His teeth chattered in her ear as they lay together, both gasping for air.

"Thank you, God," David sighed as the arms around Laurel went limp.

TWENTY

IT WAS SEVERAL MINUTES BEFORE EITHER WAS ABLE to move. David's whole body shook with cold as he disentangled his arms from Laurel. "I thought I was never going to see you again," he said. "You were under for almost fifteen minutes *after* I got my arms in front so I could see my watch."

Fifteen minutes! Laurel was instantly grateful she had freed David first instead of herself. He'd have been very dead after only five. "How did you get to shore?"

David smiled wanly. "By being very, very stubborn. I wasn't convinced I was going to make it at all. But I kept kicking and taking a breath when I could and eventually I got into shallow water." He leaned closer till their shoulders touched. "I had no idea where you were. I couldn't have even found where you were tied because the river was so dark. I just kept walking up and down the shore looking for any sign of you."

"And what if the two uglies had been waiting?" Laurel scolded.

"That was a risk I was willing to take," David said softly. A violent shiver shook his whole body, and Laurel rocked slowly to her feet.

"We've got to get you warm," she said. "You might get hypothermia after being in that water."

"What about you? You were in way longer."

Laurel shook her head. "I'm not warm-blooded, remember? Come on, let's look for something sharp to cut this rope." She bent over and started feeling around on the ground.

"No," David said. "Let's just get back to my car. I have a knife in there. That'll take a lot less time in the long run."

"Do you think you can find it?"

"I better, otherwise it won't matter that we survived the river."

They tramped wearily upstream for several minutes before things started to look familiar. "There," Laurel said, pointing at the ground. She could just see her white flip-flop sitting serenely on the bank, the current lapping at the toe. "I must have lost it when Scarface picked me up."

David paused, staring at the shoe. "How did they do that, Laurel? He picked me up in one hand!"

Laurel nodded. "Me too." And she didn't want to tell him just how heavy the two rocks had been. "The car should be this way," she said, gesturing with her head. She wanted to leave the river behind and never come back.

"Do you want this?" David asked, bending to pick up her shoe.

Laurel's stomach twisted as she looked at the scuffed white sandal. Her feet throbbed, but she couldn't bear the thought of wearing that shoe again. "No," she said firmly. "Throw it in."

With no moon to guide them, they picked their way very slowly down the path. Twice they had to backtrack, but it was less than half an hour before David knelt beside his car, searching for the spare key in the wheel well. "I told my mom this was a stupid idea," David said, his teeth chattering again. "But she assured me that someday I'd be glad she put it there." He retrieved the silver key and held it in his trembling hands. "I don't think this is exactly what she had in mind." He slipped the key into the trunk and they both sighed as it clicked and the lid of the trunk rose. "I'm buying her flowers when I get home," he promised. "Chocolates too."

David dug clumsily into his roadside survival kit and pulled out a small pocket knife. It took a few minutes to hack away the thick ropes, but it was a million times better than trying to do it with a rock. He started the car and turned the heat on full blast as they slipped into the front seats, holding their hands up to the vents and trying to dry their still-damp clothes.

"You should take your shirt off and put on my jacket," Laurel said. "It's not much, but at least it's dry."

David shook his head. "I can't do that; you need it."

"My body adjusts to whatever temperature it's in—always has. You're the one who needs to be warm." She watched

David's face shift as he warred between his chivalrous ideals and his desperate need to warm up.

Laurel rolled her eyes and grabbed the jacket off the backseat. "Put it on," she ordered.

He hesitated, but after a few seconds he peeled off his wet shirt and replaced it with her jacket.

"Do you think you can drive?"

David sniffed. "I can drive far enough to get us to the police station. Will that work?"

Laurel stopped David's hand on the gearshift. "We can't go to the police."

"Why not? Two men just tried to kill us! Trust me, that's what the cops are for."

"This is bigger than the cops, David. Did you forget how those two men threw us into the river like we weighed nothing? What do you think they'd do to a couple of cops?"

David stared at his odometer but said nothing.

"They're not human, David. And anyone who *is* human is just going to get hurt if they try to stop them."

"So what do we do?" David asked, his voice sharp. "Ignore them? Slink home with our tails between our legs?"

"No," Laurel said very quietly. "We go to Tamani."

Relieved tears stung Laurel's eyes as she passed the tree line and felt the familiar comfort of the forest envelop her. She pushed her tangled hair from her face and fruitlessly tried to run her fingers through it as she limped down the dimly lit path toward the stream. She was so exhausted, she could barely put one bruised foot in front of the other. "Tamani?" she called quietly. Her voice seemed unnaturally loud on this dark, still night. "Tamani? I need help."

Tamani fell into step with her so quietly she didn't notice him until he spoke. "Can I assume the boy in the vehicle is David?"

She stopped walking and her eyes drank him in. He wasn't in his armor tonight but a long-sleeved black shirt and fitted pants that blended almost seamlessly into the shadows. The night was so dark she could just see the outline of his face, every angle soft and exquisitely handsome. She wanted to throw herself into his arms, but she held back. "Yes, it's David."

His eyes were soft but probing. "Why did you bring him?"

"I had no choice."

Tamani raised an eyebrow. "At least you told him to stay in the car."

"I am trying, Tamani. But he was my only way to get down here tonight."

Tamani sighed and looked back down the path where Laurel had left David in the car. "I have to admit—I'm mostly just glad you're here. But the forest is full of faeries tonight— it's not a good time."

"Why are they here?"

"There's been a lot of . . . enemy activity in the area lately. We're not sure why. That's all I can say." He shot a quick look back up the path. "Let's get farther in." He took her hand and continued down the path.

The first step shot pain up her leg as a stick dug into her scraped foot. "Stop, please." Her voice was a strangled plea, but she was beyond feeling embarrassed tonight. Tears slid down her face as Tamani stopped and turned.

"What's wrong?"

But now that the tears had started, Laurel couldn't turn them off. The panic and fright of the evening washed over her as tangibly as the current of the Chetco and she gasped for breath.

Then Tamani's arms were around her, his chest warm despite the cold air. His hands stroked up and down her back until he touched the gash where she'd been cut by the window and she couldn't hold back a groan. "What happened to you?" Tamani whispered in her ear as his hands pushed through her hair.

Laurel's fingers clutched the front of his shirt as she tried to keep her balance. Tamani bent and swept his arms underneath her, lifting her off her aching feet and curling her against him. She closed her eyes, hypnotized by the graceful cadence of his feet that never seemed to make a sound. He walked a few minutes down the path and settled her onto a soft spot on the ground.

A spark flared and Tamani lit what looked like a softball-sized brass orb. Flickering light shone out of hundreds of tiny holes, filling the small clearing with a gentle glow. Tamani slid his pack from his shoulders and knelt beside her. Without saying a word, he placed a finger under her chin and turned her face one way, then the other. He moved on to her arms and legs, murmuring at the scrapes and abrasions he found. Gently, he lifted her feet onto his lap and Laurel caught the familiar scents of lavender and ylang-ylang as he rubbed something warm into her tattered soles. It tingled and almost burned for a minute before cooling and soothing the stinging ache.

"Are you hurt anywhere else?" Tamani asked after treating all the injuries he could see.

"My back," Laurel said, turning onto her side and lifting her shirt.

Tamani released his breath in a small whistle. "This one's pretty bad. I'll need to bind it."

"Will that hurt?" Laurel said slowly as warmth from the small orb seemed to wrap around her body.

"No, but you'll have to be careful for a few days while it grows back together."

Laurel nodded and settled her cheek onto her arm.

"Where did you get these, Laurel?" he asked as his soft fingers worked on the deep gash. "Faeries aren't known for being clumsy."

Laurel's tongue felt thick and slow as she tried to explain. "They tried to kill us. David and me."

"Who?" His voice was soft, but Laurel could feel the intensity behind his words.

"I don't know. Something ugly, inhuman. Men who convinced my mom to sell the land."

"Ugly?"

Laurel nodded. She closed her eyes as she told him about her dad and Jeremiah Barnes, her words starting to slur.

"A toxin?" Tamani pressed as her eyes grew heavier and his voice seemed farther and farther away.

"Papers are supposed to be signed tomorrow," Laurel breathed, forcing herself to relay the most important message as her skin tingled gently as if she were lying in the noonday sun.

A few seconds later an arm slipped around her and Laurel clung to it as Tamani's cheek settled by her hair. "Go to sleep," Tamani whispered. "I won't let anything else hurt you."

"D-d-david, he's waiting . . ."

"Don't worry," Tamani soothed, stroking her arm. "He's sleeping too. Shar will make sure he's safe. You both just need to rest now."

All she could do was nod as she nestled against Tamani's chest and let everything else slip out of her mind.

Gentle fingers trailed through Laurel's hair as she slowly stretched and rolled onto her back. Her eyes fluttered open and met Tamani's.

"Good morning," he said with a soft smile as he sat beside her head.

She grinned, then her eyes looked up at the star-filled sky and the small lamp still hanging from the branches above her. "Is it?"

Tamani laughed. "Well, it's very early in the morning I suppose, but yes."

"Did you sleep?"

He shook his head. "Too much to do."

"But—"

"I'll be fine. I've done worse." His smile dropped away and his jaw squared. "It's time to go."

"Go where?" she asked, sitting up.

"To take care of the trolls before they finish killing your father."

"Trolls?" She shook her head. Surely she'd misheard. She'd sat up too quickly, that was all. "My father? You can help my father?"

"I don't know," Tamani admitted. "But it won't matter unless we take care of the trolls first." Tamani tilted his head very slightly to the side. "Come on out, Shar. I know you're listening."

Another man stepped silently out from behind a tree Laurel would have sworn was much too small for him to hide behind. He had the same confident stance as Tamani and the same green eyes. His roots were green too, but the rest of his hair was light blond and long—pulled back away from his face. Shar had the same perfection she still wasn't accustomed to seeing in Tamani; his face was rougher though, full of sharp angles where Tamani's was soft. He was taller than Tamani— almost as tall as David—with long, wiry limbs and solid arms and chest.

"Laurel, Shar. Shar, Laurel," Tamani said without looking at the other faerie.

Laurel stared, wide-eyed, but Shar only nodded and crossed his arms over his chest, listening as he leaned back against the tree he had just stepped out from behind.

"I should have realized it was the trolls trying to buy this land. The creatures you described can't be anything else. We need to take care of them before those papers can be signed."

"Trolls? Like real trolls? Are you serious? Why would . . . trolls . . . care about buying this land? Just because you guys live here?"

Tamani glanced over his shoulder at Shar before turning back to Laurel. "No. It's because the gateway is here."

"Gateway?"

"Tamani, you go too far," Shar growled.

Tamani twisted his body back around. "Why? Don't you think she, of all fae, has a right to know?"

"That's not your decision to make. You're letting it get too personal."

"It *is* personal," Tamani said, bitterness heavy in his voice. "It's always been personal."

"We stick with the plan," Shar insisted.

"I've been sticking with the plan for twelve years, Shar. But trolls mere hours away from gaining title to this land and undoing everything we've worked for is not part of the plan either." He paused, glaring at his companion. "Things have changed, and she needs to know what's at stake."

"The Queen won't be happy."

"The Queen has spent most of her reign making me miserable. Perhaps it's best if the tide changes for once."

"I trust you, Tamani, but you know I can't hide this."

A long moment passed as the two men studied each other. "So be it," Tamani said and turned back to Laurel. "I told you once that I guarded something very special. It's not something I can pick up and move—that's why this land is so important. It's a gate to the realm. The only barrier over a gateway to Avalon."

"Avalon?" Laurel breathed.

Tamani nodded. "There are four gateways in the entire world that lead to it. Hundreds of years ago, the gateways were open. They were still secret and guarded by those who knew of them, but the fact is that too many knew. Since the beginning of time, trolls have been trying to take over Avalon. It's such a perfect piece of earth that nature is not the only abundant resource there. Gold and diamonds are as common as sticks and stones. They mean nothing to us except as decorations." Tamani grinned. "We like things that sparkle, you know."

Laurel laughed as she thought of the glass prisms she had strung across her bedroom window years ago. "I thought that was just a personal preference."

"Never met the faerie who didn't," Tamani said with a smile. "But the trolls have always tried to bribe their way into the human world with money. Some trolls spend their entire lives treasure hunting, and Avalon is too great a treasure to pass up. For centuries, it was a place of death and destruction as the trolls tried to overrun and destroy us and the faeries desperately tried to protect their home. But during the reign of King Arthur, everything changed."

"King Arthur? *The* King Arthur? You're kidding me!"

"Not a bit, though like everything else, the stories never quite got it right. I tell you this, if you want to keep a secret, turn it into a human story. They'll mess it up so badly in a hundred years, no one would ever be able to separate the truth from the myth."

"I'd take offense except, so far, I've found that to be completely true."

Tamani shrugged.

"What did King Arthur do?"

"Mostly it's what his magician Merlin did. Arthur, Merlin, and Oberon—"

"Oberon? Shakespeare's Oberon?"

"Shakespeare was hardly the first to memorialize him, but yes, that King Oberon. Together with Arthur and Merlin, Oberon created a sword that held so much magic that whoever wielded it was sure to come out victorious in battle."

"Excalibur," Laurel said breathlessly.

"Exactly. Oberon, Arthur, and Merlin led the greatest army Avalon has ever seen into battle against the trolls to banish them forever. Faeries, Arthur and his knights, Merlin and his three mistresses, and Oberon himself. The trolls never had a chance. The faeries purged Avalon of the trolls, and Oberon created the gates to guard against their return. But even for a Winter faerie, it was more magic than any living plant could bear. The greatest faerie king in history gave his life to make the gate I guard."

"It's all so incredible," Laurel said.

"It's your history," Tamani said. "Your heritage."

Shar grunted behind him, but Tamani ignored him. "That's why it's so important that this land not fall into the hands of the trolls. The gateways can never be destroyed—but the gates that guard them can. And if the gates are destroyed, Avalon will be open to anyone. Our home will become a place of war and destruction again. We have records of the terrible revenge the trolls took on Camelot, and we can only imagine the similar fate that awaits Avalon if they find their way in."

"Why now? My mom's been trying to sell this land for ages. They could have bought it years ago."

Tamani shook his head. "We don't know. Honestly, I'm almost afraid to find out. Trolls hate losing. They never make a move unless they're sure they can win. Maybe they've gotten a really big group of them together. Maybe . . . maybe . . ." He sighed. "I don't even know. But they have some kind of secret they think will give them an advantage. And unless we find out what it is, we may not stand a chance." Tamani paused. "We didn't think they even knew where this gate was."

"Why not? Haven't they been trying to get in since the gates were made?"

"Let's just say that very few trolls made it out of Avalon alive. We've suspected for many, many years that the survivors knew approximately where it was—and may have passed that information down—but until now, they've been unable to pinpoint its exact location."

"What happens if they find it?"

"If they find it, we kill them. That's why we're here. But that's not the worst that could happen. If they manage to buy the land, they can send an army of humans on some imaginary construction project to knock everything down faster than we can kill them off without attracting more human attention. The gates are very strong, but they're not invincible. A couple of bulldozers and some explosives *might* be able to bring them down. But at the very least, it would expose the gate to anyone who might want to find it."

"You said they made my dad sick?" she whispered.

Tamani looked at her for a long time, his eyes glittering with anger. "I believe they did. I also believe that because of this *toxin*—"

Shar cleared his throat and addressed Laurel. "Tamani loves to talk, but I'm sure you would agree the time is short."

Tamani pursed his lips and glanced up at the sky. "I *have* taken too long," he said. "We need to go. We want to catch them as the sky is turning pink."

"Why?"

"Trolls are creatures of the night; they prefer to sleep when the sun is up. They'll be tired and weak if we catch them at the end of their day."

Laurel nodded. She stretched one more time and hesitantly got to her feet, testing her weight gingerly. To her surprise, her feet felt almost normal. She wasn't tired or sluggish and her whole body was revitalized. "How did you do that?" Laurel asked.

Tamani smiled and pointed at the lamp. "You did say you wanted to see magic."

Laurel stared at the small brass orb. "What did it do?"

"It acts like artificial sunlight. Allows your body to regenerate as if you were out in full sun. Can't use it too often or your cells will figure out the difference, but it's handy for emergencies. Still," he said, digging into his pack once more, "you'll probably want these." He held out a pair of soft moccasins that matched the ones he was wearing.

As Laurel tied the laces, Shar stepped forward and placed his hand on Tamani's shoulder. "Good luck to you. I've already called for more reinforcements; they should be here within the hour."

"Hopefully you won't need them," Tamani replied.

"If it really is trolls and they know as much as you suspect, I imagine this glade is about to become home to many, many more sentries."

"And that's saying something, considering the last few weeks," Tamani said sarcastically.

"Are you sure you don't need someone to come with you?"

"Better if we keep it small." Tamani grinned. "Besides, there's only four of them, and one of them is a lower troll. You're just jealous I'm not letting you go."

"Perhaps a little. But really, Tam, one of them's an upper. Don't underestimate him. I don't want to come looking for your broken pulp."

"You won't have to, I promise."

Shar was silent for a moment, then he lifted his chin and nodded. "The eye of Hecate be upon you."

"And you," Tamani said softly, turning away.

As they walked quickly back down the path, Laurel was amazed at how good she felt. After the struggle to get David and herself out of the river, she had been more worn out than she could ever remember feeling before. Now she felt positively sprightly, and the gentle pressure of Tamani's hand in hers made her want to skip.

But she looked over at Tamani's grim face and decided to resist that particular impulse.

In a few minutes, they came into sight of the car. "Are you ready?" asked Laurel.

"To eliminate a bunch of trolls? Yes. To meet David? Definitely not."

TWENTY-ONE

TO HIS CREDIT, DAVID HANDLED THE MEETING FAIRLY well, especially considering he was shaken awake by a strange man who did little but glare at him while Laurel stammered out introductions. He accepted the idea of the men being trolls better than Laurel had, and Laurel wondered if he was fully awake—or perhaps in shock. Nonetheless, he was ready to play chauffeur.

Tamani got into the backseat and left the door open, his eyes inviting Laurel to sit beside him. She glanced at David— his clothes rumpled and dirty from their escapade in the river and a bruise starting to form on his cheek where she'd slapped him—and smiled in apology as she softly closed the back door and slipped into the passenger seat. Tamani didn't accept loss so easily though, and as David made his way up onto the highway, Tamani leaned forward and snaked his arm around the headrest so his hand could rest on Laurel's shoulder.

If David saw in the dim light, he didn't comment.

Laurel looked at the clock. Almost four. She sighed. "My mom's gonna freak. What about yours?" she asked David.

"Hopefully not. I told her I might stay overnight with you and she said it would be okay if I missed a day of school. But I'll call her as soon as it's late enough and tell her I'm with you."

"If she had any idea . . ." Laurel let her words trail away.

"What's the plan?" David asked, changing the subject.

Tamani answered. "You take me to this house, I take care of the trolls, you bring me back. Pretty simple."

"Tell me more about these trolls," David said. "They were the scariest things I've ever seen."

"I hope it stays that way."

David shivered. "Me too. When they took us to the river, this . . . this troll lifted me like I weighed nothing. I'm not *that* small of a guy."

"Meh, taller than me, I'll give you that." Tamani turned toward Laurel and his condescending tone disappeared as quickly as it had come. "Trolls are—well, they're almost a glitch in evolution. They're animals, like you, David—primates, even. But they're not quite human. Stronger than humans, as you discovered—able to heal faster, too. It's like evolution tried to make a superhuman of sorts, but it got a little messed up."

"Just because they're ugly?" David asked.

"Being ugly is just a side effect. The problem is that they don't match."

"What do you mean, match?" Laurel asked.

"They lack symmetry. Symmetry's what's different about faeries too. Humans, they're mostly symmetrical—as near as animals can be with their chaotic cells. Two eyes, two arms, two legs. All the same length and proportions—more or less. Impressive, really, considering."

"Considering what?" David asked hotly.

"Considering your cells are so irregular. You can't deny it; not if you're as smart as Laurel keeps telling me." The remark was made with simmering undertones, but it apparently placated David. "Laurel and me"—he stroked her neck as he said it—"we're exactly symmetrical. If you could bend us in half, every part would match precisely. That's why Laurel looks so much like one of your fashion models. Symmetry."

"And the trolls aren't?" Laurel asked, desperate to turn the subject away from her.

Tamani shook his head. "Not even close. You remember you told me Barnes's eye drooped and his nose was off-center? There's your physical asymmetry. Although it's very subtle in him. It's not normally that way. I've seen troll babies so badly misshapen that even their ugly mothers wouldn't keep them. Legs growing out of their heads, necks set sideways into shoulders. It's a terrible sight. Long, long ago the faeries would try to take them in. But when evolution has given up on you, death is unavoidable. And it's more than just the physical. The stupider you are—the worse evolution screwed you up—the less symmetrical you are."

"Why don't the trolls die out?" David asked.

"Unfortunately, they have their successes as well as failures; trolls like Barnes who can blend into the human world. Some can even exercise a degree of control over humans. We have no idea how many, but they could be everywhere."

"How can you tell them apart from humans?"

"That's the problem—it's not that easy. Nearly impossible, sometimes—though not as a sentry. Trolls simply don't respond to our magic."

"Not at all?" Laurel asked.

"Not Spring magic, at any rate. And a shame, too. Would make my job today a lot easier. There are a few signs that set trolls apart from humans, but many of them can be hidden."

"What kind of signs?" Laurel asked.

"Originally, trolls lived underground because the sunlight was too hard on their skin. With modern inventions like sunblock and lotion, they're much better off, but even so, their skin is rarely healthy."

Laurel winced, remembering the way Bess's skin had cracked and feathered around her collar.

"Along with the asymmetry, their eyes are often different colors, but contact lenses can hide that well enough too. The only way you would probably be sure is to either observe their strength or catch them eating a big hunk of bloody meat."

"Barnes was fascinated by the blood on my arm," Laurel said.

"You don't bleed," Tamani said.

"Well, it wasn't my blood; it was David's."

"On *your* arm?"

Laurel nodded. "He cut his arm coming through the window. Same time I cut my back."

"A good amount of blood?" Tamani asked.

"Enough to cover Barnes's palm when he grabbed me."

Tamani chuckled. "That explains throwing you in the river. No troll in their right mind would try to drown a faerie. He didn't know what you are."

"Why would he know?"

Tamani sighed. "Unfortunately, it's very easy for trolls to distinguish humans from faeries. A troll's sense of smell is keenly tuned to blood, and faeries don't have any. Unless you're blossoming, a troll won't be able to smell you at all. Coming upon what looks like a human who has no scent of blood would tip him off immediately."

"But David bled on me. So he smelled enough blood that he didn't suspect?"

"It's the only logical explanation."

"What about in the hospital?"

"Hospitals reek of blood to a troll. Even bleach doesn't dim the smell. He wouldn't have noticed ten faeries in a hospital."

"And at your house," David said, "I smelled like smoke from the bonfire."

"He came to your house!" Tamani said, the hand on Laurel's shoulder tightening a little. "You forgot to mention that."

"A long time ago. I didn't know what he was."

Tamani's hand tightened on her shoulder. "You've been very, *very* lucky. If he'd have realized what you were before, you'd probably be dead right now."

Laurel's head was starting to spin and she leaned back against the headrest—right against Tamani's cheek. She didn't rectify her mistake.

They neared Brookings and Tamani began grilling Laurel about the layout of the house. "It would be easier if I came with you," she protested after describing the house in every way she could think of. Which wasn't much—it had been too dark.

"Not a chance. I won't risk you—you're too important."

"I'm not that important," Laurel grumbled, sliding down in her seat a little.

"You're set to inherit the land, Laurel. Don't take that lightly."

"I could help—be a backup."

"I don't need your help."

"Why?" Laurel snapped. "Because I'm not some specially trained sentry?"

"Because it's too dangerous," Tamani snapped back, raising his voice. He sat back in his seat. "Don't make me lose you again," he whispered.

She knelt on the seat and turned around to look at him. His face was just visible in the early morning glow. "What if I make sure to stay out of sight? If something happens to you, we'll need to know."

His face didn't change.

"I won't try to fight or anything," she promised.

Tamani paused and mulled this over for a few seconds. "If I say no, are you going to follow me anyway?"

"Of course."

He sighed and rolled his eyes. "Listen to me." He leaned forward, his nose almost touching hers as he spoke quietly but with an intensity that almost made Laurel wish she hadn't brought it up in the first place. "If there's trouble, you let me go. You drive straight back to Shar and tell him what happened. You promise?"

She shook her head. "I couldn't leave you."

"I want your word, Laurel."

"It won't happen anyway. Like you told Shar, there's nothing to worry about."

"Don't try to change the subject. Your word."

Laurel bit at her lower lip, wondering if there was some way to get out of this. But Tamani was not going to leave it alone. "Fine," she said sullenly.

"Then you can come."

"What about me?" David asked.

"That's impossible."

"Why?" David demanded, gripping the steering wheel. "I'd be more of a help than Laurel—no offense," he added with a smile.

"Well, I guess you can come," Tamani said, smiling wickedly, "if you want to be bait."

"Tamani!" Laurel protested.

"It's true. Not only is he human, he's got open wounds. Barnes would smell him a hundred feet away. Maybe more. He's bait, or he doesn't come." Tamani leaned forward again and lightly punched David's shoulder in what anyone else would have thought was a friendly gesture, but Laurel knew better. "No, mate. I suggest you man the getaway car."

David couldn't argue. Not unless he wanted to insist on being bait.

They pulled off the 101 onto Alder just as the sky was pinking up. As they reached Maple and began to retrace the route she and David had taken the night before, Laurel grew more and more nervous. She'd been so confident and arrogant last night. She'd known she was right and had been determined to find answers. Now she knew firsthand just what she was up against, and her confidence was rapidly dwindling.

"Tamani?" she asked, even though she knew this was the wrong time. "How is a plant supposed to beat a superstrong troll?"

For once Tamani did not grin. His face was stony and his eyes hooded. "Stealth," he replied softly. "Stealth and speed. It's the only advantage I have."

Laurel didn't like the sound of that.

TWENTY-TWO

DAVID'S CIVIC ROLLED SLOWLY INTO THE SEA CLIFF cul-de-sac. "It's that one down at the end," Laurel said, pointing.

"Let's stop here, then," Tamani said.

David pulled the car onto the curb and the three sat looking at the large house. In the early morning light, they could now tell it had once been gray. Laurel studied the splintery curved trim on the eaves and the embellished window frames and tried to envision the beautiful home it must have been a hundred years ago. How long had it belonged to the trolls? She shivered, wondering if they'd bought the house or simply slaughtered the family and taken possession. At the moment, the latter seemed much more likely.

Tamani was pulling a belt from his pack and checking its little pockets. He handed her a leathery strap that held a small knife. "Just in case," he said.

The knife felt heavy in her hand, and for a few seconds she just stared at it.

"It goes around your waist," Tamani prompted.

Laurel shot him a glare but pulled the strap around her middle and buckled it.

"Ready?" Tamani asked. His face was serious now. The strands of hair hanging over his forehead cast long shadows that looked like stripes across his eyes. His brows were furrowed in concentration and a small crease stood out on his forehead, marring what could have been an advertisement featuring a brooding male model.

"Ready," she whispered.

Tamani stepped out of the backseat and closed the door very softly. Laurel unbuckled her seatbelt and felt David's hand on her shoulder. His eyes darted momentarily to Tamani when she looked up at him. "Don't go," he whispered fiercely.

She squeezed his hand. "I have to. I can't let him go alone."

David set his jaw and nodded grimly. "Come back," he ordered.

Laurel couldn't get her mouth to form the words, but she nodded and pushed her door open. Tamani stuck his head down and looked at David. "In about ten minutes, go ahead and pull up a little closer. If anyone in that house doesn't know we're there by that time, it's because we're dead."

David swallowed.

"Keep a very careful watch. If one of them comes to get you in the car, drive away—if they can reach you, it's too late for us. Drive to the land and tell Shar."

Laurel didn't like that part.

Tamani hesitated. "I'm sorry I can't let you do more," he said, his tone sincere. "Truly I am." He closed the door, took Laurel's hand, and walked toward the house without looking back.

Laurel looked over her shoulder and stared at David for a long time before turning around.

They made their way around the sprawling house in much the same way David and Laurel had gone the night before. Laurel felt her chest tighten as she retraced her steps and crept closer to the creatures that had tried to kill her. *Who walks willingly back to their own death?* she asked herself with a shake of her head. But she kept her eyes on Tamani's back. His confident stance, even while sneaking along the wall, gave her courage. *I'm here for him*, she repeated over and over in her mind till it started to sound reasonable.

As they approached the smashed window, Tamani's hand shot out and held her still against the peeling siding. He peeked into the destroyed window frame, which the trolls had not even bothered to board up, and dug into one of the pockets on his belt. He drew out what looked like a brown straw and slipped something small into it. He dropped to one knee and sprawled out away from the wall, exposing himself for just an instant to whoever might have been in the room. He blew on the straw and Laurel heard something whiz through the air.

Then Tamani was on his belly, crawling under the splintered sill toward the very back of the house. Laurel followed him, ducking onto her belly too. "What did you do?" she whispered.

But Tamani only held a finger over his lips and continued to creep forward. In a few more seconds, Laurel heard the soft buzz of conversation. Several feet ahead Tamani had stopped and was surveying what little he could see around the corner. He looked up at an ancient trellis, and a tiny grin touched his lips. He turned to her, pointed at the ground beside him, and mouthed, "Stay."

Laurel wanted to argue, but as her eyes found cracks and breaks in the trellis, she decided her extra weight would be exceptionally *un*helpful. Tamani scaled the trellis silently— something Laurel hadn't thought was possible with the rickety wooden web—and looked more like an agile monkey ascending a tree than anything remotely human.

Laurel crouched by the corner of the house and peeked around the side. Scarface and his friend were lounging on a dirty couch on the equally dirty porch. Their voices were too low for Laurel to catch what they were saying but, considering their conversation in the car the previous night, that was probably best.

Scarface yawned and the other troll looked close to falling asleep. Laurel heard the tiniest skitter as Tamani made his way across the roof, but apparently the two trolls were too tired or distracted, because neither of them even glanced up.

Even though she was expecting him, Laurel had to suppress a yelp of surprise as Tamani came flying down from the roof and swung to land gracefully in front of the trolls.

His hands shot out like two blurs and clunked their heads together with a dull thud. They slumped into the couch cushions and didn't move.

Laurel took one step and crunched a dried leaf.

"Wait," Tamani said softly. "Let me finish first. You don't want to see this."

It was too great a temptation. He wasn't looking at her, so she didn't pull her head back around the corner—just watched in rapt fascination, wondering what he was going to do.

Tamani braced his knee against Scarface's shoulder and held his face in both hands. By the time Laurel realized what was going to happen, it was too late. Her eyes refused to close as Tamani snapped the troll's head around and a sickening crunch assaulted her ears. Tamani leaned Scarface back onto the cushion and, as he turned his attention to the other troll, she couldn't help but look at the limp face— devoid of life and, for the first time, not wound up in a sneer.

When Tamani lifted his knee to the other troll's shoulder, Laurel quickly pulled herself back around the corner and shoved her fingers in her ears. Not that it mattered. The snap of Red's neck found its way to her inner ears and her mind filled in what her eyes couldn't see. Tamani's soft finger on her shoulder made her jump.

"Come on, we need to keep going." Tamani tucked Laurel under the arm farthest from the dead trolls, but she still peeked around him to look at the two forms that appeared to simply be sleeping.

"Did you have to do that?" she whispered, trying to remember that these men had attempted to kill her and David. But they looked so harmless in the dim morning light with their deformed faces slack and peaceful.

"Yes. One of the rules of the sentries is to never leave a hostile troll alive. It's something I'm sworn to do. I told you—you shouldn't have come."

He took an instant to grab something from his belt and sprayed the hinges of the back door. When he swung the door open, it moved silently. Laurel remembered Bess and followed Tamani very hesitantly. But she was lying limp on the floor. Tamani crouched beside her and removed a small dart from her neck. Laurel remembered the brown straw and realized what he had done.

"Is she dead?" Laurel whispered.

Tamani shook his head. "Just sleeping. The death darts are much bigger and don't work as quickly. She'd have gotten out a few good yelps and ruined everything." He was reaching into his belt again. He sighed as he unscrewed a small bottle. "These are the ones I always regret. The ones too stupid to know what they're doing. They're no more guilty than a lion or tiger that stalks their prey, at least in the beginning. But once they're taught to be vicious faerie haters that obey their masters' every order, they'll never stop being dangerous." He pulled down one of Bess's eyelids and squeezed out two drops of yellow liquid. "She'll be dead in a few minutes," he said, putting the bottle back into his pack.

He turned to Laurel and set his face close to hers so he could whisper right by her ear. "I don't know where the other one is. If we can find him and catch him by surprise, it'll be easy. So follow me, but not another word from here on out. Okay?"

Laurel nodded and hoped she could walk half as quietly as he did. She'd never in her life felt clumsy—she'd always had more grace than her peers—but compared to Tamani, she was downright stumbly. By watching Tamani's feet and stepping right in his footsteps, she managed to traverse the stairs more or less silently.

They walked by three doorways with nothing in them but sheet-covered furniture and swirling dust motes. Tamani peeked around the fourth doorway and immediately reached for his belt. Laurel could see Barnes's shadow, elongated across the floor by the sunlight from the eastern window, and somehow even the shadow profile was unmistakable. Tamani pulled out the long straw again and rose to one knee. He took a breath and aimed carefully. With a small puff the dart flew.

Laurel kept her eyes on the shadow. There was a jolt and a tiny grunt. Eternal seconds passed, then the shadow head thunked down onto the desk. Tamani pointed to the ground where Laurel was curled against the wall and again whispered for her to stay.

This time she obeyed.

Tamani crept forward and crouched behind the still troll for a few seconds. She watched in the shadows as his hands rose to the sides of the troll's head. Knowing what was coming next, she squeezed her eyes shut and placed her hands over her ears. The next sound she heard was not a crack but a loud thud that rattled the wall at her back.

"You thought your little faerie tricks would work on me?"

Laurel's eyes flew open and she flung herself to the spot Tamani had vacated only seconds before. She couldn't see Barnes, but Tamani was crumpled on the floor against the wall, shaking his head as he glared at Barnes. She watched the long shadow jump toward Tamani and opened her mouth to scream a warning, but Tamani was gone before Barnes crunched into the wall, cracking the plaster. Tamani darted around the room as Laurel tried to press farther and farther into the wall. The whole house was shaking now as Barnes lunged at Tamani over and over and Tamani continued darting just out of reach. Laurel watched their shadows dance and held her breath, afraid that every movement, every sound, might give her away.

With a yell and a mighty swipe of his long arms, Barnes caught Tamani across the chest and threw him against the south wall, directly across from the doorway where Laurel crouched. Cracks spidered over the plaster where Tamani hit the wall, and he slid onto the floor. Laurel willed him to rise and jump away again, but Tamani's head lolled to the side and he breathed heavily.

"That's better," Barnes said.

Laurel pulled her head back around the corner, but it didn't matter; Barnes's back was to her as he stood halfway across the room towering over Tamani. He leaned forward and studied

Tamani before breaking out in his grating laugh. "Look at you. You're just a boy. A baby. Are you even of age to be a sentry?"

"I'm old enough," Tamani rasped, glaring at the troll with hard eyes.

"And they sent *you* to take care of me? You faeries always were fools."

Tamani flung a leg out, but this time he was too slow. Barnes caught him at the calf and twisted, lifting Tamani from the ground and flinging him around before slamming him back against the wall with enough force to create a few more cracks.

"You want it the hard way, I'll give it to you the hard way," Barnes said. "Truth be told, I rather like the hard way."

Laurel's eyes widened as Barnes took a pistol from his belt, pointed it at Tamani, and pulled the trigger.

TWENTY-THREE

A SHRILL, DEAFENING SCREAM REVERBERATED IN LAUREL'S head as the room filled with the crack of gunfire, but somehow only a small whimper escaped her lips. As the smell of gunpowder burned her nose, a muted yell forced its way into her consciousness. Laurel's eyes sprang open and flew to Tamani. His face was contorted in pain and a groan continued to work its way through his clenched teeth. He clutched his leg and his fingers were wet with sap as he glared up at the troll.

Barnes pointed his gun again, and this time Tamani couldn't hold back a cry of agony as a bullet ripped through his other thigh. Laurel's whole body trembled as Tamani's scream seemed to invade every organized, symmetrical cell in her body, throwing them into chaos. She crawled one step forward, and Tamani shot her a look that ordered her to stay put. No sooner had his eyes met hers than they were back on Barnes. A sheen of sweat glistened on Tamani's brow as

Barnes set the gun down on the desk with a loud clunk and walked forward.

"Not going anywhere now, are you?"

Hate burned out of Tamani's eyes as he stared up at the hulking figure.

"You're here the day I'm supposed to go down and sign papers on the land holding your precious gate. I'm not stupid enough to blame that on coincidence. How did you know?"

Tamani closed his lips and said nothing.

Barnes kicked Tamani's foot, and a low growl escaped his tight control. "How?" Barnes shouted.

Still Tamani said nothing and Laurel wondered how long she could bear to watch. Tamani's eyes were tightly closed, and when he opened them he looked straight at Laurel for an instant.

She knew what he wanted. He wanted her to keep her promise. He actually wanted her to turn her back on him, walk down the stairs alone, and return to the land to fetch Shar.

She'd given her word.

But she knew she couldn't do it. She couldn't leave him. In one glaring instant, she realized she'd rather die with him than leave him to die alone.

In that moment of surrender, her eyes lit upon the gun.

Barnes had left it sitting on the desk and was paying no attention to it at all. Under lowered lids Tamani followed her gaze. He looked back at her and shook his head in such a small motion she barely saw it. Then he winced and moaned as Barnes kicked his leg again.

"How?"

Barnes crouched in front of Tamani. Laurel knew it was the best chance she was going to get. She crept forward, trying to imitate the deft strides she'd watched Tamani take all morning.

"In ten seconds, I'm going to take your foot and break every stem in your leg."

Her hands curled around the cold steel and she tried to remember everything her father had taught her about guns a few years ago. This one was a heavy, squarish pistol—the kind that almost looked like a black water gun. She looked for a safety or a hammer and saw neither. She closed her eyes for just a second, hoping with all her might that this was one of those point-and-pull kinds of guns.

"You get one more chance to give me my answer, faerie. One, two—"

"Three," Laurel finished for him, pointing the weapon at his head.

Barnes froze.

"Stand up," Laurel commanded, staying just out of arm's reach.

Slowly, Barnes stood and turned slightly toward her.

"Against the wall," she said. "Away from him."

Barnes laughed. "You really think you're going to shoot me? Little snippet of a thing like you?"

Laurel flinched as she squeezed the trigger, almost crying out in relief as her efforts sent a bullet into the wall. She pointed the gun at Barnes again.

"Okay," he said, and backed up a few paces, turning all the way around to face her. His eyes widened as he recognized her face. "I thought I had you killed."

"Think harder next time," Laurel said, proud her voice was not shaking nearly as much as her legs.

"Did my boys forget . . . Wait, no." He sniffed the air suspiciously. "You—I don't . . ." His voice faded as he turned to Tamani and gave a sinister chuckle. "I get it now. The faeries have resorted to placing changelings. Changelings!" He looked down at Tamani, his tone casual. "When are you going to learn that we trolls come up with all the best ideas?"

Laurel fired another shot at the wall and Barnes jumped. "We're done talking," she said.

The two stood together in some kind of impasse. Barnes seemed almost sure she wouldn't shoot him, and Laurel was just as sure she couldn't. But she couldn't let Barnes know that.

Unfortunately, the only way to put his doubts to rest was to actually shoot him. Her fingers felt sweaty on the trigger as she let the gun rise till the barrel covered his face, blocking it from her sight.

That was as far as she could go.

"Remember what I told you, Laurel," Tamani said very quietly. "He ordered you to be killed, he poisoned your father, he manipulated your mother . . . He'll do it again if you let him get away."

"Stop, really, you give me far too much credit," Barnes said with a mocking smile.

Loud, ragged breaths hissed in and out of Laurel's mouth as she tried to make her fingers contract. But her arms lowered a few inches and a smile tugged at the corner of Barnes's mouth.

"I knew you couldn't do it," he jeered. He dropped into a crouch and flew at her.

All Laurel saw was red-rimmed, murderous eyes and hands extended more like claws than fingers. She didn't even feel the gun in her hand as her fingers clenched and the crack of a gunshot roared in her ears. Barnes's body jerked back as the bullet tore through his shoulder. Laurel screamed and dropped the gun.

With a groan, Tamani pulled himself forward and his hands clutched at the weapon. Barnes roared in pain, but his eyes found Laurel again.

"Leave her alone, Barnes!" Tamani yelled, aiming the gun.

Barnes barely had time to focus on the gun pointed at his head. Even as Tamani pulled the trigger, Barnes leaped at the window and crashed through it, dropping to the ground below. Tamani's shot embedded itself harmlessly into the wall. Laurel ran to the broken windowsill and caught one last sight of Barnes fleeing toward the river before his bloodied form disappeared over a hill.

Tamani let the heavy gun clatter to the ground. Laurel flung herself to her knees and into his arms. He groaned in her ear, but when she tried to pull back, he held her tight against his chest. "Don't you ever, *ever* scare me like that again."

"Me?" Laurel protested. "I'm not the one who got shot!"

Her arms snaked around his neck and her whole body shook.

Her head jerked up when she heard footsteps pounding up the stairs. Tamani shifted her a little to the side and grabbed the gun, pointing it at the doorway.

David's white face appeared at the top of the stairs. Tamani sighed and let the gun fall back onto the floor, his arms limp.

"I heard the shots and saw Barnes run away," he said, his voice shaking. "Are you two okay?"

"Eye of Hecate, do neither of you know how to follow directions?" Tamani growled.

"Apparently not," Laurel said dryly.

"What happened here?" David asked, looking wide-eyed around the disaster of the room.

"We'll talk in the car. Hurry, David, Tamani needs help." They each ducked under one arm and managed to raise Tamani from the floor. Tamani was trying to be brave, but Laurel winced every time a choked moan escaped his lips. They half-dragged him toward the doorway when Laurel stopped. "Wait," she said, transferring all of Tamani's weight to David. She hurried to the desk and looked at the papers. The top layer was peppered with a fine spray of blood. *Troll blood*, Laurel thought with a grimace. But she took a breath and forced herself to sort through them anyway. Anything that mentioned her mother or the address of the land, she scooped up to take with her. Luckily, it was a small stack.

"Let's go," she said, ducking under Tamani's arm again.

They were silent as they passed the bodies of the dead trolls. The sun was out in earnest now and Laurel hoped no one would see them dragging this obviously injured person out to their car. Belatedly, she wondered if anyone besides David had heard the shots. Looking up and down the street at the other crumbling and dilapidated houses, she wasn't sure it mattered. It looked like a neighborhood where gunfire was commonplace.

David laid Tamani in the backseat and tried to make him comfortable, but Tamani brushed his hands away. "Just get me back to Shar. Hurry."

David held Laurel's door open, but she shook her head and, without looking at him, slid into the backseat with Tamani.

Laurel settled Tamani's chest and head on her lap and he clung to her like a child, groaning each time David drove over a bump. His face was pale and his black hair slick with sweat. She tried to get him to open his eyes, but he refused. As his breathing grew more and more ragged, Laurel glanced up at David, who watched her in the rearview mirror. "Can't we go any faster?" she pleaded.

David pursed his lips and shook his head. "I can't speed, Laurel. It's too risky. What do you think a cop would say if he pulled us over and saw Tamani?" His eyes met hers in the rearview. "I'm going as fast as I dare—I promise."

Tears filled Laurel's eyes, but she nodded, trying not to notice that Tamani's grip on her arms was getting looser.

The road was mostly empty, but Laurel held her breath the entire way through Crescent City and then Klamath as they passed close to several other cars. One man even looked over at her, and she wondered if his sunglasses covered mismatched eyes. Just as she felt sure he was a troll sent to finish them off, he looked away and turned down a side street.

Finally the driveway came into view and David pulled off the road. The unpaved drive was bumpy, but Tamani didn't protest as the car bounced over ruts. Laurel's breath stuck in her throat as David reached the end of the drive and shifted into park.

"Please hurry, David," Laurel begged in a whisper.

David ran around to the other side of the car and helped her ease Tamani out. They dragged him past the house and down the now-familiar path. As soon as they passed the tree line, Laurel began shouting in a sob-strained voice, "Shar! Shar! We need help."

Almost instantly, Shar stepped onto the path from behind a tree. If he was shocked, it didn't register on his face. "I'll take him," he said calmly. He lifted Tamani from David and Laurel and slung him gently over his shoulders. "You can't come any farther," Shar said to David. "Not today."

David's brow furrowed and he looked to Laurel. Laurel threw her arms around him. "I'm sorry," she whispered and turned down the path.

David caught her hand. "You are coming back, aren't you?" he asked.

Laurel nodded. "I promise." Then she pulled her hand away and hurried up the path after Tamani's limp form.

As soon as David was out of sight, other faeries stepped onto the path, adding their shoulders beneath Tamani's weight—a parade of unbelievably beautiful men, several clad in camouflaging armor. Each faerie who appeared made Laurel feel better. Tamani wasn't alone now—the faeries would find a way to make everything all right. She had to believe it. They led her down a twisted path that looked strangely unfamiliar and came to a stop in front of an ancient tree that, even in the chilly late-autumn air, had not changed color.

Several of the faeries took a turn placing a palm in a shallow hollow on the tree's trunk. Finally, Shar lifted Tamani's limp arm and placed his hand on the tree. For a few seconds, no one moved and nothing happened. Then the tree began to sway and Laurel gasped in surprise as a crack appeared at the base. It widened and grew, pushing the trunk out, molding it into an archway. The air glimmered and sparkled until it was almost too bright to look at. Then a brilliant flash shone and Laurel had to blink. In the instant it took to close her eyes and open them again, the shimmering air had turned into a golden gate snaked with brilliant white blossoms and glittering with millions of sparkling jewels.

"Is that the gate to Avalon?" Laurel said breathlessly to Shar.

Shar barely spared her a glance. "Bar her way; Jamison's coming through."

Spears crisscrossed in front of her and Laurel realized she'd taken several steps forward. She was almost overwhelmed by the urge to push through the spears and run to the shining gates, but she forced her feet to stay where they were. The gate was moving now, swinging slowly outward in an arc as all the faeries backed away and made room. Laurel couldn't see much as she strained against the spears, but her eyes found an emerald-green tree, a sliver of cerulean sky, rays of sunshine that sparkled like diamonds. The thick aroma of fresh earth rolled over her, along with a heady, intoxicating scent she couldn't identify. A white-haired man in long, flowing silver robes waited on the other side of the shimmering gate. Laurel couldn't help but stare as he made his way forward to stand by Tamani. He ran a finger down Tamani's face and looked back at several other faeries carrying a stretcher.

"Take him quickly," he said, beckoning them forward. "He's fading."

Tamani was transferred onto the soft white stretcher, and Laurel watched helplessly as he was borne into the shining light that poured from the gate. She had to believe he would be fine now, that she would see him again. Surely no one could enter a world so full of wonder and not heal.

When she looked up, the older faerie's eyes had settled upon her. "I assume this is her," he said. His voice was too sweet, too musical to be of this world. He walked toward her as if he were floating on air, and the face she looked up into was so beautiful. He seemed to glow, and his eyes were soft and blue and surrounded by wrinkles that fell not in the uneven crevices she saw on Maddie's face but in exact, even folds like perfectly hung drapes. He smiled at her gently, and the pain of the last twenty-four hours melted away.

"You've been very brave," Jamison said in that sweet, angelic voice. "We didn't think we would need you so soon. But things never go quite as planned, do they?"

She shook her head and looked back through the gate, where she could just see the top of Tamani's head. "Will he . . . will he be all right?"

"Don't worry. Tamani has always been stronger than anyone expected him to be. Especially for you. We will take good care of him." He placed a hand on her shoulder and beckoned her down the unfamiliar path. "Will you walk with me?"

Her eyes stayed locked on the gate into Avalon, but she responded instinctually. "Of course."

They walked in silence for a few minutes before Jamison stopped and invited her to sit on a fallen log. He joined her and sat close, their shoulders almost touching. "Tell me about the trolls," he said. "You obviously ran into trouble."

Laurel nodded and told him how Tamani had been so careful and brave. Jamison's eyes glimmered with respect as she described how Tamani refused to talk even after being shot. She hadn't expected to tell him about herself, but she began speaking of how she'd held the gun and couldn't bring herself to shoot the monster until her life depended on it. And even then it was mostly an accident.

"So he got away?" There was no judgment in his voice.

Laurel nodded.

"It's not your fault, you know. Tamani is a trained sentry and he takes his work very seriously. But you, you were made to heal, not kill. I think I'd have been disappointed if you were able to kill someone, even a troll."

"But he knows now. He knows who I am."

Jamison nodded. "And he knows where you live. You must be on your guard. For your parents' sake as well as your own. I am appointing you as their protector. Only you know the secrets that can keep them alive."

Laurel thought of her father lying in his hospital bed, perhaps even now taking his last breaths. "My father is dying, and in a few days there will be no one left but my mother and me. I can't be what you want me to be," she admitted in a shaky voice. Her face dropped into her hands and desperation washed over her.

The old faerie's arms were around her instantly, pressing her against his robes that cushioned her face as softly as down feathers. "You must remember that you are one of us," he whispered in her ear. "We are here to assist you in any way we can. Our aid is your right—your heritage." Jamison reached into his voluminous robes and pulled out a small, sparkling bottle filled with a dark blue liquid. "For times of trouble," he said. "This is a rare elixir one of our Fall faeries made many years ago. We create very few potions that can help humans these days, but you need it now, and you may need it again in the future. Two drops in the mouth should be sufficient."

Laurel's hands shook as she reached for the tiny bottle. Jamison placed it in her hand and closed his palm over hers.

"Guard it carefully," he warned. "I don't know for certain that we have another Fall faerie strong enough to make an elixir like this. Not yet."

Laurel nodded.

"We would also like to assist you in one more way. But," he said, one long finger in the air, "it is a conditional offer."

"Whatever you need," Laurel said earnestly. "I'll make it happen."

"It's not a condition for you. Here," he said, opening his palm to reveal what looked like an almost golf ball–sized piece of rough crystal. "I would like you to offer this to your mother." He placed the rock in Laurel's hand, and she gaped at the gem.

"Is this a diamond?"

"Yes, child. One that size should be sufficient for any need you may have. Here is our offer. You know you were placed with your human parents for the sole reason of obtaining the land upon their eventual death." When Laurel nodded, he continued. "Recent events have made your purpose so much more important, and we must see this property transfer ownership sooner. This gem is for your parents if they will put the land into a trust in your name as soon as your father's health allows. How and what you tell them is a decision only you can make." His voice became very firm. "But you *must* own this land, Laurel. And we are certainly willing to pay a fair price for that to happen."

Laurel nodded and tucked the gem into her pocket. "I'm sure they'll agree."

"I believe you are right," Jamison said. "You need to hurry, Laurel. Your father's time is measured in hours now, not days."

"Thank you," Laurel whispered, and turned to leave.

"Oh, Laurel?"

"Yes?"

"I hope to see you again soon. Very soon," he added. His eyes sparkled as he lifted his old lips into a gentle, knowing smile.

TWENTY-FOUR

IT SEEMED IMPOSSIBLE THAT THE DRIVE BETWEEN
Brookings and Orick could feel longer than when she held
Tamani fading in her arms. But alone with David—her pockets
filled with two of the greatest treasures she could imagine—
the miles crept by slower than ever. The old faerie's words
pounded through her head. *Your father's time is measured in
hours now, not days.* He had said hours, plural, but what did that
mean? And how close to the end was too late? Laurel kept
taking the bottle out and cupping it in her hands, then tucking
it back into her pocket, not sure which was her safest choice.
In the end she left it in her pocket—if for no other reason than
to keep David from asking questions she couldn't answer.

Which he hadn't so far. After hugging her when she
stumbled out of the woods, he had silently opened her door
and said, "The hospital?" He hadn't said a word since. She
was grateful for his silence. She hadn't decided yet what she
could and could not tell him. Weeks earlier she'd promised

to tell him everything Tamani said unless it was a faerie secret. But she hadn't actually expected to be made privy to such details.

Now she had. She knew the location of a gateway that any troll would kill her or her loved ones to gain access to. Perhaps telling David would only put him in more danger.

So nothing was the best thing to say right now.

He finally pulled into the hospital parking lot and looked up at the tall, gray building. "Do you want me to go in with you?"

Laurel shook her head. "We're both a mess. At least if there's only me, maybe I won't draw quite so much attention." *Not likely*, she added in her mind.

"I'll stay out here and call my mom, then." He hesitated, then laid his hand over hers. "I need to head back to Crescent City in a few hours—my mom's going to have kittens when I call her as it is. She's left me about twenty messages. But if you need anything . . ." His voice trailed off and he shrugged. "You know where to find me."

"I'll come down soon to say good-bye. But I have to go see my dad right now."

"They gave you something to save him, didn't they?"

Tears filled Laurel's eyes. "As long as it's not too late."

"Go, then . . . I'll wait for you."

Laurel leaned in to hug him before pushing the car door open and hurrying to the hospital entrance.

She tried to stay out of sight as much as possible. Her tank top was stained with mud from the bank of the Chetco River, and she'd forgotten to get her jacket back from David to cover it. On top of that, her hair was a mess, her jeans were torn over the right knee, and she was still wearing the oddly fashioned moccasins.

At least the river had washed David's blood out of her shirt. And she didn't have a face full of bruises like he did. *Not visible ones, anyway*, she thought, touching a particularly sensitive spot on her cheek.

She managed to reach her father's room without actually being approached by anyone—though she did receive several probing looks—and took a deep breath before knocking on the door and pushing it open. She peeked around the curtain and saw her mother asleep with her head on her father's thigh. The room was full of familiar sounds; the beeping of her father's heartbeat, the soft whoosh of oxygen puffing through his nose tube, the buzz of the pressure cuff inflating on his arm. But instead of being daunting the way they had for the last three weeks, the sounds brought instant relief. Her father was alive, even if just barely.

Her mom's eyes fluttered open. "Laurel? Laurel!" She staggered to her feet and ran to her daughter, flinging her arms around her. "Where have you been? I was terrified when you didn't come back last night. I thought . . . I don't even know what I thought. A million horrible thoughts all at once." She shook Laurel's shoulders a little. "If I weren't so happy to see you, I'd ground you for a month." Her mom stepped back and looked at Laurel. "What happened to you? You look awful."

Laurel rushed back into her mother's embrace—the embrace she'd been sure she would never feel again when she was trapped under the murky waters of the Chetco. "It's been a long night," she said with a shaky voice as tears threatened.

Her mother clung to her as Laurel looked over her shoulder and studied her father. He'd been lying in that hospital bed for so long, it was almost too bizarre to imagine him waking up and rising from it. Laurel stepped away from her mother. "I have something for Dad." She laughed. "I have something for you too. Never go on a trip without bringing back presents, right?" Her mother looked at her strangely as Laurel continued chuckling to herself.

She walked around to the other side of her father's bed and pulled a rolling stool up near his head. "Don't let anyone in," she told her mother as she removed the small bottle from her pocket.

"Laurel, what is—?"

"It's okay, Mom. It'll make him better." She unscrewed the top and sucked some of the precious liquid into the dropper. Very carefully, she bent over her father and squeezed two sparkling blue drops of elixir into his mouth. Then, looking at his pale face, she let one more drop fall. Just in case. She looked up at her mom. "He'll be fine now."

Laurel's mom stared openmouthed at her. "Where did you get that?"

Laurel looked at her mother with a weary smile. "You didn't ask about your present," she said, avoiding the question.

Her mom sank into the armchair beside the bed as Laurel pushed her stool around to sit next to her. She paused for a few seconds, not sure where to begin. Where do you start a story this big? She glanced at the clock and cleared her throat. "Mr. Barnes isn't coming this morning." Her mom leaned forward to say something, but Laurel continued, speaking over her. "He's never coming, Mom. I hope you never see him again. He's not what you think he is."

Her face had turned white. "But . . . but the land, the money, I don't know how . . ." Her voice faded and tears started to slide down her cheeks.

Laurel reached out to place a hand on her arm. "It'll be fine, Mom. Everything will be fine."

"But Laurel, we've talked about this. There's no other way."

Laurel pulled the diamond out of her other pocket and held it in the palm of her hand. "There *is* another way."

Her mom's eyes bounced warily from the diamond up to Laurel's face and back down. "Where did you get this, Laurel?" she asked sternly, her eyes on the rough, glittering gem.

"I've been asked to deliver a proposition."

"Laurel, you're scaring me," her mom said, her voice a little shaky.

"No, no. Don't be scared. Everything's fine. There is"—she hesitated—"someone . . . who wants the land to stay in our family. Specifically, for me to own it. They are willing to let you have this diamond in exchange for you signing the land into a trust in my name."

Her mother stared at her silently for a long time. "Your name?"

Laurel nodded.

"In exchange for this?" she said, gesturing at the gem.

"Exactly."

"And saving your dad?"

"Yes."

"I don't understand."

Laurel stared down at the diamond. During the whole drive to Brookings from Orick, she hadn't been able to decide just what to tell her mom. Now that the moment was here, she still wasn't sure. "Mom? I . . . I'm not like you."

"What do you mean, not like me?"

Laurel stood and crossed to the door. She closed it, wishing it had a lock. She walked slowly back to her mother. "Haven't you ever wondered why I'm so different?"

"You're not different. You're wonderful—you're beautiful. I don't know why you're suddenly doubting that."

"I eat funny."

"But you've always been healthy. And—"

"I don't have a pulse."

"Excuse me?"

"I don't bleed."

"Laurel, this is ri—"

"No, it's not. When was the last time I cut myself? When was the last time you saw me bleed?" Her voice was louder now.

"I . . . I . . ." Her mom looked around, suddenly confused. "I don't remember," she said weakly.

And then everything, *everything* in her life suddenly made sense. "You don't remember," Laurel said softly. "Of course you don't remember." They wouldn't have let her mom remember the dozens of times she must have suspected something was wrong. The hundreds of times something was just a little too weird. Laurel felt suddenly weak. "Oh, Mom, I'm so sorry."

"Laurel, I haven't understood a word you've said since you walked in this room."

"Sarah?" A scratchy, weak voice made both of them turn.

"Mark! Mark, you're awake!" her mom cried, forgetting her confusion. They stood on each side of her dad's bed, clasping his hands as he blinked hesitantly.

His eyes slowly came into focus and traveled around the room, taking in the myriad of medical equipment beeping and whirring all around him. "Where the hell am I?" he asked in a gravelly voice.

When Laurel walked back out to the parking lot in one of her mother's clean shirts, David was sitting on the trunk of his car waiting. "Is everything okay?" he asked quietly.

Laurel smiled. "Yeah. Or it will be."

"Did your dad wake up?"

Laurel smiled softly and nodded. "He's still kind of out of it because of all the morphine and tranquilizers they've had him on, but as soon as they wear off, he'll be good to go." She climbed up onto the trunk beside him and he wrapped his arm around her. She let her head rest on his shoulder.

"How'd your mom take it?" she asked.

David laughed. "Pretty well, considering I lied through my teeth. I told her I left my phone in the car all night and we slept in your dad's room." He looked down at the small phone in his hands. "Well, half of that is true."

Laurel rolled her eyes.

"She lectured me for a while and told me I was irresponsible, but she didn't ground me from the car or anything. That's thanks to you, I imagine. She knows I'm helping you."

"Yeah," Laurel said with a sigh. David's mom would never know the half of it.

"I don't know what she's going to do when she sees this though," David continued, pointing to the large bruise on his face. "And this," he added, looking at the gash on his arm. "In fact, considering I have no idea what was in that river, I should probably go in and get a tetanus shot or something. Stitches, maybe." He laughed morosely. "I guess I'll have to come up with something to explain that too."

Laurel stared at the wide, red gash for several seconds before she made her decision. If David didn't deserve it, who did? She removed the bottle of elixir from her pocket and carefully unscrewed it.

"What are you doing?" David asked.

"Shh," Laurel whispered, turning his head so she could reach his cheek. She dabbed one drop of liquid onto her finger and rubbed it across the purpling bruise. "This might sting," she warned as she let another drop fall into his gash.

By the time she finished stowing the bottle back in her pocket, the bruise had almost disappeared and David was staring openmouthed as the cut faded from an angry red to a soft pink in front of his eyes. In another few minutes, there wouldn't even be a scar.

"Is that what you gave your dad?" he asked, still staring at his disappearing gash.

Laurel nodded.

David grinned. "He'll be on his feet in no time. Which is a good thing," he said with feigned offense. "I'm getting pretty tired of the way you drive me like a slave in that bookstore. I have rights, you know," he added with a laugh as Laurel slapped his shoulder. He held her wrists till she gave up and they both fell into a subdued silence. "When will you come back?" David asked.

Laurel shrugged. "I can't imagine Dad will be here for too long. Maybe they'll release him this weekend."

"You're sure that stuff will fix everything?"

"I'm sure."

David grinned, looking down at his smooth arm. "I'm pretty sure myself." He paused for a few seconds. "What did you tell your mom?"

Laurel sighed. "I started to tell her the truth, but then my dad woke up. I have to tell her something. I'm not sure what though."

"I think the truth is your best bet. Well, not about everything. You may want to skim over the trolls and how your parents had a murderous monster in their house."

Laurel nodded.

"But they should know the truth about you. You shouldn't have to hide in your own home."

Their fingers twined and David squeezed her hand. "Faeries, trolls, what else is out there that I'd never have believed? Magic medicine, apparently. Thanks, by the way."

"It's only fair," Laurel replied. "I've put you through a lot. And I don't just mean the troll fiasco."

"I knew what I was getting into when I signed up." He shrugged. "Well, I guess I didn't know *everything*, but I knew you were different. From the first time I saw you, I knew there was something . . . something special about you." He grinned. "And I was right."

"Special?" Laurel scoffed. "Is that what you call it?"

"Yes," David insisted. "That's what I call it." He paused and reached for her hand, turning it over and covering it with both of his. He watched her in silence for a while, then lifted a hand to her cheek and drew her a little closer. She didn't resist as his lips brushed hers, soft as the kiss of a light wind. He pulled back and looked at her.

She didn't speak; she didn't lean in. If he was going to get involved in everything her life had turned into, it had to be his choice. She knew what she wanted, but it wasn't just about her anymore.

After a slight hesitation, David held her closer against his chest and kissed her again, longer this time. Laurel almost sighed in relief as her arms twined around his waist. His lips were soft, warm, and gentle—just like David.

When their kiss ended, he stood in front of her with her hands in his. Neither spoke. Nothing needed to be said. Laurel smiled and let her finger trail down the side of his face, then slipped off the trunk of the car.

David eased into the driver's seat, his eyes still on Laurel. She waved as she watched his car back out of the parking spot and roll quietly down the street, back onto the 101, headed to normal life again.

TWENTY-FIVE

"ARE YOU SURE YOU DON'T WANT ME TO COME WITH you?" Laurel's mom asked as she pulled onto the long, bumpy driveway.

"They may not come out if you do," Laurel said. "I'll be safe." She smiled at the dense trees. "I don't think there's any-where on earth I would be safer." She had spent the last three days convincing her parents she was a faerie and most of this morning assuring them that it was in their best interest to accept the faeries' proposition. And even though her parents were skeptical, their objections to the arrangement seemed insignificant compared to the fact that the faeries had saved her dad's life. That and the initial appraisal of the rough dia-mond, which had an estimated value of just under eight hun-dred thousand dollars.

Laurel leaned over and hugged her mother. "You are coming back, aren't you?" her mom asked.

Remembering how David had asked the same question, Laurel smiled. "Yes, Mom, I'm coming back."

She stepped out of the car into the cold, crisp air. The sky was murky with dense gray clouds that threatened rain, but Laurel refused to see that as an omen. "It's just the winter air," she muttered under her breath. Still, she clasped the bag containing the soft moccasins to her chest as if it could protect her from the bad news that might lie waiting for her within the forest.

It *couldn't* be bad news, though. It couldn't! She stepped into the shadow of the woods and walked down the path toward the river. She knew she must be surrounded by faerie sentries, but she didn't dare call out—she wasn't entirely sure she could find the voice to, even if she dug up the will.

When she reached the rushing stream, she laid the bag on the rock she'd been sitting on the first time she met Tamani. She sat on it again now, waiting. Just waiting.

"Hello, Laurel."

She'd know that voice anywhere; it had haunted her dreams for the last four days. No, that wasn't true. For the last two months. She turned and threw herself into Tamani's arms, waves of relief rushing over her as tears wet his shirt.

"I should get shot more often," he said, his arms tight around her.

"Don't ever get shot again," Laurel ordered, her cheek glued to Tamani's chest. His shirts were always so soft. Right now, she never wanted to lift her face from the smooth fabric. His hands were in her hair, stroking her shoulder, brushing a tear from her temple—everywhere at once. All the while, a soft murmuring of words she didn't understand flowed from his mouth, comforting her as effectively as any spell could have. It didn't matter to her that Tamani only had weak magic—he *was* magic.

When she finally let him go, she laughed and wiped her tears away. "I'm happy to see you, I really am. Are you okay? It's only been four days."

Tamani shrugged. "I'm a little sore, and technically I'm here for recuperation, not on duty. But I knew you'd come. And I wanted to be here when you did." He leaned forward and brushed a strand of hair behind her ear.

"I—I—I brought these back," Laurel stuttered, holding up the bag with the moccasins. His closeness always made her shiver.

Tamani shook his head. "I made them for you."

"Something else to remember you by?" Laurel asked, touching the tiny ring around her neck.

"You can never have too many reminders." Tamani's eyes circled the small clearing. He cleared his throat. "First things first, I've been assigned to ask you how our proposal was received."

"Quite well," Laurel responded in the same mock-formal tone. "The papers will be drawn up as soon as possible." She rolled her eyes. "I think they're going to make it my Christmas present."

Tamani laughed, then pulled her a little closer. "Let's get out of here," he said. "The trees have eyes."

"I don't think it's the trees," Laurel said sardonically.

Tamani chuckled. "Maybe not. This way."

He took her hand as he led her down a path that snaked back and forth but never seemed to really go anywhere.

"Is your father okay?" Tamani asked, squeezing her hand.

Laurel smiled. "They're releasing him this afternoon. He intends to be back at work bright and early tomorrow morning." She sobered. "That's why I'm here. We're all going to Crescent City in a few hours. I—" She looked down at her feet. "I don't know when I'll be coming back."

Tamani turned and looked at her, his eyes a deep well of something she couldn't quite place. "Did you come here to say good-bye?"

It sounded so harsh when he said it. She nodded. "For now."

Tamani shifted dead leaves on the ground with his bare foot. "What does that mean? You're choosing David over me?"

She hadn't come here to talk about David. "I wish it could be different, Tamani. But I can't live in your world right now. I have to live in mine. What am I supposed to do, ask my mom or David to drive me down here once in a while so I can see my boyfriend?"

Tamani turned and walked a few more steps, but Laurel followed him.

"Should I write you letters or call you on the phone? I don't have an option here."

"You could stay," he said, his voice so quiet she barely heard him.

"Stay?"

"You could live here . . . with me." He continued on before she could speak. "You're going to own the land soon. And there's a house. You could stay!"

Glorious thoughts of life with Tamani spun through Laurel's head, but she forced them aside. "No, Tam. I can't."

"You lived here before. And things were good."

"Good? How were things good? I was being constantly watched and you guys were feeding my parents memory elixirs like they were water!"

Tamani focused on the ground. "You figured that out?"

"It was the only logical explanation."

"I didn't like it either, if that helps."

She took a deep breath. "Did they . . . did they ever make *me* forget? After I got here, I mean."

He wouldn't meet her eyes. "Sometimes."

"Did you ever do it?" she asked tentatively.

He looked at her with wide eyes, then shook his head. "I couldn't." He leaned closer, his voice so low she could barely hear. "I should have, once. But I couldn't do it."

"What happened?"

He scratched at his neck. "I hate that you don't remember."

"Sorry."

He shrugged. "You were really young. I was a new sentry— I'd been out maybe a week—and I got sloppy and let you see me."

"I saw you?"

"Yeah, you were about ten in human years. I just put my finger to my lips to quiet you and ducked back behind a tree. You looked for me for a minute or two, but within an hour you seemed to have forgotten it."

Laurel stood silently for a long time. "I—I remember that. Just barely. That was you?"

Joy glowed out of Tamani's eyes. "You remember?"

Laurel broke eye contact. "A little," she said quietly. She cleared her throat. "What about my parents? Did you ever dope them?"

Tamani sighed. "A couple of times. I had to," he added before Laurel could argue. "It was my job. But only two or three times. By the time I got here, you were more careful. We didn't have to patch you up once a week. And the times when your parents got too close, I tried to assign someone else." He shrugged. "I always thought it was a lousy plan to begin with."

Laurel was silent for a moment. "Thanks, I guess."

"Don't be mad. It wouldn't be like that if you stayed now. You know everything. Your parents even know. We wouldn't have to do that anymore."

She shook her head. "I have to stay with my parents. They're in more danger than ever. I've been given the responsibility of protecting them. I can't turn my back on them now. They're human—and maybe that seems lesser to you. But I love them and I won't leave them to be slaughtered by the first troll who comes across their scent. I won't!"

"Then why are you here?" he asked bitterly.

She paused for a few seconds, trying to control her emotions. "Don't you know how much I wish I could stay? I love this forest. I love—" She hesitated. "I love being with you. Hearing about Avalon, feeling its magic in the trees. Every time I leave, I wonder why."

"Then why do you go?" His voice was louder now, demanding. "Stay," he said, grasping her hands in his. "Stay with me. I'll take you to Avalon. *Avalon*, Laurel. You can go there. We can go together."

"Stop! Tamani, I can't. I just can't be part of your world right now."

"*Your* world."

Laurel nodded weakly. "My world," she relented. "My family is depending on me for too much. I have to live my human life."

"With David," Tamani said.

Laurel shook her head, frustrated. "Yes, if you must know. David is very important to me. But I told you, this is not about choosing between you and David. I'm not trying to decide who's my one true love. It's not like that."

"Maybe not for you."

His voice was quiet—barely audible—but the intensity hit her like a tangible blow.

"What does it take, Laurel? I've done everything I can think of. I got *shot* to protect you. Tell me what else to do and I'll do it. Whatever it takes, if you'll just stay."

She forced herself to meet his eyes—deep pools of an emotion she'd never been able to identify. Her mouth went dry as she tried to find her voice. "Why do you love me so much, Tamani?" It was a question she'd been longing to ask for weeks. "You scarcely even know me."

Above their heads the sky rumbled. "What if—what if that wasn't true?"

They were on the edge of a cliff, she could feel it. And she wasn't sure she had the strength to jump. "How could it not be true?" she whispered.

Those fiery eyes still burned into hers. "What if I told you our lives were entwined long ago?" He slipped his fingers through hers, holding up their joined fists.

Laurel stared at their hands. "I don't understand."

"I told you that you were seven when you came to live with the humans. But in the faerie world, you were mentally much older, remember? You had a life, Laurel. You had friends." He paused, and Laurel could see he was trying to maintain control over his emotions. "You had me." Tamani's voice was barely above a whisper. "I knew you, Laurel, and you knew me. We were just friends, but we were such good friends. I . . . I asked you not to go, but you told me it was your duty. I learned about duty and responsibility from *you*." He looked down and lifted her hands to his chest. "You said you'd try to remember me, but they made you forget. I thought I would die the first time you looked at me and didn't recognize me."

Laurel's eyes filled with tears.

"I lied—about the ring I mean," Tamani said, his voice soft and serious. "I didn't just give you a random ring. It was yours. You gave it to me to keep until the time came to return it to you. You thought—you hoped—it might help you remember your life before you came here." He shrugged. "Obviously it didn't work, but I promised you I'd try."

Cold rain dripped down Laurel's arms as she stood silently.

286

"I never gave up on you, Laurel. I swore I would find a way back into your life. I became a sentry as early as they would allow and called in every favor I could to get assigned to this gate. Jamison helped me. I owe him more than I could ever repay." He lifted her hands up to his face and brushed a soft kiss across her knuckles. "I've watched you for years. Watched you grow from a little girl to a full-grown faerie. We were best friends when we were little, and I've been with you almost every day for the last five years. Is it so unreasonable for me to have fallen in love with you?"

He laughed very quietly. "You used to come out here and sit by the stream and play your guitar and sing. I would sit up in a tree and just listen to you. It was my favorite thing to do. You sing so beautifully."

His bangs were soft, damp tendrils now, hanging down across his forehead. Laurel let her eyes travel the length of him: his soft black breeches tied at the knees, the fitted green shirt hugging his chest, and the symmetrical face that was more perfect than any human boy could ever wish for. "You waited for me this long?" she asked in a whisper.

Tamani nodded. "And I'll wait longer. Someday you'll come to Avalon, and when that time comes, I'll show you what I have to offer you in my world, *our* world. You'll choose me. You'll come *home* with me." He held her face in his hands.

Tears stung Laurel's eyes. "You don't know that, Tamani."

He licked his lips nervously for just a second before a forced smile cut across his face. "No," he said hoarsely. "I don't." His hands on her face, stone-cold a second ago, now seemed to warm with the heat in his eyes as his thumbs traced her cheekbones. "But I have to believe; I have to hope."

Laurel wanted to tell him to be realistic—not to hope for what might never happen. But she couldn't force the words out of her throat. Even in her mind they sounded false.

"And I'll wait, Laurel. I'll wait as long as I have to. I have *never* given up on you." He pressed his lips to her forehead. "And I never will."

He pulled her close and held her, and neither spoke. For a perfect moment, no one else in the world existed outside of this tiny space on a wooded path. "Come on," Tamani said, squeezing her one more time. "Your mother will be worried."

They walked hand in hand, farther down the curvy path until Laurel began to recognize where she was. "I'll leave you here," he said, about a hundred feet from the tree line.

Laurel nodded. "It's not forever," she promised.

"I know."

She lifted the thin silver chain holding the seedling ring and studied it—its significance far more compelling now. "I'll think of you, just like I promised."

"And I'll think of you, just like I have every day," Tamani said. "Good-bye, Laurel."

He turned and walked back down the curving path and Laurel's eyes followed his back. Each step he took seemed to take a piece of her heart with it. His green shirt was about to disappear behind a tree, and Laurel squeezed her eyes shut.

When she opened them, he was gone.

And it was as if the magic of the forest had left with him. The life that she could feel all around her—the magic that seeped through the gateway. The trees around her felt lifeless and empty without it.

"Wait," she whispered. She took a step after him and her feet began to run. "No!" The cry ripped itself from her throat as she pushed branches out of her way. "Tamani, wait!" She rounded another corner and her eyes searched for him. "Tamani, please!" Her feet pressed onward, desperate for a glimpse of that deep-green shirt.

Then he was there, turned half toward her with a guarded expression etched across his face. She didn't stop or even slow her step. When she reached him, she grabbed the front of his shirt in both fists, pulling him to her, pushing her mouth up into his. Heat swirled through her as she pulled his face closer, tighter. His arms wound around her and their bodies melded with a rightness she didn't bother to question. Her lips filled with the sweetness of his mouth, and Tamani held her against him as if he could somehow pull her inside of him, make her part of him.

And for a moment, she did feel like part of him. As if their kiss bridged the gap between two worlds, even if only for that one brief, sparkling moment.

A sigh that held the weight of years shuddered out of Tamani as their faces drew apart. "Thank you," Tamani whispered, almost too quiet to be heard.

"I . . ." Laurel thought of David, waiting back home for her return. Why, when she was with one, could she think only of the other? It wasn't fair, to feel so torn all the time. Not to her or David or Tamani. She looked up, forcing herself to meet his eyes. "I don't know what's going to happen. But my parents are in danger. They need me, Tam." Laurel felt a tear slide down her cheek. "I have to protect them."

"I know. I shouldn't have asked."

"If it weren't for them, I . . ." *I'd what?* she thought.

She didn't know the answer.

"The little faerie who gave you her ring, I don't remember her, Tam. I don't remember you. But something . . . some part of me does. Something inside me cares about you from back then." She lowered her head. "And I care about you now."

Tamani smiled a strange, melancholy smile. "Thank you for that glimmer of hope, however fleeting."

"There's always hope, Tamani."

"There is now."

She nodded, forced her fingers to release Tamani's shirt, and turned back the way she had come.

ACKNOWLEDGMENTS

AN AUTHOR IS ONLY ONE SMALL PART OF THE PROCESS involved in creating a book, and there are a lot of people who deserve my unending gratitude. To my incredible agent, Jodi Reamer; where in the world would I be without you? To Tara Weikum, my editor; I am convinced there is no one else who could have molded this book more perfectly than you. Huge thanks for Erica Sussman's continued assistance; I appreciate you sticking with me. Thanks to Tara's assistant, Jocelyn Davies, whose bright smile and helpfulness are so noticed and appreciated. The entire team at Harper has been beyond extraordinary. A special thanks to Melissa Dittmar, Liz Frew, Cristina Gilbert, Andrea Pappenheimer, and Dina Sherman, who all went out of their way to make me feel welcome. And to Laura Kaplan, for all the work she's already done, and the mountain of work she'll do in the future. Harper is truly the place to be.

Where would I be without old friends who have been with me from the beginning? Thanks to David McAfee, Pat Wood, Michelle Zink, and John Zakour, all of whom believed in me more than I ever believed in myself. Stephenie, you have opened so many doors for me; I will always be grateful. Thanks. And, of course, new friends—Sarah Rees Brennan, Saundra Mitchell, and Carrie Ryan, plus the rest of the incredible Debs at www.feastofawesome.com. You are all awesome like whoa. A huge thank-you to my incredible fiction instructor at LC—as well as fellow author—Claire Davis; the foundation of my writing skills I owe to you. A special shout-out to the Carson girls, Hannah, Emma, and Bethany, for being my betas. You guys are priceless!

Finally, to my amazing family, who also head up my fan club. Duane, Trina, Kara, Richard, Emily, Corbett—thanks. To my awesome kids, Audrey, Brennan, and Gideon, who are miraculously low maintenance, and even when they aren't, are the sunshine of my life. And more than anyone else, thank you, Kenny. Without you, none of this would have been possible.